Colin A

Colin was born in Cambridge and raised in Dumfries. He attended university in Edinburgh before embarking on a series of what he now describes as 'proper jobs.' He moved to Bedfordshire in the mid 1990's and has lived there ever since.

Having always had a passion for reading and occasionally writing short stories, circumstance and a desire to do something different with his life led to the decision to try writing full time.

He has co-written three children's books with long-time friend Spike Breakwell. Published by Cambridge University Press all three sell around the globe.

Colin decided in 2019 to embark on his first full length novel, Foreign Bodies, which was published in 2020 and continues to sell worldwide. His second book, Bipolarised, is a collection of short stories of varying genres and styles, encapsulating Colin's versatility and breadth of imagination.

Two Weeks in the Sun, his second full length novel and opens the new Rose McPhail series.

He is currently working on the sequel to Foreign Bodies.

He has two children and he and his fiancé Roz live with a snake, two cats and a gecko all of which keep him busy and out of mischief.

Praise for Colin A Millar and Foreign Bodies

"Totally gripped from the get go!! Fabulously written with intriguing psychological elements to keep the reader on his toes!"

"Great first novel, I was hooked from the start… I couldn't put it down!"

"What a brilliant book, five stars is not enough… Colin is just brilliant, I just could not put this book down."

"If you're a fan of Ian Rankin's Rebus or Michael Connelly's Bosch you'll love Colin A Millar."

"Compulsive reading. Gruesome. Thoroughly recommend."

"Gripping from the first page, a well written, clearly extensively researched, intelligent psycho thriller, interspersed with a true shock factor when you least expect it!"

"Colin is a real talent, with an eye for detail and the ability to weave plots and characters seamlessly into gripping and intriguingly gruesome tales."

Other Books by Colin A Millar

Foreign Bodies, published 2020.

Bipolarised, published 2021.

Dedication

As always this is for Roz, Caitlin and Bryony. Without their support and encouragement this book would simply not have happened.

Thank you to Tracy Starreveld for her excellent and professional copy-editing.

A special mention needs to go to Douglas Monaghan and Sim Harris for their constructive and useful input and initial proofreading.

Prologue

The dog just wouldn't come to heel. It would take a few bounding leaps back towards her when she called but would then halt and spin back to the thicket of bushes. It was wet and muddy, and the leaves of the trees dripped steadily on her head. She was getting fed up. The dog, which had been a pristine blonde retriever when they had left the house, was now a black and brown muddied mess. She called it again, and again it refused to come, instead rummaging its snout about in the bushes and occasionally giving a low growling bark. It was getting dark and she was keen to get home; the woods were not somewhere she liked to be at night.

After her third attempt to get the dog to obey her call, she gave up and went to fetch it. She angrily grabbed at his collar as soon as she got near enough. The dog managed to pull away and returned its attention back to the bush. She tsked in exasperation and bent to grab the collar once more.

It was as her head came nearer to the bush that she spotted what the dog was worrying at.

It was a human hand.

She looked more closely and could make out the arm it was attached to disappearing further into the bush. It was very pale, almost green in colour. The tips of the fingers had been chewed off and there were chunks of flesh missing above the wrist, such that the bone showed through the ragged flesh. She realised her dog had probably caused some of the bite marks she could see.

Spinning quickly away, she vomited on the path, the dog now whining and pawing at her. Pulling out her phone with shaking hands she managed to dial emergency services.

Oh I do like to be beside the seaside …. oh I do like to be beside the sea … da de dum de da de dum …. Da de dum da de dum …. beside the seaside …. beside the sea.

'The first one I offed was more 'n twenty years ago now. Right smelly old tramp 'e was. Did him with the garrotte, up close and personal like. God, 'e stank to high heaven. But it was good, you know, to see the garrotte work proper for the first time. I'd looked it up on the internet, see, you gotta get the knots in the right place, crush the larynx and some of the main veins and arteries. Subdues 'em quicker. Worked a treat. The old cunt was out for the count in less than a minute – mind, he was off 'is tits on bog cleaner or whatever. But they're not dead then, see, so then I held on for another three minutes, you know like it said – the internet that is – and Bob's your fanny fuckin' Aunt he was gone. Checked 'is pulse and stuff to make sure, but the smell of shit gave it away – well 'e stank of shit anyway but it got worse, y'know what I mean?

Then I did the prozzie. Knifed her. Now, was she on the same holiday? Or was that the next one? No, no, she was the next one. I remember now, she was in Liverpool – the old fucker was in Oxford. I remember now 'cos I got a personal best carp when I was down Oxford. Got bugger all up Liverpool way. Cor, that was a bewt, nearly thirty pounds it was. Lovely spot too – gravel pit, like – but they done the lanscapin' lovely. All trees and bushes an' nice grass an' that. Anyway, I spodded out a big bed of hemp and then got the old spod full of, like, crushed boilies an' nuts and pulses, you know the sort of thing? Then a little splash of the old vanilla essence – carp love the sweet stuff they do. Anyway, I'd barely got me indicator set and the bloody thing roared off. Bloody screamed away it did. Took me near half an hour to get that fucker in, lovely it was though. Twenty-eight pound common carp – beautiful scales.

So yeah, the old tramp 'e was Oxford and then the prozzie was Liverpool.

'Course I wasn't staying in Oxford – well not the city, like – I was out in the sticks, near the fishin'. Smart enough to have me phone on me all day then left it at the B&B before I went looking for me first victim, as it were. Found him quick enough. See though, the thing with him was it was all a bit too easy, you know? Not that much of a thrill. Well, I say that, but it was good, you know, being the first one and all that. I got a big rush at the time – fuckin' marvellous it was – almost creamed me pants! Thing was though, I was all excited after but then I had to remember to pick everything up, leave no trace an' all that. Think I got everything though. I knew that from watchin' them crime documentaries on Sky. You know the kinda thing? With whatsisname? Fred someone. You know, they tell all what the coppers did and what stupid mistakes the psycho made an' all that kind of fing. 'E used to be on telly a lot, you know, like, years ago an' then he just seemed to disappear. Made me think a bit about what I was doing first, you know? Oh what was 'is name? Nah it's gone.

Lovely city Oxford, all them colleges and places of learning. Wasn't that Inspector Morse from Oxford? Sure it was there. Thought I saw a couple of bits there that had been on the telly. Nicer than Liverpool that's for sure.

It was all right, Liverpool that is, I went round the Tate and The Cavern an' all that kinda fing, but not the same as Oxford. Well I say that, but I liked the Tate – that was sort of interesting. All that modern art an' stuff. Stayed not far from there, actually, nice place, lovely breakfast. Then I went further out, you know edge of town, so's I'd be further away from me phone an' me car. Got buses and stuff, you know? So yeah, I found 'er up this manky-looking street – proper red-light district stuff. Anyway, that's me getting ahead of meself again – that was the second 'oliday, not the first.

See, the first one was alright, but I was just learning then. More into house-breaking an' car theft an' that sort of fing .....

What was that bloke's name? My fucking memory, I tell ya.

So, car-breaking and house stuff – that's what I did first off, like. Just a bit o' fun really. Used to pop out of whatever B&B I was in and test meself with different locks and types of car, you know? Never took nothin' – it's all just for a bit of excitement. Got the old ticker going, you know?

Anyway, most of that's pretty irrelevant now. All things considered. Funny combo though innit? Fishin' and killin'. Funny as well 'cos I've never killed a fish in me life – just people. Funny how it is. Care deeply about fish. Couldn't give a fuck about people.

Don't get me wrong – I don't mean everyone. Your mum don't count o'course – or you two. You lot are alright.

Well, more 'n that I suppose, you know what I mean don't ya? But the rest? Well – fair game in my opinion.

See the fing is most people are just twats – not a brain cell among 'em in my view. Did the world a favour I reckon. Mind, that's not totally true, did for a few more select types, like. There was this businessman-type I remember – can't fink where that was just now – but 'e was all pinstripes and bowler hat an' that. Weird in this day an' age to see that kind o' fing. Oh, what a bloody mess 'e made. Blood an' guts an' stuff everywhere. Squealed like a little girl an all. The great nonce. Proper effete – if you know what that means? Funny the words you pick up when you're out and about in't it?

God, way ahead of meself again. Proper muddle I'm getting in. Stick to the subject Charlie you old git – your mother was forever sayin' that to me. "Stop bloody wandering about all over the place – always the bloody same, start talking about one thing and before you know it it's off on somin' else." God, she went on.

So, in her memory I'll tell you some more about Oxford ....

DINENAGE, that's the bugger, Fred Dinenage. Oh, I liked 'is programmes on the old Sky Crime channel. Brilliant they were. Used to make me think about this stuff. Long before I did anything about it.'

Chapter One

The rain pelted at the branches and leaves of the trees for the second day in a row. The ground beneath the trees was slick with mud and sodden autumn leaves. Dark, detritus-filled puddles rose steadily in the dips and ruts of the path that wound its way through the woods. The air was heavy with the dank smells of rotting vegetation and peaty soil.

Detective Chief Inspector Rose McPhail picked her way gingerly toward the cordon of police tape, the lack of daylight making the going harder. Fortunately lights had been set up on stands around the scene which at least gave some illumination to the uneven and root-gnarled ground. The tape wound around trees and bushes taking in an irregular area of perhaps twenty square metres. This was a large area to search, with the torrential rain and the nature of the ground making searching properly and thoroughly difficult. Evidence could easily be missed and trampled into the mud or washed away into the little stream, twice its normal width and depth and running at three times its usual rate. It would be a balancing act between not losing evidence to the elements and the dark, and having enough light to see things properly. She would have kept the ground search back until dawn had it been dry but with the weather the way it was she had opted for an immediate sweep. A fingertip search would be carried out as soon as there was daylight.

As she ducked under the tape, Rose nearly slipped on a slick tree root but managed to keep her feet. She did not want to spend the rest of the evening with mud stains all over her suit. At first, she couldn't make out where she actually needed to be – all she could see was a large bush filling the gap between two trees. Just as she began to move around the trees a white-suited Scene of Crime Officer's head and shoulders appeared above the far side of the bush.

'Evening, Chief Inspector,' he said, from behind the mask he wore. 'Easiest way round is to your right, there's a gap in the undergrowth which'll bring you out this side.'

She thanked him and began to look for the path he had described. It was, indeed, just a gap in the undergrowth and Rose cursed her lack of foresight at leaving her wellingtons in the car. She picked her way around the puddles and dodged sodden branches and bushes until she emerged on the opposite side of the bush she had been looking at when she arrived.

The woods opened up into a grassy clearing beyond the bush, an almost circular area bounded by large mature trees, with the gaps between them filled with brambles and yet more bushes. She had no idea what type of plant these bushes were but had already formed the opinion that they provided excellent cover from the main path. It would be possible, providing you were quiet, to commit any sort of crime in this spot and be completely undetectable by casual passers-by.

The clearing didn't feel as secluded as she entered it. Uniformed officers were searching the surrounding area with flashlights and a dog handler was leading his German shepherd around the perimeter. The area around the bush she had just circumnavigated held two SOCO and the pathologist. Rose was pleased to see it was Dr Stephanie Matheson, someone she considered to be a 'proper' pathologist. Matheson did the job required and gave straight answers without trying to waffle her way through anything she didn't know.

Matheson looked up from her kneeling position beside the bush. 'Ah, Rose,' she said quietly, 'this is an interesting one I must say.'

Rose nodded her greeting and moved to stand beside the doctor. The body of the man lying on his back was half in and half out of the bush. He looked like he had been dragged into the bush by his left arm but that whoever had dragged him there had only got so far before abandoning their attempt at concealment. His head was turned to the right, making his face fully visible in the lights; his jaw was hanging slack, dark curly hair plastered to his forehead by the rain, his eyes open and glassy. There were no marks or bruises on his face. He was probably in his late twenties, maybe early thirties, and in Rose's opinion – quite a handsome man. He was bare-chested and as Rose scanned down to his torso her eyes widened and her mouth fell slightly open.

'Is that actually pinned to his chest?' she asked, pointing down at the body.

'Yes,' Matheson said, not looking up from swabbing the man's fingers. 'Large safety pin pushed through the skin and muscle and out the other side. Whoever killed this guy didn't want their message to get lost.'

Rose shook her head and hunkered down for a better look. Pinned to the man's chest was a sheet of A4 paper sealed into a clear document wallet, with a trickle of blood running from the entry and exit wounds made by the pin. Although Rose hadn't seen anything like that before it was what was on the paper that drew her attention. There was a single word printed in large bold lettering:

'RAPIST'

'Christ,' Rose said in a hushed tone, then slightly louder, 'Do we have an ID and cause of death?'

'No ID,' Matheson replied, 'but cause of death is straightforward enough – gunshot, just under the left armpit. No exit wound so I'm assuming the bullet ricocheted off a rib and is somewhere in the torso. He would have died pretty quickly, I would say. I'll know more about that when I've got him on the slab.'

Rose leaned over the body, careful not to touch it or the note pinned to the chest, and peered at the area under his left arm. A small ragged hole could be seen a few centimetres below his armpit. There was a small amount of blood running down his torso towards his back.

'There's less blood than I'd expect,' Rose said, manoeuvring herself back to kneel beside the doctor.

'Rain's probably washed a lot of it away. He would have bled quite profusely at the time.' Matheson had finished swabbing fingers and was placing her final swab into the small vials used to store and transport them.

Nodding her understanding, Rose stood up, sweeping her soaked hair away from her eyes. 'Anything else you can tell me?' she asked whilst looking around the clearing.

'Not really at this stage,' Matheson replied, also standing up. 'Time of death is anywhere from twenty-four to forty-eight hours ago. Again, I might have a better idea after the PM. He was dragged into the bush post mortem, at a guess. Your forensic guys picked up a smear of blood on the grass starting just behind you. I would say the note was pinned to him before he was shot, judging by the blood that's left on his chest.'

'That'd smart,' Rose said with a frown. 'The victim would likely have made some sort of noise and very probably a scream when that safety pin was pushed through him and the gunshot wouldn't have been quiet.' she said mostly to herself. But there had been no reports of either from the houses that bordered the small woods, as far as she knew. First job when I'm back at the office, she thought.

'Well, thanks Stephanie,' Rose said, still scanning the clearing, then looking back at the doctor and smiling, 'let me know when you've completed the PM.'

'Will do,' Matheson said and bent to collect her bag and samples. 'I should be done tomorrow late afternoon.'

'Great,' Rose said as she moved off across the clearing. She had spotted one of her sergeants talking to one of the uniformed officers.

'What have you got, Rod?' she asked as she approached.

'Evening, ma'am,' he replied stepping towards her. 'Not very much, I'm afraid. Weather and lack of light's hampering the search so no real joy with that. Dog handler says there might be something over the far side of the clearing, behind the victim, but the area's full of scents the dog might pick up – the rain's washing them all together, sort of thing.'

Detective Sergeant Rod Laing was tall and wiry. His frame and long limbs had earned him the nickname 'Crouchy' from the rest of the team, after his resemblance to the footballer Peter Crouch. His slightly thinning hair was plastered to his scalp, making it look even sparser than it actually was. Rose tried not to focus on the dew drop that hung precariously from his slightly hooked nose.

'OK, not entirely unexpected,' Rose said. 'Can you hang around until the area's been fully swept, please? We'll do another one in daylight. I'll be at the office for an hour or so and then back at home if you need me. Get yourself home when you're done and get some rest. The rest of the team's in at eight so we'll have a briefing then.'

Laing nodded, making the dew drop wobble, and grumbled, 'Sure, I don't think I could get any wetter anyway.'

'I always think of you as something of a wet bloke anyway, Rod,' Rose replied with a wink. 'See you at eight.'

She left Laing chuckling, tutting and huffing all at the same time and gingerly made her way back to her car.

Back at the office, she immediately got on her computer and double-checked that there hadn't been any reports of either a disturbance or gunshot in the last two days from anywhere near the woods. There were none. Just to be thorough, she checked two days further back and for the whole town of Milton Keynes. Again nothing.

She checked her watch; it was nearly half past ten. She had been at home when the call had come in and had spent the following three quarters of an hour coordinating with a counterpart in uniform to ensure the scene was secure, and then calling out Rod Laing to attend ASAP. The woman who had found the body had made the call at five past eight and Rose was on scene by nine twenty. She was pleased with the response; it couldn't have been much quicker.

There was very little else she could do at the office at that time of night so she jotted a few notes down ready for the morning's briefing, sent a text to Rod to thank him and remind him to be in for eight and, finally, emailed her boss with a quick update. Turning out the light she headed home, knowing that she would get precious little rest with so many questions about the scene and the victim left unanswered.

***

Her prediction had been wrong; she had slept soundly that night after getting home. A hot shower, cup of hot chocolate and a brief chat with her husband had left Rose drowsy and ready for bed. She still hadn't expected to get much sleep so was surprised when the alarm woke her at six. A full seven hours, she thought, *I need more murders in my life!*

She was in the office by seven thirty and had hit the ground running. She had already worked out the roster of duties and assignments and formed a solid idea of the sort of information her team would need to assemble. The Scene of Crime officers had already emailed her the pictures they had taken of the body and surrounding area so she had already begun putting the printed pictures on the crime board as her team filed in.

'Wakey, wakey, Louise,' Rose teased a very sleepy looking Detective Constable Louise Carney, who had just slouched through the door with a takeaway coffee in her hand. 'Not another date surely? Didn't you have one Monday night?'

'No, just round a mate's house, ma'am. Lost the time,' Carney shrugged and yawned.

Rose gave a mocking tut and shook her head. She knew that as soon as the work began Louise would be as sharp as a knife and faster on the uptake than most of her colleagues.

A quick glance round the room told Rose that most of the team were there.

'OK, guys and gals,' she shouted, clapping her hands, 'we have a murder on our hands. So, make sure you can see the board. I want you all awake and alert and straight onto this, OK?'

There was a general murmur of ascent from the room.

'Rod will fill us in on most of the detail, but in essence we have an unknown male, shot in the woods in North Loughton Park. The body was discovered by a woman walking her dog, a Mrs Helena Warwick, at around eight last night. As you know, the weather was filthy last night so the on scene officers had a hard time gathering what evidence there was. Rod, can you fill us in on anything that was found?'

Rod Laing stood up from his desk. 'The short answer is not much. We're hoping that a daylight search will uncover more. But in essence, it looks like our man was shot where we found him and only partially dragged into some bushes. There was little or no attempt to conceal the body. As you can see,' he said, pointing to one of the pictures on the board, 'the body was only partially clothed and we have, as yet, to discover the whereabouts of the remainder of his clothing, a wallet or phone. SOCO and uniform are on site again now so hopefully there'll be more for us later today, although a full and thorough search of the area will take several days.'

'Thanks Rod.' Rose opened her mouth to continue but stopped when the door to the open-plan office was opened and DC David Baker made his way sheepishly into the room. Rose gave him a hard stare, one she knew the young man would feel extremely uncomfortable under.

'Thanks for joining us, Davey,' she said coldly and then turned her attention back to the room. 'We don't have an ID yet for our victim so that's number one priority. Louise and Chris, can you two get on that, please? Chase up SOCO for fingerprints, check missing persons etcetera, you know the drill. You'll all have noticed this,' she said, pointing to a picture of the note pinned to the victim's chest. 'Whoever killed this man believed he was a rapist. If he is, he'll likely have form. Start with that, you two, OK?'

Louise looked over to DC Christine King and nodded. Christine nodded back and made a couple of notes in the jotter on her lap.

'We need door to door across the whole area. There've been no reports of gunfire or a disturbance but that doesn't mean that people didn't hear something and chose not to report it. David, you're on this with Anna.'

Baker nodded and did his best not to show he had been given the bum job. DC Anna Hagan was glaring at him across the room but he steadfastly avoided her gaze.

'Sandra,' Rose continued, 'can you pay a visit to Mrs Warwick? See what, if anything, she can add to her account. Then can you catch up with David and Anna and coordinate the rest of the door to door.'

Detective Sergeant Sandra Adams nodded and glanced over at David then at Anna whom she gave a sympathetic, tight-lipped smile to.

'Gareth, you're office liaison. Put all the information coming in together and report it back to me as soon as you have anything. Also, while you're waiting for that to happen, chase the labs on the samples that have been sent off already and prime them on what's likely to be coming in through the course of the day. We should at least have a bullet for ballistics after the PM's been completed – I want this stuff fast-tracked.'

DC Gareth Exley turned immediately to his computer and began opening a case log. He was the most experienced officer on the team, having served for over fifteen years in uniform. He had only been in the Serious Crime Unit for a few months and Rose was still deciding how he fitted in and what his strengths were. His years on the job meant he knew his way around reports and sifting information so that was where she tended to put him.

She turned to Rod Laing. 'Rod, you go back to the scene and coordinate the searches. I'll join you there after I've seen the Chief Super. Now everyone, listen carefully, I do not – I repeat, not – want this hitting the media right now. So, if you're asked you know nothing. Understood?'

There was a round of ascents and then for the next five minutes the office was a hive of activity. Those with assignments that were taking them out of the office were pulling on coats and collecting bags, those with internal jobs were firing up computers and in Louise Carney's case collecting another cup of coffee. Rose wove through them all on her way to see the Chief Superintendent. She wasn't happy that she would have very little to report, but report she must.

Rod caught her up in the corridor. 'I have an uneasy feeling about this one, Rose,' he said as they walked.

'Yeah, me too. Are we both thinking the same thing?' she said quietly.

'I can't read minds, but I'm suspecting you're thinking that this might not be the only body we have to deal with. That note – it's weird and in my view reeks of vigilante.'

'Well,' Rose said and stopped walking, 'you could be right. But until we know otherwise keep that well and truly under your hat.'

'I don't wear a hat,' Rod said, deadpan.

'Pass the Sellotape, my sides are splitting,' Rose said, just as dryly. 'Now, I seem to remember I gave you a job to do.' She made a shooing motion with her hand. Rod took the less than subtle hint and moved off with a smile. Rose shook her head and with a sigh made her way to see her boss.

Chapter Two

The rain had only become heavier since daybreak and the search team were slipping and sliding around the cordoned-off area of woodland when Rod arrived on site. He spotted a uniformed sergeant he knew and made a beeline in his direction.

'Dylan? Anything turn up yet?' Rod asked the barrel-chested sergeant, who was bent down on his haunches, gently moving fallen leaves and detritus from an area under a tree.

Dylan looked up and round at the sound of his name, 'Oh, all right Rod? Nah, nothing much. There's a shoe print over there,' he said, indicating an area about twenty feet from where the body had been found. 'SOCO have taken a cast and photos – could be something or nothing. And the bullet casing was found near there, again that's with SOCO, so looks like we can be fairly sure whoever it was, they were standing in that spot. Other than that, naff all.'

'Right,' Rod replied, sniffing. 'Well that's a couple of things we didn't have last night. Still no sign of the victim's clothes or wallet anything that could help with an ID?'

'Nope.' Dylan had returned his attention back to the tree roots.

Rod sighed and looked around. 'We're gonna have to widen the search then. We need an ID – there might be a wallet or something. Maybe the gunman took it then dropped it somewhere. And the victim's clothes, again maybe taken further away by the assailant. I think it's time we went from one end of the woods to the other, don't you?'

17

Dylan grunted his approval, then stood with a slight groan and pushed his hands into the small of his back. 'Right you are, Rod, let's get the line sorted then.'

They moved off together to collect the other officers, and Dylan got on his radio as they walked to request reinforcements so that the line could be as thorough as possible.

Half an hour later, a line of uniformed officers began a slow and meticulous walk from one side of the woods to the other. Rod watched them set off then, deciding he had had enough of the rain, walked back towards his car.

As he was opening the door, Rose's Vauxhall Astra pulled up behind his car. He re-shut the door and walked slowly over to the Astra. Rose indicated the passenger side door and he climbed in. He was very pleased that Rose had left both the engine and the heater running.

'Anything?' she asked as soon as he was in the car.

He told her about the shoe print and the bullet casing and that he had ordered the woods to be searched top to bottom. Rose nodded thoughtfully.

'Yep, right call,' she said still nodding.

'How was the Super?' he asked, still shaking water off his coat, hair and hands.

'You're soaking my carpets, stop it. The Superintendent is just fine and dandy,' she said, looking mournful. 'He wants up dates as soon as they come in – as if we didn't have enough to do – but then I suppose we don't get many shootings to deal with. He wants a speedy resolution so we're going to have to go all out on this. Not that I'd expect us to be anything else.'

Rod appeared to be about to speak when Rose's phone began to ring.

'McPhail,' she said when she answered. She listened for a second or two, then said, 'Right, I'll head back now.' She turned to Rod. 'We have an ID.'

'That was quick,' Rod said, raising a questioning eyebrow.

'Seamus Harding. He's got form for flashing and voyeurism. He's been on the sex offences team's radar for a while now.' Rose put her phone back into the inside pocket of her jacket and placed her hand on the gear stick and pushed into first gear.

Rod took the hint and placed his hand on the door handle ready to leave. As he climbed out of the car, he looked over his shoulder. 'Nothing for rape though?'

Rose shook her head. 'No,' was all she said and Rod shut the door.

She was back in the office in fifteen minutes. Only Louise, Christine and Gareth were in there now and the room was quiet.

'Are you sure it's our victim?' Rose asked as she approached Louise at her desk.

'Certain. Fingerprint match,' she replied, lifting a piece of paper off her desk and handing it to Rose. It was a picture of a young man looking nervous and it was definitely their victim.

'Records show he was last arrested for indecent exposure two years ago,' Louise continued. 'Nothing really since although he was picked up six months ago after a complaint that someone was lurking outside their house. Patrol car picked him up about two hundred yards away – he reckoned he was just out for a walk. Not much they could do to prove he had been hovering about so he was released at the scene. Nothing after that.'

Rose was staring at the picture. You were a bit of a naughty boy but you certainly weren't a rapist, she thought. She looked back at Louise. 'Address? Next of kin?' she asked.

Louise handed her another sheet of paper which Rose accepted with a nod.

'Age twenty-eight, mother, Stella Harding, no father or siblings,' Rose murmured. 'Address in Oldbrook – that's not that far from where he was found.' She turned back to her colleague. 'Good work Louise.'

Rose turned away and began walking toward her office whilst saying to no one in particular, 'I'll organise a family liaison officer and get over to tell the mother.' She stopped in her tracks and turned back to Louise. 'He hasn't been reported missing?'

Louise looked to Gareth who was busy typing. When he didn't look up, she said, 'Gareth? Has our man been reported missing, do you know?'

Gareth looked up, his expression half annoyed and half startled. 'No, it was the first thing I checked. No record of him missing. Mind, depending on when he was killed, he might not have been missed yet.'

Rose nodded. 'True. Right, Louise you head for the mortuary to see if you can't chivvy up the PM. Christine, you go and help David and Anna with the door to door. Gareth you keep manning the fort.' With that she turned on her heel and walked briskly the rest of the way to her office.

It took her five minutes to organise a family liaison officer and then she was moving again. She passed Louise and Christine pulling on coats and gathering their things together. Both nodded with tight lips as Rose passed; they knew how difficult her visit to the mother would be and were glad she had the responsibility and not them.

The liaison officer was waiting by Rose's car when she emerged from the back of the station. She was an experienced PC called Meredith Watkins. Rose had worked with her before and liked the way she had with grieving relatives. More than once she had uncovered vital evidence with her way with people and ability to pry into memories and recollections of the victim's last hours or days that would otherwise have been lost in the fog of their grief.

Rose waved her greeting and unlocked the car. It was only once they were seated in the car that Rose turned to speak to her. 'Victim's name is Seamus Harding, mother is the only relative called Stella. Seamus was shot in the woods in North Loughton Park sometime in the last twenty-four hours. The mother hasn't reported him missing yet but then he is twenty-eight and it's likely that she might not have begun to worry.'

Meredith nodded. 'Could be a real shock for her then.'

'Yep,' Rose said as she turned the key in the ignition. 'Christ I hate these visits. Doesn't matter how many you do they never get any easier. How the hell do you do it all the time?' She glanced over to Meredith and then turned her attention to pulling the car out of the station and on to the busy road.

'I look at it as a vital part of policing and it means I play a crucial role in any investigation. Families need to know what's going on and understand what we're doing about it. So, I guess I see myself as the face of the force and the voice for the victim's family. I wouldn't say I enjoyed it exactly but I do get a real sense of satisfaction from my work.'

'Well, rather you than me is all I'll say.' Rose smiled across to Meredith and then turned her attention back to the road.

The Harding residence was a small, neat semi-detached house in a quiet cul-de-sac. Rose pulled the car up outside and let out a sigh as she undid her seatbelt. She was glad of Meredith's calming and reassuring presence a step behind her on the short walk up the path to the door.

She rang the bell and stood back to wait. The door was answered in a matter of seconds. A short, plump woman, who Rose guessed would be in her fifties or sixties, stood in the doorway looking both wary and worried. It was clear she had immediately seen Meredith in her uniform and this had put her on her guard.

Before she could speak, Rose had produced her ID and said, 'Mrs Harding? I'm Detective Chief Inspector McPhail and this is PC Watkins. May we come in?'

The woman hesitated for a second and then nodded, 'Yes, I'm Stella Harding but it's Miss actually. Is it about my Seamus? He hasn't done something silly again, has he?' She had a pronounced Irish accent, Belfast or thereabouts, Rose guessed. She had tucked a loose strand of her greying hair behind one ear while she spoke and now looked very nervous.

'We don't think so, Miss Harding. Please may we come in?' Rose kept her voice soft and reassuring as she spoke. This was not a conversation for the doorstep.

'Yes, sorry, yes come in.' Stella Harding stood to one side and opened the door further to allow the two officers in.

Once inside, they were ushered into a small, cluttered, living room. As Rose looked round at the many photos on the walls and every available horizontal space,

Stella Harding said, 'Would you like some tea or coffee?' She was already making her way towards the door to the right of the room.

'Why don't you sit down, Miss Harding?' Meredith said quietly. 'I'll make the tea – through here is it?'

Miss Harding looked from one officer to the other. Her expression said she now knew that bad news was coming and her bottom lip quivered slightly as she said, 'What's happened?'

'Please, Miss Harding,' Rose said more firmly than she had intended. She softened her voice. 'Please sit down. I am afraid I have some bad news.'

Stella Harding slumped down on the nearest sofa, a tear rolling down her cheek. She looked pale and her mouth hung open slightly.

'Miss Harding, I'm afraid to say your son has been murdered.' Rose knew from experience it was best to simply say outright what had happened. In her younger years she had tried to soften the blow but that always ended with the relatives in even more of a state.

Stella shook her head. 'What do you mean, murdered? There has to be some sort of mistake. Who would murder Seamus? He's harmless. Oh, my boy. My boy.' She began to weep gently and repeated, 'Oh, my boy. It can't be true.'

'I'm afraid it is, Miss Harding,' Rose said softly, as Meredith came back into the room bearing a tray with teapot, cups, milk and sugar. She immediately put the tray on the coffee table and sat down next to Miss Harding, taking her hand.

Rose moved and sat down on the other couch in the room. She took a deep breath before saying, 'He was found in North Loughton Park – he had been shot, we think sometime in the last twenty-four hours but we can't be certain yet.'

'Shot?' Miss Harding wailed, before sobbing loudly. She took a long sniffly breath. 'How do you know it's Seamus?'

'From his police record,' Rose said, sitting forward and clasping her hands together. 'You didn't report him missing. Does he often stay out for whole days at a time?'

Miss Harding sniffed again. 'Yes, that wasn't so unusual. Why would someone shoot my Seamus?'

Rose ignored the question, partly because she didn't have an answer and partly because she had other questions she wanted to ask. 'When did you last see him, Miss Harding?' she asked instead.

'Yesterday morning. He leaves for work at about eight. I always make him some tea and toast ready for when he gets up and then we spend an hour chatting together before he goes.'

'Where does he work?' Rose asked, pulling out her notebook and jotting down a few lines.

'He works for Maitland's the builders. He's a roofer.'

Rose jotted that down. They would be her next port of call. If Seamus had made it to work that day it would narrow down the time of death.

'Did he have a group of friends he saw regularly? You know, down the pub or whatever?' Meredith asked. *Good girl*, Rose thought.

'There was only really one – John Denning. That was where I thought he was. They play those console things together. Sometimes he plays here with John on the phone, or however they do it, others he goes over to John's place.'

'What about girlfriends? Or boyfriends?' Meredith asked, her voice was calm and quiet but the questions were stated in such a way that ensured they got an answer.

'He wasn't gay,' Miss Harding stated firmly. 'But there was no girlfriend as far as I knew. That's not to say he didn't have one, mind. He was a private boy, even with me.'

Meredith nodded and then looked over to Rose.

'Can I take a look in his room?' Rose asked.

Miss Harding nodded and reached for a box of tissues on the coffee table. Meredith took the opportunity to pour the tea.

'Which one?' Rose asked, standing up.

'First on the right,' Miss Harding replied blowing her nose.

Rose left Meredith to look after Miss Harding, knowing she would get the address for Seamus' friend. The stairs were narrow and led to an equally narrow landing. Two doors faced each other across the landing and another was straight ahead. Rose guessed the door on the left to be the bathroom and the door at the end to be Miss Harding's room. She checked the door on the left to be sure. She had been wrong; it was Miss Harding's bedroom. Turning to the door on the right she made her way into Seamus Harding's bedroom.

The small room was extremely neat and tidy: a single bed was against one wall with an Arsenal duvet cover; there was a single wardrobe and a chest of drawers along the opposite wall; and in the corner a small table with a flat-screen TV on it. Below that there was a Playstation 4 and plumped next to the table was a bean bag which also displayed the Arsenal badge and colours.

Rose opened the wardrobe which held a number of shirts, one suit and a couple of jackets, one predictably Arsenal-emblazoned.

'Three nil to the Arsenal,' she muttered to herself as she bent to check the bottom of the wardrobe. This held several pairs of trainers and one pair of smart shoes. With nothing else to check, she turned her attention to the chest of drawers.

She rifled through each drawer. The top two smaller drawers held socks and underwear and nothing else. The next two were full of neatly folded t-shirts and jumpers and again nothing else. As she bent to search the final drawer something caught her eye on the underside of the little table with the TV on top. Moving a little closer she could see it was the corner of a piece of tape hanging down from the underside of the table where it had come unstuck. Dropping to her knees she reached under the table and carefully peeled the tape away. It came away easily and by the colour of the tape she could see it had been stuck there for some time. As the tape came away a USB memory stick fell to the floor next to the Playstation.

'Well, Seamus, what's hidden on here?' she said quietly, picking up the memory stick. It was white and there was no logo or writing on it. She stood back up and looked around the room again, tapping the stick against the palm of her left hand. There was nothing in the room that she could see that would be able to take the memory stick – no laptop or computer, and from her admittedly limited knowledge Rose didn't think the Playstation would accept it either.

She put the memory stick in her inside jacket pocket then realised she hadn't finished checking the last drawer. Opening the drawer, she saw there were several pairs of very neatly folded jeans. She took out one pair at a time and checked the pockets. When the final pair were out, she was disappointed that there was nothing in the drawer and all the pockets were empty. She wasn't sure what she had expected to find but felt she must have missed something. Why had Seamus hidden a USB stick and yet have nothing to view its contents on?

She put the jeans back more or less as she had found them. Taking one last look around the room with a sigh and feeling none the wiser she left and closed the door behind her.

As she arrived back at the bottom of the stairs, she could hear Miss Harding was still crying. She didn't want to hang around much longer and badly wanted to avoid talking to Miss Harding again but she needed to ask one final question. She opened the living room door and stepped inside, positioning herself so that she was just inside the door, ready for a quick exit. Miss Harding and Meredith both looked up as she entered.

'Thank you, Miss Harding,' Rose said. 'I don't need to bother you any further. Meredith will look after you from here on in and will keep you appraised of the investigation as it progresses. Just two final things: do you have an address for Seamus' friend, John was it? And also, do you know if Seamus owned a laptop or a computer of any sort?'

Miss Harding blew her nose on another tissue – adding it to the small but growing pile on the arm of the sofa – before saying, 'Yes, John lives over in Fishermead. I've got his address in my phone, if you can hold on a moment.' She bent to pick up her handbag that was sitting on the floor next to her feet. Retrieving her phone, she tapped the screen a few times then proffered it to Rose. 'Here you go,' she said as Rose moved over to take the phone.

Rose juggled phone and notebook for a few seconds as she jotted down the address, then handed the phone back to Miss Harding. Realising she had moved further into the room she began to back off; she really couldn't stay with this grieving mother any longer.

'Right, Miss Harding, thank you. I'll be in touch through Meredith here if I need anything else. Be assured we are doing everything possible to catch whoever did this.'

Miss Harding nodded absently and dropped her head as Rose began to turn away. Then she looked back up as though she had just remembered something.

'No, he didn't,' she said flatly.

Rose turned back around. 'I'm sorry? No, he didn't what?' she asked.

'He didn't own a laptop,' Miss Harding replied, looking down as she screwed another tissue around in her hands.

'Ah right, yes,' Rose said, and gave the top of Miss Harding's head a tight-lipped smile and nodded once before turning and making quickly for the front door.

Chapter Three

Davey Maitland was what could only be described as looking every inch the builder: large with an impressive beer belly and hands the size of shovels. He paled and pulled his hands down the side of his face when Rose imparted the news that his employee had been killed.

'Jesus,' he said quietly, 'he was a good kid. Who would want him killed?'

'We don't know at this stage, Mr Maitland. What time did Seamus finish work yesterday?' Rose asked, straining her neck in order to look directly at Maitland's face.

'About four, four thirty. I let the lads go as soon as they've finished whatever needs to be done for that day.' He had started to regain some colour but his voice was still shaky.

'Was that a fairly regular thing? Seamus finishing early?' Rose asked.

'Yeah, fairly. He was a good worker, got through stuff pretty quickly,' Maitland replied, shaking his head. 'I can't get my head round it. Murdered?'

'Yes I know,' Rose said, putting some sympathy into her voice. 'These things are very hard to comprehend. Thanks for your time, Mr Maitland. Much appreciated.'

'Not at all, not at all,' Maitland said, shaking his head again.

Rose walked back to her car, feeling that at least now they had a time frame for when Seamus was murdered.

That's a start, she thought, as she pulled out and headed in the direction of the station.

***

David trudged to the entrance of a block of flats. This was the third block he had to visit since arriving to do the door to door enquiries with Anna. She was on the other side of the street and he realised now that she had suggested she take that side as it was predominately houses and only one block of flats.

He was about to push several of the buttons on the security panel, hoping one would answer and let him in, when his mobile began to ring. Pulling it out of his pocket he saw it was Rose calling. He took a breath, readying himself to receive his reprimand for being late, and answered.

'Getting anywhere?' Rose asked with no preamble.

'No ma'am. There's quite a few places with no one in, given the time of day. We've noted the addresses so we can come back later. Those that have answered the door so far didn't hear anything.'

'OK, well keep on it. I can't believe a gunshot went completely unnoticed,' Rose said.

'Yes will do ma'am, I'll call you if we get anything,' David replied, feeling a little relieved that he hadn't immediately had a strip torn off him as soon as he had answered. Maybe the DCI saw putting him on door to door as enough of a punishment.

'Good,' Rose said firmly. 'Christine should be joining you shortly, if she's not already there, and I'll be diverting uniform from the search when they're finished to help out as well. So, you should all be finished at some point this evening.'

David sighed quietly. I'll be lucky to get home for nine at this rate – that's another game I'll have missed, he thought but said, 'Right you are ma'am.'

'Oh, and David?' Rose said before he could hang up.
'Yes ma'am?'

'If you're late to a briefing again I'll string you up by your balls. Understood?'

'Yes ma'am,' David said with some relief. If DCI McPhail made even the slightest joke when she was unhappy with someone it usually meant the matter was officially dropped. Providing there were no further misdemeanours.

He hung up and turned his attention back to the flat's security panel.

***

Rose put her mobile down on the desk and smiled. David was a pain sometimes but generally a very good officer and it was unlike him to be late. But then she thought that anyone could be late for a multitude of reasons and that on this occasion she was happy to be lenient with him. Dismissing the thought, she turned her attention back to the memory stick in her hand.

'Right, let's see what dirty little secrets you hold, eh?' she said as she inserted the stick into the USB port in her computer.

It took a few seconds for the memory stick to show up on her screen and a few more seconds to load its contents. There were three folders on the stick: one labelled 'Seamus', one 'John' and the final one was simply labelled 'New folder'. Rose clicked on the folder labelled 'Seamus'. When the folder opened, she sat back and whistled.

'Well, well, Seamus, you sneaky little devil,' she whispered as she moved closer to the screen and began to scroll down the images in the folder.

Each one was clearly taken quickly on a mobile phone and all of them were upskirt shots of young women. All appeared to be in public places and on public transport.

Each one was essentially a pair of thighs in different positions: some where the subject had clearly bent over to pick something up and others where they were sitting on bus or train seats and perhaps a little off guard. In a lot of the shots Seamus had managed to capture a glimpse of underwear and in one or two no underwear at all.

'I bet you were proud of this one,' Rose said as she looked at one such shot. The subject was probably in her twenties by the way she was dressed in short skirt and top – a hot day likely, Rose surmised. She was bending over the boot of a car clearly putting shopping away; a gust of wind must have blown the back of her skirt up, with the picture showing her shapely legs and bare bottom.

There were over a hundred such images in the folder. Rose shook her head and moved to the folder marked 'John'. Again, there were well over a hundred images of girls and women. Some were similar types of upskirt images to the ones Seamus had taken but others were simply of the women walking along the street or sitting on a park bench. The only connecting factor was that they were all wearing short skirts. Rose supposed that these were probably test shots or failed attempts. Either way it was all in very poor taste, to say the least. She would have more to ask John about than simply the last time he had seen Seamus now.

The final folder had only three images in it but they were all worse in a way than the other folders. They were taken with a better camera, for a start, and from some distance away it seemed. All three images were of women in their early twenties, maybe late teens – the shots all taken through bedroom windows with the curtains open. Two were women in their underwear and the final one showed a young woman naked with a towel wrapped around her head. None of the subjects appeared to be aware of the camera.

'Filthy little buggers,' Rose said as she got up from her seat, grabbed her phone and walked into the main office. The photos did not reflect well on either Seamus or his friend John and if looked at in the context of Seamus' record could be considered very sinister. It was looking possible that Seamus and John were scoping out potential victims for sexual assault. But then it could just be that they got a cheap thrill from these pictures and had no plans to take things any further. Either way they needed to find out.

Gareth was the only one in the office. He looked up as she moved past him.

'DS Laing has just called in, ma'am,' he said, making her stop and turn. 'They've found the rest of the victim's clothes, they think – a t-shirt and a workman's hi-viz jacket, found about fifty yards from where the victim was found. He's taking them direct to the lab.'

'Good,' Rose said nodding. She turned to start walking away again and then stopped and turned back. 'Actually, can you get back hold of him and say to meet me at this address? Tell him to get one of the uniforms to drop the clothes at the lab.' She wrote down the address for John Denning on a jotter on Gareth's desk, then turned and walked briskly to the office door.

'Will do ma'am,' Gareth said to her, retreating back before picking up the phone.

'What's the score with this John Denning guy then?' Rod Laing asked as he manoeuvred himself into Rose's passenger seat. They were parked outside John Denning's address; Rod had arrived five minutes after Rose. She filled him on the memory stick and its contents.

'Hmmm, maybe there is something in the rapist tag after all?' Rod said quietly and thoughtfully.

'Could be,' Rose replied. 'We'll need to see what sex crimes have on both of them when we're back at the station. But let's get Mr Denning in first, eh?'

Rod nodded and got out the car.

'Think he'll be in?' he asked, as they made their way towards the door of the small terraced house.

'He's in,' Rose replied. 'I called when I was on my way, just to say that I needed to speak to him about Seamus. He has no idea we're about to ask him to accompany us to the station so be on your toes when we're in.'

'Right you are,' Rod said as he reached for the doorbell.

A man of around thirty answered the door. He was tall and overweight with thinning sandy-coloured hair. He was wearing a well-worn Arsenal top and a pair of grubby knee-length shorts. With at least two days stubble on his chin, he looked like he had just got out of bed.

'John Denning?' Rose said raising her ID. 'I'm Detective Chief Inspector Rose McPhail and this is Detective Sergeant Rod Laing.'

Denning looked from one to the other. 'This is about Seamus, right?' he asked in a voice that was higher than his frame suggested. 'His mum's just called me. It's awful. Just dreadful.' He shook his head but made no move to let Rose and Rod in when they stepped closer to the door.

'There are some questions we need you to answer for us,' Rose said, noting that Rod had moved so that he could catch the door should Denning decide to shut it on them. 'I need you to accompany us to the station to answer them.'

'What?' Denning said, looking shocked. 'But why?'

'You'll find out in due course,' Rod said as he pushed past Denning and into the house.

'Hey, you can't just barge in here,' Denning protested, trying to push Rod out. There was a good few stones of difference in weight between the two of them but Rod was easily the stronger of the two and held his ground.

'Now, now,' he said, 'you can either agree to come with us voluntarily or we can arrest you and take you out of here in cuffs. What would you prefer?'

'What the hell is all this?' Denning said angrily. 'Arrest me? What the fuck for? You're not trying to say I had something to do with Seamus, are you? That's just wrong and fucked up. He was my best friend.'

'Did you have anything to do with Seamus' death, Mr Denning?' Rose asked.

'No, of course bloody not,' Denning shouted.

'Right, then you've not got too much to worry about then,' Rose said, joining Rod and Denning in the now cramped hallway. 'There are some things we need to discuss and they need to be discussed at the station. So, grab your coat and keys and let's go, shall we?'

'Fuck sake, ok, ok, whatever,' Denning said, shaking his head and sighing.

'Good lad,' Rod said, patting him on the shoulder.

Denning shrugged the hand off and strode into his living room, with Rod following closely behind. Denning grabbed a denim jacket off the back of a chair and a set of keys from the coffee table in the middle of the messy room. Rod took the keys off of him before he could put them in his pocket. Denning scowled at him.

'We might want to have a look around later, so I'll keep these for now,' Rod said, his tone tolerating no argument.

Denning appeared to be about to complain and then gave up, just nodding and moving back out the room. They left the house and Rod made sure to lock up behind them.

'Anyone else live with you?' Rose asked, as she opened the rear door of her car for Denning to climb in.

'Nope,' he said sullenly.

'Good, good,' Rose said shutting the door and moving to get behind the wheel. They were about to pull out when her phone rang. It was the office.

'Ma'am it's Gareth,' Gareth said, sounding a little breathless. 'We've got another one.'

'What do you mean, another one?' Rose asked, taken aback. She had never heard Gareth sound anything other than calm before.

'Another body ma'am. With a note attached,' he said calming slightly.

'Jesus,' Rose said and closed her eyes, raising her face to the underside of the car roof.

Chapter Four

DC Louise Carney was feeling confident and happy as she made her way out of the mortuary. Not only had she managed to cajole the report from Dr Mathieson sooner than expected, she had now been assigned to interview John Denning in Rose's absence.

The pathologist's report had not really said much that they didn't already know, but at least the bullet had been retrieved. It had entered through the right of his torso just below the armpit, grazed a rib on its way through and finally come to rest, lodging in the victim's shoulder blade. It had punctured his left lung and nicked the aorta and the resultant internal bleeding had killed him. It hadn't been a particularly quick death but quick enough that the victim hadn't moved much after being shot. The bullet itself was low calibre, probably a .22, hence it hadn't penetrated the whole way through the body. It had been sent to ballistics to be certain of the calibre and to see if there was a match on the database of known weapons.

Dr Mathieson surmised that due to the placement and angle of the entry wound and track of the bullet that the victim had likely been standing with his arms raised – execution-style – with the killer standing slightly to one side. She raised the question of whether the ground was lower where the killer likely stood or whether it was level with the place the victim was found. The thinking being that if the ground was level then the killer was likely shorter than the victim, and if lower then the killer was either of a similar height or possibly taller. It wasn't a great deal to go on but Louise had related the question to Rose when she had called. Rose said she would have it checked.

Time of death had been put at anywhere from twenty-four to thirty hours from the time the body was found. Again, not hugely surprising and the information simply meant that the victim's timeline for the past thirty hours would have to be ascertained. And that had been all Louise could tell her boss. Rose had thanked her and then explained that she would have to take on the Denning interview. Louise had been pleased she had been chosen but immediately shocked that there was another potential victim.

Getting into her car she mentally rehearsed how the interview would go. She had, naturally, been in on tens of interviews in the past but she had always been accompanied by a senior officer, usually one of the sergeants. She only conducted interviews on her own for the more minor cases she worked solo – burglaries and the like. And now Rose had trusted her with this one. As a result, she was determined to get it right; it could be crucial to a major investigation, with murder still being relatively rare in Milton Keynes.

This could get her the attention she felt she was due. She knew she was a damn good copper and her work was always highly professional and accurate. She had a very high arrest and conviction rate and she believed that she got on well with the other members of the team. She felt strongly that at thirty-four she was overdue for a promotion to sergeant. It irked her a little that Rose seemed to think differently but there was little she could do about that for now. In the meantime, she would keep pushing to be noticed, if not by her immediate superior then by the Detective Chief Superintendent. One way or another she would get the promotion she was due.

She entered the station with a steely expression, ready to find out what dirty little secrets John Denning was holding and what light that would shed on the death of his friend. DS Laing was just exiting as she walked in.

'He's in interview room two,' he said, stopping to hold the door for her. 'Has Rose filled you in on what's going on and what we need from buggerlugs in there?' He nodded down the corridor towards the interview rooms.

'Yep,' she said, moving past him. 'I know what I'm doing Rod.'

'I know you do,' he said, not unkindly, and then moved off towards the exit and his car.

Louise walked the short way to interview room two, paused and took a breath at the door and then put her hand on the handle. She stopped short of opening the door; she hadn't yet seen the photos for herself and hadn't got any printouts; neither had she collected note paper and a file to put it all in. Chiding herself for nearly walking into an interview completely unprepared she turned and made her way to the office.

As soon as she walked in, Gareth was holding several photos out towards her on top of a brown folder. He didn't look best pleased.

'Want me to join you in there?' he asked, without any opening pleasantries.

'No, I'll be fine,' Louise replied airily. She opened her briefcase and pulled out a brown folder not unlike the one Gareth had just given her. 'PM report for logging.'

Gareth took it with a perfunctory nod. They had not got on from the day he had joined the team a few months back. Louise didn't really know why, although she suspected it was to do with him acting and thinking he was somehow her superior by dint of experience, even though they were the same rank and she had more years in serious crime.

'I don't mind sitting in with you, you know?' he said absently, pretending to be engrossed in the post mortem report.

'No, Gareth, I'm fine. And, besides, you have to get on with logging that. We need to be moving fast on this, especially now there's another one due on the slab.'

He harrumphed and turned his attention to his computer. Louise smirked slightly at the back of his head, turned and headed back for the interview room, flicking through the photos as she went.

***

Rod Laing pulled up as close as he could to the piece of open ground not far from Wolverton rail station. Going into his car boot he pulled out a white forensic suit and a pair of plastic overshoes. He would have to walk the rest of the way and was thanking his lucky stars that the rain had eased. He walked out on to the grassy parkland and looked about for the police cordon and forensic tents that should have been up by then. It didn't take long for him to find it. The cordon went around some low scrubby bushes and took in some of the open ground around them. The white tent was erected just behind the bushes from where Rod stood; it was clear that the area could be approached from any direction but would also be secluded from any of the others. He paused at the tape and pulled on the suit and overshoes.

He made his way round the cordon until he was the right side of the tent then ducked under, acknowledging one of the uniformed officers on its periphery as he did so. Rose was making her way out of the tent with a grim look on her face. His long stride covered the yards between them in short order.

'Is it another one?' he asked as soon as they were face to face.

She nodded and pursed her lips. 'Certainly looks like it,' she said with an exhalation of breath. 'This one looks to have been here longer than Seamus Harding. To my eye he's been here maybe a week – the doc's taking a look now. Whoever it is had done a real job on this one. It's pretty horrific.'

Rod looked at her with a twist to his mouth. 'It's not like you to use words like horrific. It must be pretty bad. What do you mean 'did a real job'?'

'Go look for yourself. I'll be in my car.' She moved past him and he watched her walk off in the same direction he had approached from.

Taking a deep breath Rod pulled a mask over his face and made his way into the tent. The body was almost impossible to see through the SOCO team and the pathologist crouching over it. All he could make out was a foot in a sock but no shoe and a hand lying straight out from the body. He made his way around and past the various white-suited figures such that he could peer over the shoulder of the SOCO photographer standing at the victim's feet.

Rose had not been wrong. The body had certainly been in the open for quite some time longer than that of Seamus Harding. The skin looked almost green and there were obvious animal bite marks in several places over the body. The lips were pulled back over the teeth in the horrible death grin he had seen many times before. The corpse appeared to be that of an older man. By Rod's estimation the victim was around sixty years old. But it was the state the body had been left in that caught Rod's breath.

The man was unclothed save for the one sock Rod had seen as he'd entered the tent. The man's genitals had been cut off and pinned to his chest by means of what looked like a knitting needle. Along with the genitals there was the note:

'Paedophile'

The large needle pierced right through the man's flabby chest. It had been pushed through then out again to pin the note and his genitals and then back through so that it emerged to the side of his chest. Rod drew in a whistling breath.

'Please tell me that happened post mortem,' he stated to no one in particular.

Dr Mathieson looked up from nearer the body's head. 'I wish I could,' she said flatly.

'Cause of death?' Rod asked, although he had already spotted the wound on the man's temple.

'Single shot to the head,' Mathieson said, pointing to the temple. 'I'm pretty sure the other injuries – which aside from the obvious also appear to include a broken arm – were very likely peri mortem. He would have died in agony and had he not been shot would have bled to death in a very short space of time.'

'So, he would have made plenty of noise and why shoot him if he was going to die anyway?' Rod asked, looking to the body's right arm. He had only seen the left arm – the one thrown out from the body – from his original vantage point. The right arm did indeed look broken; about halfway down the forearm twisted and sat at an angle away from the rest of the limb. It would have been excruciatingly painful at the time.

'I can only speculate on that,' Mathieson said. 'It's probable the killer didn't realise he would die soon enough, or shooting their victims is an integral part of their MO. That, my dear sergeant, is for you to figure out. I'll get on him first thing in the morning. PM report should be with you early afternoon.'

Rod nodded and moved away. He had seen enough. As he was about to leave the tent he turned and looked at the Dr again. 'Who found him?' he asked.

Mathieson shrugged. A SOCO who was standing nearby looked over. 'Two PCs were investigating a report of kids running amok on a motorbike – they came across him.'

Rod nodded his thanks.

'Oh, and sergeant?' Mathieson called out as he was about to leave the tent. He turned back towards her. 'Don't send someone round to chivvy me up this time. The report will be ready when it's ready.'

'Gotcha,' Rod said and left the tent with a smile she couldn't see through his mask.

***

Feeling fully prepared and ready for whatever John Denning decided to try, Louise pushed open the door to interview room two. She marched over to the chair on the door side of the desk, directly opposite Denning. She placed the manila folder down on the desk in front of Denning; it now contained the photos as well as a blank A4 notepad, making it look impressively full. She counted to five in her head, allowing Denning to properly take the folder in. He looked appropriately unnerved.

'Look, I've been in here ages. What the hell is going on?' Denning said before Louise could begin the interview.

'Do you know the phrase "helping the police with their enquiries"?' Louise asked flatly. Denning nodded. 'Well, that's what you're doing.'

'Right, so I'm not under arrest, then?'

'No, not at this time.' Louise deliberately kept her voice light and unthreatening.

Denning's eyes widened a little. 'Not at this…..?'

Louise interrupted him, 'Look, John, can I call you John?' Denning nodded and she continued, 'We have a number of things we need to clarify with you about Seamus. Depending on what answers you give will then determine what happens after that. OK?'

Again, Denning nodded mutely.

'Good. Right, one more thing, I'd like to record this interview if that's all right? It's easier than me trying to remember what you've said or keep up with my notes.' She gave him a tight-lipped smile.

His nod was more cautious this time.

'The camera up there records the whole time, mainly to assure fair play and to check that no rules have been broken, so it's there as much for your protection as it is for me to have a record of what's said. OK?' She tried her best to sound reassuring but wasn't sure she had managed it. She paused for a second or two before pulling the notepad out from the folder and a pen from her jacket pocket.

'Right,' she said in a decisive tone. 'Let's start with how you knew Seamus Harding.'

'I've known him for years,' he answered in a quiet voice. 'We knew each other at school but weren't really mates then. Then we met up again after school – we both worked in the Amazon warehouse for a bit – and we got talking about gaming. Turned out we both loved the same games so started hanging out playing them.'

'OK, but you don't work with John now?'

'No, he got qualified as a roofer and went to work for that building firm up the road.'

'And you?' Louise knew one way to get people talking was to ask the easy questions for as long as possible until they relaxed into giving the trivial minutiae of life. Then you hit them with the sucker punch.

'I'm still at Amazon. Just never got round to leaving.'

'You and Seamus were gamers? What games did you play?' She had to make a conscious effort not to stress the word 'games'. Easy girl, she thought, don't get him on edge yet, let him talk.

'Call of Duty we play a lot. We started on that and worked our way up through all the variations and consoles. We still play that loads, Black Ops, you know?'

Louise didn't but nodded anyway. She had vaguely heard of it but was no gamer herself. She just couldn't see the point in them.

'Any others?' she asked, seeing Denning warm to his subject.

'GTA was always a favourite. And Seamus especially liked to play FIFA. I wasn't so good at that but it was good when we played as a team and as Arsenal, of course.'

She really didn't know what GTA was but had heard of the FIFA football game. Her ex-boyfriend used to play it a lot. She picked up on the Arsenal tag; Rose had said Seamus' room was all Arsenal.

'You and Seamus both supported Arsenal?'

'Yeah, it was something else we found we had in common after we left school. He was a mad gooner – I'm more of a casual fan, if you get my drift?'

'Yeah sure.' She felt it was time the questions became a little more to the point. 'When did you last see Seamus?'

He paused for moment. She supposed he was trying to remember.

'Do you mean actually saw him?' he asked eventually.

She was about to ask what he meant and then realised that as gamers they didn't need to be in the same country, never mind the same room these days, to play their games.

'Yes, actually saw him.'

'That would be Tuesday last week. We met at The Rattler pub and then went back to my place for a few more drinks and a blast on Grand Theft Auto.'

Ah, GTA! You really have to catch up on this shit. She considered what to ask next and then realised the question was obvious.

'And when did you last hear from him?'

'That would be Monday of this week,' he said, drawing the 'Monday' out to show he was having to think about when it was exactly. Monday was three days ago.

'You haven't heard from him since Monday – was that unusual?'

'Well, maybe a bit. I mean we didn't always speak to each other all the time, you know?'

'A lot of the time though?'

'Yeah a lot, but...' Denning shrugged.

'OK,' Louise said, letting her voice harden just a little bit, 'what else did you two get up to together?'

Denning looked slightly shifty but didn't give much away in his body language. 'Not a lot really. You know? Just hung out.'

Louise sat back in her chair and eyed Denning for a moment, then sat forward and leant her elbows on the table.

'So, you didn't go around finding young women and try to take compromising images of them?' She had decided it was time to go in for the kill. Denning flushed ever so slightly. Gotcha!

'What? No. What do you mean?' He stammered slightly when he spoke.

'Images like these,' Louise said as she started pulling out the printouts of the photos found on Seamus' memory stick. She held back the more compromising and damning ones of the women taken through their bedroom and bathroom windows.

Denning shifted in his seat as she placed the images on the desk. He looked at them sideways, refusing to look at them directly.

'No, we never done anything like that,' he said, looking away from her.

'Really? That's interesting. You see these were found on a memory stick in Seamus' bedroom. There are three folders on there – one called Seamus, one called John and one unnamed. These ones,' she said, indicating the photos she had already put down, 'these are from Seamus' folder.'

'Well, there you are then they're his, he must have took them,' he interrupted, his voice rising slightly.

'Well, that is our assumption too but what about these ones?' She produced some more images. 'These are from the folder named John. Why would Seamus have a folder named John if they aren't images that you have taken?'

Denning was no master criminal; he had no record for anything that Louise could find, and he wasn't the sharpest knife in the drawer. She watched him visibly and mentally collapse as he realised he would not be able to lie his way out of this.

'OK, OK,' he said, shaking his head, 'so we enjoyed taking a few sneaky shots of women? So what? It was nothing, just a bit of fun. A bit of upskirt action never hurt anyone. You can't see who they are and we never posted them online or nothing.'

Louise could feel her temper rise – he dismissed this violation of someone's privacy far too lightly for her liking. She allowed herself a count of ten to calm down then sat back again in her seat. Then she reached into the folder and produced the more damning images.

'And what about these ones? They don't look like they've been taken by a phone, unless you have a bloody good one, and these are not just casual shots of women's knickers, are they? What was the purpose of these photos?'

'They were all Seamus,' Denning said quickly. 'I never took any like that.'

'But he showed them to you, didn't he? You're not particularly surprised to see them, are you?'

'Yeah, he showed them to me,' Denning said, lowering his head and running a hand through his hair.

'Was there ever talk of the two of you taking this a bit further? Maybe cornering one of these women and sexually assaulting them? Anything like that get discussed?'

Denning's head snapped up. 'No!' he almost shouted the word. 'No, we never talked about anything like that. I wouldn't, I mean, I couldn't do –' he waved a hand over the photos – 'that kind of thing.'

She believed him; he had been too outraged at the thought. But she got the feeling he was hiding something, maybe something about Seamus that they didn't know about.

48

'John,' she said, moving her head so she was making eye contact, 'did Seamus say he was going to do something? Maybe on his own?'

'I dunno,' Denning said, shaking his head, then drew in a deep breath. 'He told me once that he sometimes followed women, stalked them kind of thing. But he never said he did anything to them. Maybe these girls are the ones he used to follow.'

'Did anyone else know about this?' Louise asked slowly.

'Not that I know of, no,' Denning replied. 'I can't tell you any more than that. Honest, I don't know any more than that. Is this why someone shot him? Did some woman's husband find out or something?'

My thoughts exactly, Louise thought but said, 'That's what we're trying to find out. Thank you for your time Mr Denning. We'll be in touch if there's anything else.' With that she rose from her seat.

'You mean I can go?' Denning asked, looking relieved.

'For now. The officer at the desk will let you out,' Louise said and left the interview room.

Chapter Five

Rose had told Rod to go home. It was getting late and she had already told those doing door to door to call it a day. They had garnered nothing – no one in the area appeared to have seen or heard anything. The search of the woods was being wound down for the day. They would continue to scour the area metre by metre tomorrow but so far the only find had been Seamus Harding's clothes. Louise had reported in that John Denning had admitted to some of the photos but said the worst ones were not his doing. She had speculated that these images, and Denning's belief that Seamus had been stalking those women, could perhaps be related to his killing. Rose had agreed to the possibility. The PM report raised questions but yielded little by way of answers.

And now they had a second body, with the victim killed in a similar fashion but much more brutally and with the same type of label pinned to their chest. They had no ID and it was getting too dark for a search. It was best that it was also called off and resumed in daylight.

Everyone was shattered and the investigation would be best served if they got some rest and recuperation ready for the next day.

After the flurry of calls she decided to take her own advice, despite her near overwhelming desire to return to the office and go through the meagre evidence they had all over again, especially the transcript of Louise's interview with John Denning. But she too was exhausted and knew when to call it a day. She turned the ignition and steered the car for home.

Home was a nice four-bed detached house in the village of Aspley Guise, a quiet little place thirty to forty minutes' drive away from the murder site. She took the time to think. Driving always calmed her, even in heavy traffic. She selected an AC/DC CD from the glove box and pushed it into the player. She found the relentless and raucous rock music helped her clear her mind and let thoughts drift in and out of her consciousness. Those fleeting and ethereal thoughts often threw up new ideas and angles she might take with a case.

She never played any of the CDs she had tucked away in her glove box when any of the team were in the car with her. She knew they were incongruous to the image she portrayed and the rank she held. She had no problem with admitting she loved her rock and heavy metal but knew the others probably didn't share her passion. Her day-to-day appearance was one of a suited, smart professional, but inside she was still the rocker she had been in her youth – all long back-combed hair and leather jackets, hanging out with bikers and fellow metal heads in the bars that played non-stop rock music. Her tastes didn't go much past the late nineties, aside from those bands that had survived the crazy, heady days of the seventies and eighties. She still kept her hair long but these days it was neat and invariably tied up, hiding the few grey hairs that betrayed her age.

The music kept her young at heart if not in reality. At forty-eight she knew that time had caught her up and that she found herself tired and sometimes emotionally drained by her work. But a good blast of Metallica, Iron Maiden or – as was the case now – AC/DC brought out the teenager in her and she would find herself regaining the energy and enthusiasm of that era in her life.

She nodded her head along to '*Hells Bells*' and allowed her thoughts to clear. Traffic was relatively light at that time of night and the easy driving aided her thinking process. The image of the unknown 'paedophile' drifted across her mind. It had been a horrible death, if – as the pathologist believed – he had been mutilated and 'labelled' prior to his death, only to finally be shot through the head. At least it had been quick at the end, she thought. They had no idea who the man was and as such had no clue as to whether he actually was a paedophile or not. That was a question for the next day; sex crimes would have to be quizzed yet again.

She had already realised that they were dealing with some form of vigilante killer; the pattern was obvious even with only two killings. But right now there was nothing to tell them how the victims had been selected or how the killer knew or believed they were what they had been labelled as. Is there a connection between the two victims? Again, this was a question for the following day. They had to identify victim two before they could investigate that possibility. Then she realised she would have to think of victim two as actually being victim one. He had been found second but had been killed first. There were too many unknowns at the moment, for her liking.

Then there were the two sites. They were not that far apart and both were secluded and under-used areas. The killer was probably local or at least knew the area well, maybe having grown up there but now living elsewhere? Rose thought it likely that they were local rather than traveling into the area but decided to keep an open mind at this stage.

Be honest with yourself, Rose, you know jack shit at the moment and with two bodies now in the mix you are going to have to come up with some answers pretty fast or the Superintendent will be on your case.

She realised she was home when she pulled into the drive of her house; she had driven most of the way on autopilot. She found that happened a lot these days and chided herself for not taking more care and concentrating on the road rather than on whatever case she was working on.

She walked through the front door and called out that she was home. Samantha, her eldest daughter, appeared from the kitchen door at the end of the hall, smiling at her mother.

'Dad's been called out. Big pile up on the M1 apparently. So, I've made you dinner,' she said, her smile broadening.

'Oh, bless you Sam,' Rose said, giving her daughter a hug.

At sixteen, Sam took responsibility for the household whenever both her parents were out, which could be frequently given Rose's position and her father's job as a trauma consultant at Milton Keynes General Hospital. She was a tall girl, which always surprised Rose who was only five feet three and her husband, no more than five eight. Their parents had not been tall either. She often wondered where Samantha got it from.

'Where are the other two?' she asked, taking her jacket off and hanging it over the banister. It would stay there until she could summon the energy to go upstairs and change, which usually meant when she was heading for bed.

'Kelly's in her cave,' Samantha said, raising her eyebrows.

Kelly was thirteen and an Emo. Rose didn't know exactly what that was but recognised the black goth clothing and black makeup from the goths that had haunted the clubs and pubs she had frequented when she was young. Kelly would spend hours hidden away in her room listening to music that Rose would describe as introspective if she was feeling kind and depressing if she wasn't.

'And Michael's in the living room watching Harry Potter, of course.' Samantha gave another role of her eyes.

Rose smiled at her daughter. It was a running joke that Michael could recite every word of every Harry Potter movie. He was ten and like many ten-year-olds he obsessed on certain things – in his case, Harry Potter and rugby. He was built like his father – on the short side but stocky and, for his age, muscular. He had started rugby at school and if he wasn't engrossed in a film would talk incessantly about rugby. Fortunately, his father Gordon was also a rugby enthusiast and had played to a relatively high level as a young man, representing his university and then playing for a local club.

She went through to the living room and ruffled Michael's hair.

'Bedtime soon, young man. School tomorrow,' she told him.

'Aw, Mum, can I at least watch the end of the movie? It's only got half an hour to go.' Michael always challenged bedtime but rarely put up much of a fight when she eventually put her foot down.

'OK, half hour, no more. If it's not finished by then it's bed regardless.'

He nodded absently and returned his attention back to the screen. Rose was proud of her children; they were all doing well in school and in general very well behaved. She rarely had trouble from any of them with the exception of the odd spat between Samantha and Kelly.

She ate her dinner in the dining room with Samantha sitting with her at the table. They chatted a little about her schooling and Rose allowed all the sixteen-year-old gossip to pass over her head. She really couldn't keep up with who was going out with whom and which set of 'best friends' had since fallen out. After dinner, it was time to get Michael to bed and then she sat with the TV on but not watching it and tried to relax with a glass of wine.

The case kept rolling round in her head but she came up with no new answers. She tried to put it out of her mind but failed. She knew she tended to obsess on her work often to the detriment of her family which she always regretted. She felt she was as good a mother as she could be but that wasn't actually much of a mother at all, especially when a big case was on her mind. She tried to comfort herself that she had great kids that were well adjusted and used to the rigours of their parents' jobs. They had grown up with them not being around much and being preoccupied when they were.

When Gordon hadn't arrived home at midnight and the bottle of wine was finished, she gave up and wearily climbed the stairs to bed. Her jacket stayed where it was.

Chapter Six

'Right, we now have two victims. There's no doubt that the murder of Seamus Harding and this unknown individual have been committed by the same person. The second victim was actually killed before Seamus, early suggestion is anything up to a week ago, so from now on he is victim one and Seamus victim two. As you can see, he was badly mutilated and again the early suggestion is that this happened prior to his death. Now, the clear priority is to find out who this man was and if he indeed has a record for any child sex offences. We also have to keep on it with the Seamus Harding murder and follow up all and any leads, no matter how tenuous. Rod and Christine, I want you to have another go at John Denning to see if there's anything else he can tell us or something we've missed.'

Rose saw Louise bristle at the suggestion that she may have missed something but was not inclined to placate her at this time. Louise was good but it was easy to miss a hint or separate line of questioning when interviewing a subject. Even the most experienced officers could do it. She moved her gaze away from Louise and directed it at Anna.

'Anna, you liaise with the child protection unit, see if they know who victim one is. David, I want you trawling the database to see what you can find, either on victim one or if there have been any complaints about stalking, voyeurism or similar in recent weeks – we think Seamus may have been actively following the women he photographed.'

'Louise, you'll be with me. We're going to check both areas for CCTV and see what footage we can pull together. Let's see if we can't spot our victims and maybe anyone they're with. The rest of you, back on door to door in the vicinity of the Harding murder. Gareth, office liaison again please.'

Gareth raised his eyebrows then scowled. I'm going to have to let him out sometime soon, Rose thought.

'Oh, and Rod?' she said, as a thought struck her. 'Get the names of the pubs Denning and Harding frequented, and check them out. See who knows them and what they know about them.'

'Hah, with pleasure,' Rod said with a chuckle. Rose gave him a half-cocked smile and shook her head.

'Do you want us to bring Denning back in ma'am or keep him at home this time?' Rod asked to offset Rose's lack of humour at his pub joke.

'His place. I want him at ease this time, not sweating on what we know. Right, you all know what to do so get on with it.'

Louise approached Rose who was readying to leave. 'Just a tick, Louise,' Rose said and moved over to Gareth's desk.

'Actually, Gareth. While you're wating for anything new to come in you could check with all the local stations and other nearby forces, you know, Bedfordshire and maybe out to Hertfordshire up to Oxford. See if any of them have had minor run-ins with Seamus, same sort of stuff we know he got up to here. I just want to try and get a picture of how far out we need to be looking for any potential husbands and boyfriends with a grudge that might just be our killer.'

'Right you are, ma'am,' Gareth replied, looking happier.

'Thanks,' Rose said then turned to Louise. 'OK, Louise, let's go.'

There was a general movement for the door, aside from Gareth, Anna and David who were already picking up

57

their phones. Rose, as was her habit, waited until the rest were out the door before leaving herself, Louise in tow.

Louise offered to drive but Rose insisted. As she turned the ignition Metallica's 'For Whom the Bell Tolls' blared out the speakers in the car. Rose cursed herself for forgetting to turn the stereo off or switch it to the radio – and turn it down – before leaving the car that morning. Louise flinched and raised her eyebrow at Rose.

'Bit of a passion of mine,' Rose mumbled, turning the stereo off.

Louise chuckled, 'Didn't have you down as a headbanger, ma'am.'

'I was in my younger days,' Rose said, pulling the car out of the station carpark, the look on her face telling Louise that that would be the end of subject.

After five minutes of driving, Louise turned to Rose. 'I didn't miss anything with John Denning. I got enough for him to have got a caution at the very least and I found as much as he knew about Seamus Harding.'

'I know you probably have,' Rose said, glancing over. 'But sometimes it pays to double up on these things. Bear that in mind when you're in charge of an investigation – double-check as much as possible.'

'It came across to the others like you didn't trust my work or judgement,' Louise said, failing to keep some of the anger from her voice.

'Look, Louise. You're a good detective but you still have a lot to learn. I know you think you should be sergeant already and that you're a lot better than some if not most of the rest of team, which, by the way, I think you probably are. But you have to grow a thicker skin. You've got to learn to lead and part of that is ignoring perceived slights.' Rose gave her another glance and then turned her attention back to the road.

Rose kept quiet but Louise didn't say anymore. She gave it five minutes before she spoke again. 'Keep at it, learn as much as you can now. You'll get there, trust me.'

Glancing over she caught Louise nodding and saw her visibly relax. Pep talk over, she thought but didn't say.

Rose pulled the car up in the same spot as she had two evenings before to see the site where Seamus Harding had been murdered. Unbuckling her seat belt, she said, 'This is going to be a lot of walking and driving around. There's no point looking in the park or the woods, we know there's no cameras there. We need to work in concentric circles out from here and see if there are any cameras on the streets and buildings round about the site. Maybe we'll get lucky.'

She looked over to the woods and thought she could just make out a couple of uniformed officers pacing carefully through the trees, eyes down, scanning for anything that might be important. *Please, please come up with something*, she thought and turned away.

They walked and drove around for the best part of the day. Their efforts afforded meagre fruit. Most of the streets around both sites were residential with only a few cameras pointing at driveways. North Loughton Park, where Seamus had been found, was also bordered by two of Milton Keynes' much praised through roads – the A5 to the west and A509 Portway to the south. They would yield nothing but a stream of cars caught on traffic cameras. They found a couple of pubs near the Wolverton site where victim one was found that might yield something, but Rose didn't hold out much hope. By late afternoon they had covered all the ground around and between the two sites.

It was as they were climbing wearily into the car not far from the Wolverton site that Rose spotted a familiar figure walking towards her. Medium height and medium build, he walked with a slightly exaggerated swagger. She closed her eyes and shook her head, whispering, 'Oh Jesus, that's the last thing I need.'

Scott Ellis approached the car with a wide smile on his face. He was a local journalist who also occasionally managed to get pieces in national papers and online news sites. He was probably of an age with Rose but looked older by quite some way. As an individual Rose quite liked him – he could be funny and charming when he wanted to be. As a professional she loathed him. He was tenacious to the point of annoyance and if he got a whiff of a story he wouldn't hesitate to publish, even if expressly forbidden. He was like a terrier with a bone, when he had a story on the go. He just would not give up on it. Rose knew that the fact he had tracked her down so close to a murder scene meant he had, somehow, got wind of the killings. She swore inwardly and threatened all sorts of bloody murder on whoever had leaked it to him.

'Rose,' he greeted her and nodded to Louise, 'and the lovely Louise. Fancy bumping into you here.'

'Yes, fancy that, Scott,' Rose answered, face and voice deadpan. 'What are you doing around here?'

'Oh, you know,' Scott's voice was all light and airy, juxtaposing Rose's cold greeting, 'just taking a wander around your murder site, wondering why you hadn't been in touch about a double murder that's happened here on our doorstep.'

'Who told you that? Right now, I have nothing I can tell you.' Rose's voice remained ice cold.

'So, there have been two murders? Thanks for the confirmation. C'mon Rose, just a little quote. Something about reassuring the public? You have things in complete control? That kind of thing.'

'Look Scott, I don't want this getting out just yet. We're at very early days and right now I don't need my phone lines jammed with crackpots and busy bodies thinking they've seen the killer dressed as Jack the Ripper marauding about Oldbrook. I'll bring you in as and when we get to the public appeal stage but, please, do me a favour and keep a lid on it for now, eh?' Rose folded her arms when she had finished and looked the journalist in the eye. He promptly shifted his gaze away from hers.

He pretended to think about it, studying his shoes. 'I'll tell you what Rose,' he said eventually. 'I'll hold off for a couple of days, maybe three, but –' he held up one finger – 'I want to stop by the station tomorrow and for you to fill me in on what you have so far. You know, so I have the background stuff ready for when I do go to print. And you know damn fine I will at my earliest opportunity – people have a right to know.'

'Ok, anything to keep you out of my hair for a few days. I'll fill you in, but, and it's a big but –' now it was Rose's turn to hold up a finger – 'you are not to publish anything until I say so, understood?'

Scott held up three fingers and saluted, 'Scouts honour', then turned on his heel and walked away.

Louise looked at her boss and seeing the ire on her face decided it was best to say nothing. Instead, she took the safe option and climbed into the car, slipped her seatbelt on and sat looking straight ahead. After a minute or so Rose joined her in the car, slamming the door shut behind her.

'If I find the bastard that talked to him, I'll string them up by whatever bit is most painful for them,' Rose growled, then gave Louise an accusing stare.

'Don't look at me,' Louise protested. 'I barely know the man.'

Rose visibly calmed. She shook her head, 'He would have found out soon enough anyway.'

Chapter Seven

Back at the station, Rose sat in her office, her feet feeling swollen and aching, legs likewise and her head throbbing. Her day's work had yielded the grand total of zero results. Fortunately, the team had faired a little better. They now had a name for victim one, Evžen Souček, a Czech national who had lived in the area for over ten years. He had been reported as missing by his wife eight days ago. He had been caught up in a scandal surrounding a private school where he had taught maths and physics. A number of teachers had been accused by an ex-student of abusing pupils. Souček had been named as one of the teachers who were not involved directly but had turned a blind eye to the abuse. He had been brought in for questioning and released without charge. There was no direct evidence he had been involved but some of his answers led investigating officers to place him on their watch list.

Rose considered this. There was one dead man labelled a rapist who wasn't really a rapist and another labelled a paedophile who wasn't really a paedophile. It was possible the killer knew something about these men that the police did not. Or, and this worried her, the killer had access to the dead men's files and had extrapolated their crimes from minor incidents into horrendous ones. If that was the case then the investigation would have to start looking internally as well as externally. Rose did not like the idea of another copper being involved.

There was no discernible link between the two victims other than that they had been shot and had a label pinned to their chest. Souček lived on the other side of town to Harding and they were very different people. Souček was middle-aged – he would have been fifty-three the following month – while Harding was in his twenties. Souček was married and had two children. Harding was single and lived with his mother. No other possible links had been found as yet.

Gareth had done sterling work checking in with their neighbouring forces and their colleagues from Thames Valley Police stations in the surrounding towns. He hadn't garnered much except that Harding had been cautioned at Bedford police station for apparently following a young girl around the town centre. He had denied it, saying he had just been browsing the shops and it was coincidence that they had both been moving in the same circuit. With no way to prove otherwise, Bedfordshire Police had taken the same course as Thames Valley – cautioned him and sent him on his way. Again, maybe not useful right now but one that may prove so in the future. Gareth was waiting for information from the other forces on Souček.

Rose thought about this further. Why label Seamus Harding a rapist? He was a bit of a pervert and something of a nuisance but a rapist? No, she couldn't see it. And Souček? He was only on the watch list; there was no evidence he was a paedophile. So why such a violent and horrendous attack? Did the killer have information on both these men that they didn't have? Was the murderer the link between these two seemingly unconnected men? Rose's head thumped with the constant bombardment of questions she couldn't answer.

There was a sudden eruption of raised voices coming from the main office. Rose's head gave another throb of pain. She couldn't make out what was being said but she would not tolerate rows between members of her team, so with gritted teeth she stood up and marched into the main office.

Gareth, Louise and David were on their feet. David looked calm but Louise and Gareth's faces looked like thunder. Rose caught the gist of the row as she entered the office.

'...wouldn't have happened if you had let me come in with you,' Gareth was saying through gritted teeth.

'C'mon Gareth, that's not fair, the boss...' David was saying calmly and quietly.

'Oh, Mr I-know-how-it's-done!' Louise ignored him and continued to shout straight into Gareth's face. 'If you're so fucking brilliant how come you're still only a DC? All those years of so-called experience and no promotion? Yeah right.'

'Enough!' Rose shouted over the noise. 'What the hell is going on here?'

The room fell silent. Gareth's face was still red with anger while Louise looked at the floor, clamping and unclamping her jaw. David, who seemed to have been trying to be peacemaker, gave a half-smile and raised his hands in a 'Christ if I know' gesture.

'You two, my office,' Rose said stiffly, pointing to Gareth and Louise.

This was not the first row between these two but Rose was determined it would be the last. She turned on her heel and stomped back to her office, not looking to see if they were following. Sitting down at her desk she glowered at the two of them as they entered. She kept up her angry stare for nearly a minute, saying nothing. The two officers soon became discomforted and both looked at their feet.

'I am not going to sit here and listen to who said what or why it was their fault,' she said at last, her voice quiet but full of authority. 'What I want to hear is sorry ma'am, it won't happen again ma'am, do you understand?'

Gareth gave a barely perceptible nod.

'He continually tries to undermine me. And he…' Louise stopped talking as soon as Rose raised her hand and glared at her.

'Are you deaf Detective Constable? Or just plain stupid?' Rose said, her voice rising slightly. She had no intention of playing arbiter in this stupid spat.

'No ma'am,' Louise replied quietly, going red in the face.

'Right, then you understood what I said, then?' Rose said, voice still raised and with a face that would have no truck with any backchat.

'Yes, ma'am,' Louise responded, her voice even quieter than before.

'Good.' Rose calmed herself and her voice dropped to its more normal level. 'If I hear you two bickering again, there will be a disciplinary waiting for both of you. Understood?'

Neither officer replied. 'Understood?' Rose said loudly and with real steel in her voice.

'Yes, ma'am,' both replied together.

'Now get out there and do your bloody jobs.'

The two officers turned in unison; Gareth gestured Louise through the door first and then crept out behind her.

'And shut the bloody door,' Rose shouted at his retreating back.

He turned and meekly closed the door behind him.

Chapter Eight

Dion Myers walked confidently to his car. The car park was near deserted and it was quite the walk to where he had parked. Car parks in central Milton Keynes were plentiful and large which meant there was always a good chance of finding a space but also often then entailed a long walk back. Dion didn't mind – he always felt the stroll back to his car let him reflect on his day's work. And Dion was often very satisfied with what he achieved each day.

He ran a small firm that sold ownership of plots on green belt land. The customer typically bought from one to fifty square metres. The investment was sold on the premise that the plot would skyrocket in value when developers eventually turned their greedy eyes on the land. Customers paid around £250 for each square metre – more if his guys did their jobs right. Dion loved counting up the money they had made at the end of a busy day or, more importantly, the money his team had made for him.

The company's offering in itself wasn't illegal; there were plenty of others that offered much the same thing. The illegal nature of Dion's business was that they didn't own any of the land they sold. They simply used Google maps to source likely-looking pieces of land and then, using their high-res' printer, printed valid-looking certificates for each 'plot'. The point was a customer could wait years for their investment to mature, if it ever did, and Dion's salesmen made sure the customer knew that. He worked on the premise that by the time any of his clients realised that their lovely certificate of ownership was worth less than the paper it was printed on he and his company would be long gone. In fact, he was already thinking of winding things down. They had been trading for over a year and that was about as long as he liked to keep any of his ventures going.

He never allowed himself to recognise that what he was doing was illegal. He just saw it as entrepreneurial in spirit if not in practice. He had owned and operated several similar businesses in the past and felt pride in them all. He had made a considerable amount from people's gullibility and his sales ability. And there was always a long line of hungry young men, eager to learn the art of selling and make a killing along the way.

The part of the car park he was walking through was quite dark; the street lights were on but only along the edges and the central dividing paths. Dion liked to walk in the near darkness; it was like a shroud to him, letting him reflect without distraction. He always walked right in the middle of the parking bays so that he was in the darkest part possible.

He heard a car start up somewhere behind him but it sounded some way off and over to his left so he paid it no mind. He thought it a little odd that having walked for a further five or so yards he still hadn't seen any headlights. Nothing had passed him and there was no sign of any lights directly behind. He looked around but could see no sign of the car and yet he could still hear an engine quietly ticking over.

Suddenly he was blinded by the brilliant white light of halogen headlights on full beam. The car had been in front of him not behind. He only had time to register that it was a black car before the engine was gunned and he smashed into the bonnet with a sickening thud. He rolled off the bonnet and smacked onto the concrete. A searing pain streaked up his leg. He couldn't feel his right arm – he had landed on his elbow when he had fallen. He wondered if that was broken too.

Laid out on the ground, he heard the car door open and close above the sound of his own groaning. Someone – he couldn't see through the glare of headlights – approached. He expected an immediate apology and offer of help; instead, he received a swift and violent kick to the stomach. He bent double, foetal-like, gasping for air. Feeling sick he tried to roll over onto his back but received another kick to the stomach for his troubles.

He lay, blinded by the lights, groaning and moaning when he felt hands gripping under his armpits. He was roughly turned onto his back and dragged to the rear of the car. He tried to look over his shoulder at the person dragging him but with his night vision shot by the headlights and the tears of pain stinging his eyes he could only make out a blurry, shadowed figure.

The rear door of the car was opened and he was unceremoniously hauled and dumped inside. Another roaring pain ran up his leg as it hit the edge of the seat and he passed out.

The next thing he knew was a jolt and more pain as the car came to halt. His mouth was dry and sticky, pain from his broken leg – and he was sure now it was broken – screamed back into life. He groaned and tried to speak. He wanted to know what the driver thought they were doing and also to make sure they knew he was alive. He had begun to form the opinion this was some sort of crazy hit-and-run driver intent on dumping his body on some waste ground to avoid being caught.

The driver climbed out of the car ignoring his rasping attempts to speak. The rear door was opened and he screamed as he was pulled out by his feet. He passed out again.

He came to with no idea how long he had been unconscious. It was almost pitch black and the ground smelt musty and damp. It reminded him of woodlands – that smell of rotting vegetation, bark and mud. Then his vision cleared and he saw he was close to a large bush and could just make out several trees. Woodland it was then.

He mustered all his strength to try and speak. When he managed to get some words out his voice rasped in his ears.

'Look,' he stammered, 'I don't know what you think you're doing but there's no need for this. I've got quite a lot of cash on me you can have it and I won't say any more about it. I need an ambulance, please, just drop me near a main road and I'll say that I didn't see who hit me, which I haven't, so, please let's just sort this out?' He felt exhausted after gasping out each word. *This is probably the hardest and most important sales pitch you have ever made, Dion, old boy,* he thought. But there was no reply, nothing to work with.

After a minute or so of silence, save the wind rustling the leaves of the bush and trees, he heard quiet and careful footsteps coming towards him. He couldn't quite make out which direction they were coming from until they stopped somewhere near his left arm. He could feel rather than see them. The pain in his leg and right arm were dulled by a surge of adrenalin. His heart thumped in his chest and his breathing grew shallower and more rapid.

His attacker – he could think of no other word to describe them – started to pull at his suit jacket. So, they are going for the money then. He was confused when they started to haul the jacket around and behind his shoulders and then pulled it down and off his right arm. Maybe they don't want to rummage for my wallet. His confusion rose when his assailant bent over and ripped his shirt open. With a swift and painful tug, they ripped the shirt from his back. The earth was cold against his skin and he began to shiver, but more from fear than the cold.

He still hadn't really seen the person who was doing this; the woods were darker than the car park and they appeared to be wearing black and possibly a balaclava. They moved away from him for a moment or two and then approached him again, this time from the right. They bent over his chest and he could make out what looked like an A4 piece of paper in their hands.

He screamed as they pinched the skin on his chest and drove a large safety pin through skin and muscle. The person then messed around with the paper and then he screamed again when the sharp pin was driven back into and then out of his chest. They clamped the pin shut and moved away again. He tried to look down at his chest to see what had been pinned there but he couldn't strain his neck far enough.

The person approached again and shoved their hands back under his armpits. He was dragged, screaming and cursing and sobbing to a nearby tree where he was propped up, his back to the rough bark. He gulped wracking, heaving breaths into his lungs and yet still felt he was not getting enough oxygen.

'Look, just tell me what you want,' he sobbed, but his attacker stayed silent. 'Please, I won't say anything about this, I promise. Just let me go. Take whatever you want and let me go, please.' His last word came out long, jarring and shrill.

The last thing he heard was a sharp thwack.
Then blackness.

'Cor! What a scorcher!'

'It's funny 'ow these things come about, ain't it? I mean, me and yer mum, we were tight as hell for years and years. It was only as you two got a bit older that things started to go a bit outta sorts, sort of fing. Like we still loved each other, 'an that, but somehow we'd never been further apart. I started to think it was, like the familiarity, kinda like we'd got so used to each uver that it just di'n't work properly no more. Maybe that was what also got me to finking about the other stuff, y'know?

Anyways, you kids were still little nippers when we hit on what was a brilliant idea. See, 'er mum lived down in Devon by then, she'd moved like ten years before, and we always went down to visit for our holidays. Fing was, when you lot started getting older it was bloody obvious all she wanted to do was see you kids, she di'n't give a shit about seeing me an' yer mum. Then one year yer mum hit on a fucking corker of an idea. She said, "Why don't we send the kids to me mum's and we go somewhere proper for a couple of weeks? Kids are old enough to go and stay on their own wiv 'er, now."

And I thought, fuck it, why not? Y'know? Might rekindle the old 'orse 'n' carriage. So, that's what we done that first year. Di'n't turn out too bad really, all fings considered. But it di'n't really do much for the two us in terms of the relationship, if you get me meaning? We both just realised the old spark was gone for us. Not to mention we both missed you two. So, that was that for a bit. Back to trampin' dahn to fucking Devon to see the mother-in-law.

But the idea stuck. A holiday without the kids. Give us both a break, sort of fing. Thing was I had got into me fishin' good and proper by then. Me and me old mate Charlie used to go for a day here and there before. But never very regular or nuffin'. But one day we went, lovely day it was, now, where was it? Was it that syndicate pond up near Harlow or was it the big fishery down in Kent? One of the two. Anyway, we had a fucking cracker of a day. One fucking beauty after another, or so it seemed. Stayed there for over twelve hours, we did.

Thing was, Charlie had all this top-notch gear and was proper into it. 'E used to go like every chance 'e got. I was just like a fair weather type at this time. Anyway, that got me back into it all proper. So, I started to get meself some decent gear and started dreamin' of those monster carp and big tench an' all that. It becomes a sorta obsession after a bit. Always looking at new recipes for boilies and new rigs, new methods. Oh, when The Method came out, I was over the fuckin' moon.

Where was I? Got talking about me an' Charlie di'n't I? Come off subject, again. I wish I di'n't waffle so much.

Oh yeah, me an' yer mum's 'olidays. See, I wanted to go places with great fishing and she wanted to go places with sun and beaches. Now, I don't mind a bit of sun, dun't do much for the fishin' but it's nice sometimes to catch the rays, y'know? And we still wanted to 'ave you lot along, most of the time. So, there was a compromise needed, weren't there? Which was when we 'ad our second brilliant idea. We would 'ave a family 'oliday for three years in a row and then

– oh, the fuckin' beauty of this – she could go away for 'er two weeks in the sun and I could bugger off wherever I wanted and have two weeks fishin'. And you two, got packed off to yer granny's. Win fucking win.

You were still quite young, and so were we, kinda. Young enough to still want to do stuff, y'know? Anyway, that was that, all sorted. And that's what we done. Every four years we all went our separate ways. I know you might fink it was all a bit selfish of us, but, really, it meant you got the best of us. It was only once every four fucking years.

I couldn't wait when that time come round, I can tell ya'. The car would be loaded to the gunnels, what wiv my gear, yer mother's bloody two months' supply of clothes for two fuckin' weeks and all your stuff. But, once I'd dropped 'er off at Heathrow and you three in Devon, it was just me an' the motor and two weeks' peace and quiet and some brilliant fishing. And me bit of fun, o' course.

It's funny looking back, now. I think I already knew what the 'other' part of me holiday would be. I reckon I'd been finking about it for a long time. Long before I actually ever got to go and do anyfing about it. I think it was in me 'ead for fucking years if I'm bein' honest. Probably from before I met your mum.

I'm still not really sure why. Maybe it was me dad. 'E was a brutal cunt when 'e wanted to be. Used to batter me an' me bruver, your Uncle Stan, somink rotten. Black an' blue we were more often as not. 'E was a sly old fox as well, never marked the face or below the cuff, y'know? Anyway, maybe that was it or maybe I just 'ave it in me. Probably never know, now. But it was there from the off, I knew it would 'appen as soon as I dropped you off and headed for me fishin'.

So, that first 'oliday I did for the tramp, like I said.'

Chapter Nine

Rod put the two drinks down on the table, sat down and sipped his pint of real ale while watching Christine over the lip of his glass. She was staring at the table, her vodka, soda and lime all but ignored, brow creased. Rod let her think for a bit before interrupting.

'Penny for them?' he asked, eventually.

There was a pause before she looked up slightly, appeared to notice her drink for the first time and took a sip. Finally, she looked up at him.

'I'm not sure,' she said slowly. 'Did you notice he slipped something under his chair, really quickly, with his foot, just as we walked into the living room?'

Rod shook his head. They had just left a rather fruitless second visit to John Denning. He hadn't told them anything new, just recited the same story he had told Louise. He was sorry they took the up-skirt shots but they never did anything more. The photos through bedroom windows were all Seamus' doing and he knew nothing about whether Seamus had taken things further. He was adamant that he didn't believe Seamus had the inclination or the guts to do anything about it in the first place. And that he, Seamus, had never told him about doing anything really serious.

'No,' Rod said after another sip, 'but he was very nervous, don't you think?'

'Yeah, he was.' Christine paused and her brow creased again. 'He definitely hid something. I couldn't see what it was and he was quick, but I caught his foot moving as soon as he sat down. I think there's something more going on there than we know. I wonder if he and Seamus aren't in a bit deeper than he's saying.'

'Could just have been a porn mag,' Rod said, chuckling.

'Do people still buy those? I thought it was all online videos, you know, what's that one you and the lads sometimes joke about?' She smiled at him slyly.

'Porn Hub,' he said, refusing to blush.

'That's it – you lot seem to know an awful lot about it.' With the smirk never leaving her face she took a drink.

Rod laughed loudly. 'Not telling.'

They both chuckled and looked around the pub. It was one that John Denning and Seamus Harding had hung out in, according to John. Rod had already checked with the barman when he had bought the drinks and he had known the names but said he didn't know them very well. It was a tidy, pleasant place. Very much a local, with the regulars sitting at the bar and a smattering of couples and families.

'Nice place,' Rod said after a while. 'Not exactly a den of iniquity.'

'What did you expect? It's just a local pub. Doesn't mean those two didn't sit in a corner and plot their pervy goings on.'

Rod finished his pint and nodded, 'True. Another?'

'OK, yeah I will. Then I have to get off,' she replied.

'Sure. I'll sort you a cab when you're ready. This place is almost local for me too – think I'll leave the car and have a couple more and walk home.'

'Won't your wife wonder where you are?'

'She left with my liver long ago,' he said rising and walking to the bar.

It was his turn to sit and think after he had brought the drinks back to the table. As he had before, Christine let him think. They had worked together for the best part of five years now and they both knew when to let the other have a bit of head space.

'I think you're right about Denning,' he said, eventually. 'There's something more there than we've seen so far. I'll talk to the boss tomorrow to see what she wants to do.'

Christine nodded and then changed the subject away from work. They chatted for another half an hour and then he called her a cab. After she had left, he bought himself another pint and sat scrolling through his phone for a while.

He had bought the fourth pint before he really knew it. And the fifth. He knew that would be him for the night; the sixth would swiftly follow and then he would find himself ordering a short, usually whisky. He would roll home at closing time and open another bottle when he got in. The same pattern had repeated itself for many months now, since his wife had left him. Or was it that she left because of his drinking? He didn't really know anymore, or care.

I'll give it a break tomorrow, he thought. Then – *yeah right, 'course you will.*

Chapter Ten

If Scott Ellis did one thing it was to hold to his promises when it came to crime reporting. He never broke an embargo – well not often – generally keeping stories under his hat until the police were ready to release it to the public. It kept them sweet and maintained a level of goodwill between him and senior investigating officers. But then, he thought, for this particular case, no one had actually put an official embargo on reporting. And it wasn't like this was run-of-the-mill crimes: house-breaking, muggings or assaults. This was two murders. And they were pretty gruesome ones at that, by all accounts. He was experienced enough to know that most of the really bad and brutal killings were usually classed as domestic – a husband losing it with a wife over a perceived wrongdoing, or the other way around. So, two gory – he broke his train of thought and pulled out his notebook and jotted down the word 'frenzied' ... two stranger murders in the space of a few days was big news. The public should be told about them as soon as possible.

But he had promised Rose McPhail that he would hold off until she was ready. He had agreed that as long as she met him that morning and filled him in. Unless she reiterated that this was not to go out, he fully intended to file the story that afternoon. It would be on the website by this evening and in that week's print edition on the Thursday. With any luck a national would pick it up on the Friday. *Big time*, he thought with a smile.

The other thing Scott Ellis was, was punctual. And so, he was standing outside his car in the police station's car park waiting for Rose to arrive. It was eight in the morning and he knew she usually arrived between eight and eight thirty. He hoped it would be nearer eight – it had started to drizzle again and the sky promised more heavy rain. He considered waiting in his car but then he was likely to miss her and he would have to fight the desk sergeant to get to see her. So, he waited it out, pulling his collar up against the rain drops that grew steadily larger.

She was, of course, late. The rain was running off his sodden hair and down the back of his jacket when she pulled in at around eight forty-five. He waited with less patience than he had wanted for her to get out of her car and gather her things. She had had the foresight to wear a waterproof coat and he cursed gently to himself for not having done the same. He cursed again when he realised she had spotted him when she had driven in, and was now taking her time walking his way. He was sure he could see a slight, crooked grin on her face as she walked.

Eventually, she drew level with him. 'You're late this morning, Detective Chief Inspector,' he said, aiming for light and cheery and coming over as wet and miserable.

'It was one hell of a day yesterday and I don't officially start until nine so, actually, I'm early,' Rose replied as she kept walking past him. He gave a little skipping run to catch up and then fell into step beside her.

'Have you got anything new since our little chat last night?' he asked, keeping the hunger for news out of his voice. He needed her chatting, not feeling like she was being interviewed.

'Let's save it until we're out of the rain,' was all she said as she dug in her bag for her pass card.

Her team were filing in as Rose led Scott through to her office. She scanned their faces looking for signs of guilt at seeing the journalist, but they all just glanced in their direction. She knew it could easily have been one of the uniformed officers that had tipped him off but she was still mad that he had found out in the first place and wanted to take it out on someone.

She closed the door behind them and gestured for Ellis to sit down. He did so after gently teasing his soaked trousers away from his legs.

'Don't drip on my floor,' she said as she sat down on her side of the desk.

He gave a small laugh, 'I'll try.' She smiled back at him.

'No offer of a cup of tea?' he asked when they were settled down.

She sighed and got up again, opening the office door and calling into the main office, 'Two teas in here, please,' before shutting the door again.

'Thank you,' he said. 'So, what have you got for me?'

'You know just about all of it already. But I'll give you the run-down on what we have, on one condition…' She lifted her finger to emphasise her point and waited until he had nodded. 'You can put this out tonight but –' she jabbed the finger towards him – 'minimal details, just the basics. I want no indication that at this time we know the victims are linked or any hint, whatsoever, that they might be the victims of a vigilante. Understand?'

He raised his eyebrows. 'Some of that is news to me. All I really knew was that there have been two murders, neither of which appeared to be domestic. The victims are linked?'

'Yes, they are,' Rose said rubbing her eyes. 'That is to say the killer is the link and we think it's some sort of vigilante thing. We haven't got any connection between the victims themselves, as yet. But there are several very strong similarities between the two deaths.'

'Care to elaborate?' he asked, sitting forward in his seat. This was juicier than he had expected.

'No,' was all the reply he got.

There was a knock at the door and David walked in carrying two mugs of tea. He glanced furtively at Scott as he placed the teas on the desk but Rose spotted it. Hmmm-mmm.

They waited in silence until David had left the room.

'So, I can say there's been two murders and not much else, is that what you're saying? Can't I at least say that you are looking into the possibility that they're linked?' Scott asked as soon as the door closed.

'No,' Rose said emphatically. 'I suspect that whoever is behind this is a narcissist and given there appears to be a vigilante element wants to be recognised by the press. I don't want to be rewarding them right now. And I don't want them to think we know very much, which admittedly we don't, but the less they know about our thinking at this stage the better. They might get sloppy.'

When she spoke passionately or in anger Rose's long beaten down Northumberland accent showed through. She had been born there and had lived there until the age of ten when her parents had moved south. The accent had morphed into a generic southern one over the years of schooling and college that followed. But occasionally it snuck through the veneer.

Scott nodded thoughtfully. 'Yes, sure,' he said eventually. 'I'll go more with the shock of two murders in a week and leave details vague. Do you want me to mention you don't have many leads? Like you say, it might make them sloppy.'

'I don't want them knowing anything about the investigation at all, right now,' Rose said more evenly. 'And I really don't want them trying to get you to give them a name – you know, something bloody stupid like the Milton Keynes Avenging Angel, or something daft. I don't want to be in a position where they're contacting you and not me. Understood?'

'Loud and clear,' Scott said with a little mock salute. 'Promise I'll run just a straight, shock horror, two slayings in a week type thing.'

'Good man. And I promise I'll keep you in the loop and when we're ready to go public with the vigilante angle you'll be the first to know.' With that Rose stood up. 'Now, I have to get my team briefed and out to work.'

Scott stood with her and they shook hands. Rose gestured to the door and he turned and moved out into the main office, Rose close behind.

'See you later, Scott,' Rose said quietly and waited in silence until she was sure he was well on his way out and out of ear shot.

'Right everyone,' she said loudly to the room in general, 'what have we got this morning? Anyone give me a piece of good news?'

'Not exactly good news, ma'am,' Rod said from his desk, 'but Christine and I both think that there's something John Denning is holding back. Christine's certain he hid something when we walked into his living room and I just felt there was something he was holding back. He was very nervous and as evasive as he was with Louise.'

'OK,' Rose said, brow creasing in thought, 'what do you want to do about it? I'm not sure we have enough for a warrant to search his property quite yet.'

'No, ma'am, I agree,' Rod said. 'But I do wonder if he was hiding something and if he starts to really feel the heat he might try to dump whatever he was hiding. I think we should go pay a visit to his work, and visibly so, then tail him at the end of the day. If tries to dump anything we'll see and be able to grab whatever it is.'

'He might have dumped it already – if he's worried,' Sandra said.

'I took the liberty of going and checking his place early this morning. He left for work at around six thirty and he wasn't carrying anything with him. He works at Amazon so I figure he'll do twelve hours. They do four days of that and then have three off, I believe,' Rod replied.

'OK, you and Christine stay on that,' Rose nodded to Rod. 'Sandra? Did you get anything more from Mrs Harding? Or the door to door?'

'No, afraid not, ma'am,' Sandra said looking at the other two. 'Unless David or Anna had something before I joined them? Miss Harding had nothing new to say.'

Rose looked over to David and then Anna. 'Well?' she asked.

Both of them shook their heads. 'Nothing,' David said.

'Likewise,' from Anna.

Rose nodded. 'Gareth, what have we had back, PM? Ballistics? Forensic reports?'

'The PM you have for Harding, Souček's I got this morning. Nothing much to say – he was shot, which is what killed him. Mutilation was peri not post mortem so the poor bugger suffered. The pathologist speculates that he was kneeling when he was shot; there's slight markings on his knees and there were grass stains on the knees of his trousers.

Also, the bullet entry was on a downward trajectory. Other than that, not much else.'

'Anything else back in?' Rose asked.

'Yeah, ballistics are in,' Gareth continued. 'Both were shot with a .22 calibre hand gun. They are sure it was the same weapon used in both murders. Nothing new from forensics.'

'Right, thanks Gareth. So, everything still points to one killer and we have to assume the motive to be either revenge or that this person sees themselves as a vigilante. Either way it's unlikely they are going to stop now, so it's vital we start getting somewhere. I want more on the two victims, but it's definitely time to get to work on Souček. I'm going to go to the school he taught at. Anna, you're with me. Gareth, can you pull all the gun licence holders in the area and feed that to David and Louise – you two check them out. Rod, you and Christine, stay on Denning. I like your thinking so let's see what comes of it. Sandra, there must be some gun clubs around here – find them and check them out, you know, no weapons missing that kind of thing. Rod, can you and Christine go see Mrs Souček before you go over and watch Denning's place. Family Liaison have already been in but see if there's anything she can tell us, especially about his movements, habits – where he would likely have been over the last week. He was out of work but he must have gone somewhere and done something with his days. Get to it guys.'

Rose gave a 'one minute' signal to Anna and turned back towards her office. As she passed Rod, she gestured for him to follow her in. He got up from his desk and fell into step behind her. Once in she closed the door.

'Had a few drinks last night, Rod?' she asked quietly, keeping her voice light and friendly.

Rod didn't react to the question in any visible way, instead replying flatly, 'I had a couple after we finished, yeah. Don't most of us?'

'It's just the extra strong mints aren't quite cutting it this morning,' Rose said, voice still calm. She didn't want to get into a tit-for-tat who had drunk what the night before, but Rod was giving off a distinctive smell of alcohol and she knew he had had more than just 'a couple'.

He bridled slightly but said nothing.

'Look, Rod,' Rose said softly, 'I don't want to make a big thing about it, and God knows this job is notorious for driving people to drink, but you need…'

'I'm fine ma'am,' Rod interrupted stiffly, 'I had a few last night, nothing out of the ordinary. I'm fine this morning as I always am, so, if this is leading to asking whether I need help or want assistance from HR then the answer is no, I do not.'

Rose pursed her lips and gave herself a few beats to decide how she wanted this conversation to go. In the end she opted for the path of least resistance. 'OK, Rod, if you say you're fine then I accept you're fine. But let's not have to have this conversation again, OK?'

'Sure,' was all he said in reply.

There was an awkward silence for a second or two; Rose switched into business mode and her demeanour visibly changed.

'Right, well, you see what more you can dig up on John Denning. I'm not sure where it'll get us as there doesn't appear to be a connection to Souček, but it might give us more insight into Harding.'

'Right you are, ma'am,' Rod said and swivelled on his heel.

Rose watched as he marched through the office and gestured for Christine to follow him out. She had to scramble to get her belongings together and catch up, cursing as she went. Rose stepped out of her office and called to Christine before she was out of the open-plan area.

'Christine, you're driving today, OK?'

Christine turned, nodded and hurried after Rod.

The office was its normal morning buzz of people getting ready to leave on their various enquiries and assignments. Gareth was firing up his computer and looking glum. I need to mix things up a bit, Rose thought and, on a whim, changed her plans.

'Gareth, you'll be with me today – Anna, I want you to run office liaison. Get the names of the gun licensees first then follow up on anything else that comes in.' She watched Anna visibly slump and put her bag back down with a thump. Gareth smiled the smile of a winner and gathered his raincoat from the back of his chair. To her credit, Anna said nothing else and immediately fired up her computer to call up the information required by David and Louise.

Gareth rose from his desk at a nod from Rose and they followed the others out.

Chapter Eleven

It took about half an hour to get to the school Souček had worked at prior to the scandal hitting. Rose nearly missed the sign that pointed out the 'Cedars School for Boys' was on the right. The drive was long and twisting, winding through well-tended gardens, cricket, football and rugby pitches, and finally ending in a sharp right-hand bend. Having manoeuvred her car around the bend, she now had a clear view of the large school building – a grand affair which held all the hallmarks of an expensive private school.

Rose parked in one of the visitor's spaces near the front entrance. She and Gareth walked over the gravel car park and climbed the sandstone steps to the main door. A brass plaque near the door bore the name of the school and, underneath that, a white plastic sign pushed between two wooden holders proclaimed the head teacher to be a Dr Gerald Sterling.

The door didn't move when Gareth pushed it and Rose pointed to a metal intercom, mounted on the wall to his right. He lifted his chin in acknowledgment and pushed the call button. There was a buzz and then a short delay, filled only by a crackle from the intercom.

'Yes, can I help you?' a woman's voice asked, her voice sounding tinny and distant through the small speaker.

'Detective Rose McPhail and DC Gareth Exley,' Rose announced, leaning across Gareth in order to be heard. 'Thames Valley Police, we'd like a word with the headmaster.'

'Come in,' the woman said after another short delay and crackle from the intercom.

There was a buzz and the door clicked open a few centimetres. It swung in easily at a slight push from Gareth. Once inside, the wide hall area was marble-floored with a couple of marble pillars reaching the high ceiling from the centre of the hall, spaced a couple of metres apart. Their shoes echoed off the stone floor as they walked in, looking about for an office or someone to greet them. Gareth spotted an unimposing sign next to a door on their left, stating that the main reception office was through there.

The office was small compared to the imposing entrance hall, with only a couple of filing cabinets and a woman – the one who had answered the intercom, Rose assumed – sat behind a small desk. There was a wooden partition running across the front of the desk with a counter top which the woman had to peer over to see them.

'May I see some identification? she asked as they approached. Rose noted her name badge proclaiming her to be Laura.

Rose and Gareth produced their ID simultaneously. Laura reached out and took both from them and appeared to check them thoroughly before handing them back.

'The headmaster is in a meeting with one of the parents at the moment but shouldn't be too long,' she told them, whilst noting down their names in a visitors' book.

'That's fine,' Rose said, 'we're happy to wait.'

'Of course,' Laura replied. 'Could you please fill in these visitor badges and can I ask you to wear them at all times during your visit?'

They both took the white, oblong pieces of card with a lapel fastener stuck to the back, filled them in with the pens provided and clipped them to their jackets. Gareth looked around for somewhere to sit down but there were no seats in the office.

'There's a couple of benches in the entrance hall if you would like to wait there?' Laura said, reading Gareth's gesture.

The benches were polished wood with leather-clad cushions built in. They were reasonably comfortable but Rose decided she would not want to be sitting on them for longer than was necessary; she had the feeling her backside would go numb after about ten minutes. They were clearly not intended for visitors to sit on for any length of time, she concluded.

In the end, it was fifteen minutes before a short man in a blue-grey suit and black gown appeared in the hallway accompanied by an immaculately dressed woman of middle years. The man nodded to Rose as he guided his guest towards the front door.

'A pleasure to see you again, Mrs Turner,' he said as he shook the woman's hand. 'And rest assured, Charles will receive the additional attention required to get him through the Biology exam.'

The woman smiled and nodded, 'Thank you, Mr Sterling.' With that she turned on her expensive-looking heels and clip-clopped across the hall and out the main entrance.

The headmaster turned his attention to the two police detectives on the bench.

'Gerald Sterling, headmaster,' he announced, striding towards them and offering a hand. Rose and Gareth stood up from the bench and Rose took the head's hand and shook it.

'DCI Rose McPhail and this is DC Gareth Exley,' Rose said, reaching for her bag and her ID within.

The head shook his head and waved a hand, 'No need for me to see identification, I know Laura will have checked it when you arrived or she wouldn't have given you one of our visitor badges.'

Rose smiled and released her bag to sit back at her side. The headmaster's voice was cultured and smooth with a slight accent Rose couldn't quite place.

'Shall we?' the head asked, gesturing to one side of the large stairs.

They followed him past the stairs to where two solid-looking wooden doors were set in the walls. There were plaques on both of them, one proclaiming it to be the office of the headmaster and the other that of the deputy head.

Sterling's office was large with three walls taken up, floor to ceiling, by bookcases; the other had a large window which took up most of the available wall space. There was a large desk with two comfortable-looking chairs in front and a high-backed, leather swivel chair behind. The desk itself was neat and uncluttered. Sterling gestured the detectives to the two seats and moved around the desk to take his own.

'So,' he said when he was seated, 'what can I do for you, officers? I hope it's not anything to do with one of my pupils?'

'No, Mr Sterling,' Rose replied, 'we're here to ask about Evžen Souček.'

Sterling sat back in his seat at the mention of the name. He steepled his fingers under his chin and looked gravely at the two officers.

'I see,' he said slowly, 'what would you like to know? Mr Souček hasn't taught here for some time, but I will tell you what I can. Have there been any more … accusations? Damn terrible business. I've never had to deal with anything like it in thirty years of teaching.'

'No, Mr Sterling,' Rose said quietly. 'Mr Souček was found dead a couple of days ago. He was shot. And as far as I know there were no accusations against him other than he may have known what happened here and turned a blind eye. Our investigations have showed he knew very little of what actually went on, only that he had vague suspicions.'

'Yes, yes, quite,' Sterling replied quickly. He appeared to be unmoved at the news of Souček's death.

'So you knew Mr Souček wasn't involved?' Gareth asked.

'Yes, we were told that he was completely innocent of any of the accusations,' Sterling replied coolly.

'Then why did you dismiss him?' Gareth asked, sitting forward slightly.

Sterling took a breath and steepled his fingers again. 'The whole affair was ghastly and we took the decision that should the allegations prove to be true then Mr Souček had failed in his duty of care by not reporting what he suspected. It was felt that the school should distance itself from all those involved – no matter what their involvement.'

'So, you were protecting the school's reputation?' Gareth pressed. He seemed to be a touch too aggressive to Rose, so she decided to quickly ask another question before the headmaster could answer.

'How long was Mr Souček with you? And what can you tell us about his time here, Mr Sterling?' she asked, glancing at Gareth.

'He was with us around seven years,' Sterling replied, appearing grateful that he hadn't been required to answer Gareth's question. 'He was respected by the staff and the boys, but I wouldn't say he was liked, as such.'

'Why was that?' Rose asked.

'He was a little aloof, I suppose you could put it. Or maybe just very private. Either way he didn't really mix with the rest of the staff. I wondered if perhaps it was because of his background – you know, a different cultural point of view – that he found little in common with the other masters.'

'I see,' Rose said. 'I have to say Mr Sterling that you don't appear to be overly shocked or perturbed by the news of his death.'

Sterling raised an eyebrow. 'Oh, I am deeply shocked to hear the news, Chief Inspector, I assure you. It's just that after thirty years in a classroom you learn to hide your emotions very well. I hope I haven't come across as callous?'

'No, just a little unmoved, was all,' Rose said.

'He was shot, you say?' the headmaster asked, taking his cue to be concerned.

'Yes, and we believe that he was killed in connection with what happened here. What can you tell us about the period when the accusations came to light? How did Mr Souček react?'

The headmaster was quiet for some time, with a serious look on his face and brows creased.

'As I said, the whole affair was horrendous and very, deeply concerning. To think such things could be going on at this school, under our noses, so to speak. It was just awful, especially for the boys involved, of course. Until the allegations came to light there had been no rumours, nothing to indicate that anything was amiss. I can honestly say I was shocked to my very core.'

'And Mr Souček?' Rose prompted.

'He was very quiet on the subject. He didn't proffer any opinion in the staff room or to me privately. It was only when the boys concerned said that they believed he knew something and had said nothing that I had any inclination that he might have done.'

'Do you think he knew?' Rose asked.

'I'm not sure. But, of course, it's completely possible he did,' Sterling replied.

'Why do you think he said nothing, prior to the allegations coming out?' Gareth asked, appearing to have calmed down from whatever had been bothering him previously.

'I don't know,' Sterling replied evenly. 'He was, as I have mentioned, very quiet and reserved. Perhaps he felt it wasn't his place or that he didn't want to accuse a fellow teacher with very little or no evidence.'

'So, he definitely didn't speak to you before and you decided to keep quiet for the sake of the school?' Gareth asked, his early forthrightness coming back to the fore.

'No, most certainly not,' Sterling replied hotly. 'If I had heard anything from any of my staff that a master was … abusing his position of trust, I would have investigated the matter thoroughly and if I thought anything untoward was going on, I would have informed the police immediately. The reputation of the school is one thing but the welfare of the boys is another matter entirely. That is at the forefront of our ethos.'

'Do you think he was involved?' Gareth asked.

'The police found no evidence that he was,' Sterling replied having calmed a little.

'That doesn't answer my question – do you think he was involved?' Gareth asked, sitting forward again.

'I don't believe so, no. He was guilty of negligence if indeed he did know what was happening, but I don't believe he was actually involved, no. Was that a more satisfactory answer?' Sterling was clearly becoming upset at Gareth's forthright questioning.

'The boys involved – did they stay at the school afterwards?' Rose asked.

'No, their parents, understandably, pulled them out, along with a number of others, unfortunately.'

Rose nodded and tried to think of anything else she could ask but drew a blank.

'Well, Mr Sterling,' she said, 'I don't think we have anything else to ask at this time. Thank you for your time. If there is anything else that comes up, we'll be back in touch.' She got up from her seat, with Gareth following suit.

Sterling looked relieved that the questioning was over. 'Anything I can do to help,' he said standing up with them. 'Such a terrible business.'

Rose couldn't decide whether he meant the allegations of abuse or the death of Souček but she left the question unasked.

Sterling showed them out with handshakes and further promises of being available to help at any time.

As they climbed back into the car, Rose asked, 'Did we learn anything new there? Other than that you have a problem with public schools.'

'I don't have a problem with them,' Gareth said, on the defensive. 'I just don't think money should buy you an improved chance of success, which let's face it these places do. I'm not sure we learned much, though.'

Rose nodded with a half-smile on her lips, 'I didn't think you were such a Bolshevik, Gareth. But you're right, I'm not sure we learned much more – other than it confirms our suspicion that Souček was not involved and certainly didn't deserve to die in the way he did.'

Gareth snorted, 'I'm no Bolshevik.' He appeared to be about to say something else when Rose's phone began to ring.

There was a brief conversation and then she hung up.

'Louise ...' she said as she put her phone away. 'They have one .22 rifle from the gun licences. They've brought it in for examination. She's not convinced the owner is responsible – he gave the gun up too readily. But we'll see.'

Rose put one hand on the steering wheel and the other on the key in the ignition. She was about to turn the key when she appeared to have another thought.

'I may as well phone Sandra now and see if she's got anything,' she said more to herself than to Gareth. She pulled her phone back out and called up Sandra's number.

After another brief conversation she hung up again. 'Nothing,' she said, the disappointment evident in her voice.

She hit the steering wheel with her palm. 'Jesus, we have to get something soon. There has to be a connection between the two victims. How else is the killer choosing them?'

Gareth stayed quiet; he had no answers for his boss and knew better than to offer that assertion. Rose turned the ignition and they began the drive back to the office.

By day's end, Rose was back at her desk feeling frustrated and dismayed at their lack of progress. With the gun owners and gun clubs coming up blank, that avenue seemed to have closed. Ballistics had already confirmed that the rifle David and Louise had seized was not the murder weapon. They were convinced that the weapon used was very likely a hand gun rather than a rifle; the bullets had not passed through the bodies which said to them that the velocity of the bullet would have been comparatively low – much more in keeping with a pistol. Anna had done as thorough a job as possible on background checks and cross-referencing them between the two victims – nothing, no connection could be found. Rod and Christine were watching Denning's house; Rod thought Denning looked rattled when they had appeared at his work but thus far, they had nothing else. Likewise with their chat with Mrs Souček; she had nothing to add and could think of no one who would wish her husband harm. She had given them a detailed run-down of his likely movements and habits which might yield something once they had more CCTV in.

Rose made a note in the writing pad on her desk to have someone check out the boys who had made the allegations at the school and their parents. It was worth checking, but somehow she didn't think they would be involved. She was running out of lines of enquiry and was now resigned to the fact that they would probably have to wait for another victim and hope the killer made a mistake. It was a horrible thought but one she knew she would have to grimly accept.

Turning to her computer she opened the email she had received from Scott Ellis. Much to her surprise he had sent her a copy of the story he had filed with the local paper. She was also surprised to see that he had stuck to his word and only written the bare essentials.

With nothing more she could do, she decided to head home.

It's going to be Slayer on the way home tonight, she thought as she left the office.

Chapter Twelve

David was sitting, waiting impatiently, at the restaurant table. Louise had agreed that they would meet at eight but it was already twenty past. This was only the second meal they had had together – David considered them dates but was unsure how Louise thought about them and on both occasions she had been late even after agreeing that she was fine with the time.

He was just about to give up when she appeared in the door. He tried to appear relaxed and unbothered by her tardiness but knew she would probably spot his irritation. She approached the table as if she had arrived only a few moments after him and sat down, flicking her long brown hair back over her shoulder.

She caught the fleeting look on his face and smiled, 'Sorry.'

He smiled back, 'It's OK, I haven't been here that long.'

'Liar,' she laughed. 'I bet you were here at eight sharp. You're never late – well apart from the other morning but then you had a reason.' Her smile broadened as she spoke.

'Not one I could say to the boss though, was it?' He looked somewhat embarrassed. The night before he was late he and Louise had met up for the first time. They had been chatting quietly for some time whilst on a post-work drink with some of the team and had decided that they would go on and have something to eat together after the others had left. After dinner they had gone back to her place and had a few more drinks and one thing had led to another. The following, awkward, morning they had agreed that it was best they kept things very quiet and, at that stage, casual.

'True,' was all she said.

'You were all right. You were already home and could shower and change. I had to get home first. So, you managed to stay in the boss's good books – as always.' He grinned as he spoke, letting her know he was only teasing.

'I'm not always in her good books. I certainly don't try to be, it just so happens I'm bloody good at what I do.' Another broad grin.

David laughed and shook his head. He didn't really want to get into talking shop but realised they didn't really know each other very well and as such had very little else to talk about.

'Did you hear the gun was a no?' he said, failing to come up with anything else.

She nodded. 'Yeah, and a no-go on the ranges and gun clubs. Do you think the boss is starting to sweat? We've got nothing.'

'I bet she is,' he replied. 'I'm not sure what else she can be doing though. I mean, there's very little else for us to follow up on. I wonder if the investigation might get shelved.'

'I doubt it – I reckon she's waiting for another one. It's all we can do.' She looked around as she spoke and caught the eye of a waiter who promptly came over to the table. 'Are you ready to order? I'm starving.'

'You haven't even looked at the menu,' David complained as he picked his up. He had idly looked through it while he had been waiting but hadn't really paid much attention and certainly hadn't decided what he wanted.

'Four poppadoms and dips, please,' Louise told the waiter. 'There now, you've got time to decide but we can eat while you're doing it.'

'You still haven't looked at the menu,' he said in mock complaint.

'I've been here before – I know exactly what I want,' she said, smiling again.

'Fair enough.' He poured her a glass of wine from the bottle he had ordered when he had arrived; he had already had a glass while he was waiting and was halfway through his second.

'Listen,' she said, suddenly serious. 'As nice as this is, I think we should take things easy. Let's not have a repeat of the other night and just see how we go. I really don't want any gossip back at the office.'

'Agreed,' he said, taking a sip of wine. 'That would be too awkward and you know what Rod and Gareth can be like when they get going.'

'Uh, Gareth. That man drives me up the wall.' Her face took on a sour look.

'He's all right. He gets the job done and his experience is useful.'

'His experience is mainly on the beat. He's a community bobby in a suit playing detective.' Her voice took on a hard edge as she said this. 'Look at what he said yesterday – the fucking cheek of the man. Like that interview would have gone any better with him in the room. Denning would probably have clammed up the second Gareth opened his mouth.'

'He was unfair then, that's true,' David said softly.

'Well,' she said, 'thanks for sticking up for me, anyway.'

'Welcome.' He raised his glass and they clinked.

The waiter appeared with the poppadoms and set them on the table. They fell into the copper's habit of shutting up when anyone was near the table.

After the waiter had left, Louise said, 'Do you think it's someone on the force?'

David looked surprised and then thoughtful. 'It hadn't really crossed my mind, but now you mention it...' he trailed off.

'I reckon the boss is thinking it too,' Louise said, when it was clear he wasn't going to say any more.

'You seem to know a lot about what the boss thinks,' he said, crunching a poppadom.

'I reckon I think like her,' was all she said, with a shrug of one shoulder.

'Do you think it's someone on the force?' he asked.

She sat for a moment, chewing and thinking, then eventually nodded. 'Yeah I think it could be. They seem to know a lot about the victims and that information is highly unlikely to be in the public domain. Let's face it, neither man had really done very much wrong and certainly not anything that would be reported. How else would you get that info other than off the PNC?'

'True. I don't know though – I'm not sure I can see it really,' he said, shaking his head.

'Not all coppers are goody two shoes like you, you know?' she said with a giggle. 'Mind you, you weren't such a good boy the other night.' She raised her eyebrows provocatively a couple of times and grinned. She laughed when he blushed.

The waiter returned and they ordered, and to David's surprise they found quite a number of other things to talk about.

They shared a taxi home with the intention of spending the night apart but without thinking they both got out at his place.

Chapter Thirteen

Rose was about to tuck into a Chinese takeaway with her husband when her phone rang. With a sigh she picked it up, catching Gordon's eye and raising a weary eyebrow. She looked at the screen and saw it was Rod calling.

'Rod?' she said answering the call.

'Rose, we might have something,' Rod said, a little out of breath.

'Go on.'

'We spotted Denning leaving his house about half an hour ago – he tucked a carrier bag under his jacket as he was leaving. So, we followed him on foot. He eventually dumped the bag in a bin about a mile from his house. It's got about half a dozen memory sticks and a couple of CDs in it. He ran when he saw us but we've got him now. We're about to bring him in. Do you want to come down the station or leave it to us?'

Rose thought for a moment. 'Hold on, Rod,' she said, turning to her husband and covering the phone. 'Rod and Christine have got something. I need to go down the station – are you on call tonight? I lose track.'

'No,' Gordon replied, 'you go ahead.'

She lifted the phone back to her ear. 'I'll be along in about half an hour. Let him sweat until I get there and check out those memory sticks.'

'Will do,' Rod said and hung up.

Rose bolted as much chow mein as she could manage in ten minutes and got ready to leave.

'I'm not sure when I'll be back,' she told Gordon as she pulled on her coat.

He just nodded and picked up the TV remote, gathering another mouthful of noodles onto his fork.

Between their two jobs they rarely got to spend any time together, and after all the years they had been married they had got used to their evenings being interrupted. It felt, in some ways, good that they both understood the importance of each other's work but also, in a way, she felt it a shame that there were no longer any complaints that they would miss an evening together yet again.

She arrived at the station exactly half an hour after her conversation with Rod. She made her way into the office to find Rod and Christine squeezed together at one desk peering at the computer screen.

'What have you got?' Rose said as she walked in. 'Oh, and good work by the way, I appreciate you both putting in the extra hours.'

Both of them turned and nodded their appreciation. 'There's hours of stuff on here,' Rod said, turning back to the screen. 'We've only got through about twenty minutes on one stick so far, but it's already proving to be quite the find.'

Rose moved over to the desk. 'Let's have a look then.'

Rod moved his chair out of the way and Rose pulled another one over from a neighbouring desk. Christine operated the mouse and pulled up another of the many video files listed on the memory stick. It showed grainy, night-time footage of a street; the image moved and jolted around making it hard for Rose to make out exactly what she was looking at. After a couple of minutes, the back of a woman came into view several yards away from the camera. The distance and the constant movement meant she was often only a blurred image appearing somewhere in the mid-ground.

After another minute of this, the woman appeared closer in the shot and the camera had steadied somewhat. Rose assumed the earlier jogging about was the person taking the video moving quickly to get closer to the woman and now they were in position they had steadied the phone. The person taking the video didn't approach any closer but slowly moved the camera up and down, taking in the woman from head to toe. It was very hard to tell but Rose got the impression she was looking at a woman in her twenties, judging by her clothes. She could, of course, be older but from the back it was very hard to tell. She had a good figure whatever age she was, in Rose's opinion.

Then, after another few seconds, a very quiet voice could be heard over the footage.

'Another potential here,' a male voice whispered. 'Lovely legs. And look at that arse.'

The video came to a shaky end just after that. Rose straightened her back and took a breath. The video was sinister and disturbing but could be interpreted as voyeurism and nothing more – very similar to the videos she had found in Harding's bedroom.

'The next one is a bit more telling,' Christine said, selecting the next file down.

Again, the footage was initially shaky and blurred but steadied much sooner than the previous one. It showed the same woman, this time walking along a canal tow path. She was much harder to make out with the very low light but appeared to be about to walk under a bridge.

The camera made it to the same spot about a minute or so later and the video went virtually black as the operator went under the bridge. Then the shot gained more clarity as whoever it was emerged from the other side. The camera swung to the left and for a second it was completely impossible to make out what it was now looking at. After a second or two the shot panned back to show an area of waste ground, steeply sloped with low shrubs and high grass. The operator had clearly stopped moving and was running the camera up and down the embankment.

The voice spoke again: 'This is the third time she's taken this route. I figure this would be an ideal spot.'

Another male voice, unheard until that point, then spoke: 'Yep, perfect I'd say. She is definitely worth following up.'

Shortly after that the video came to another shaky halt.

Rose looked grimly at Rod then Christine.

'Clearly mobile phone footage,' Rod said. 'Makes for pretty damning watching, doesn't it?'

'Do either of you recognise either of the voices?' Rose asked. Her eyes were fixed back on the screen even though there was nothing further to see.

'The second one you hear could be Denning, but given the quality and how quietly they're speaking it's very hard to tell.'

'Are the others you've watched the same?' Rose gestured to the folder which held probably twenty files.

'The ones we've watched are all varied,' Rod replied. 'Some are on streets, a couple in parks, one or two in woodland. They all show women and, in the ones where you can see their faces, they're aged between about eighteen and thirty. There's not much talking on the others, just the occasional word like "nice" or "perfect" – that kind of thing.'

'We can pull the dates these were taken,' said Christine, speaking for the first time since Rose had arrived. 'We can cross-reference that with any complaints about being followed and also look for sexual assaults, attempted abduction, that kind of thing. Might throw up who some of the women are and if these two actually followed up.'

'Yes, good call,' Rose said quietly. 'We'll get Gareth on that first thing. I think we can be certain that Denning is one of the people filming, given he was trying to dump this lot.'

Rod nodded, 'I think it's time we had a word with matey, don't you?'

'No, let him sweat a bit longer, maybe even until morning. Arrest him tonight on charges of harassment, voyeurism and anything else you can think of. That might shake him up a bit. We've got time on the clock, given the hour we pulled him in, to do the interviews in the morning, I want him to have a bad night's sleep,' Rose said, rising from her seat. 'In the meantime, we need to have gone through as much of this footage as possible. Who's on duty tonight?'

'Sandra from our team and DC Hanigan, I think, from DCI Reid's lot. Sandra's out on a burglary just now,' Christine answered.

'Right, call her and give her the rundown. She can work on them when she's back in. I take it you haven't handled the other stuff in the bag?' Rose asked, gesturing towards the large evidence bag with the carrier and its contents sitting on the desk.

'We used gloves on this one and haven't touched the others,' Rod replied.

'Good – get one of them through to forensics and see if you can fast-track finger prints. I'm pretty sure Denning's prints will be on them but let's dot the i's and cross the t's. When you're done the two of you, get yourselves home. Good work tonight.'

Rod rose from his seat. 'I'll charge Denning, Christine can you brief Sandra and get a stick off to the lab?'

'Yep,' Christine said, already reaching into a desk drawer for a fresh evidence bag and a pair of gloves.

'Good, I'll leave you two to it,' Rose said and pulled her coat from the back of the chair she had been sitting on.

Rose decided that it would need to be something quieter and more melodic on the way home. She selected an old Marillion CD from the glove box and slotted it into the player, after carefully putting the Slayer CD back in its case. As she drove some thoughts occurred to her: it now looked like Denning and Harding were actually up to something far more nefarious than voyeurism but how had the killer known that? Also, they still had no idea how they had been tracked down. And finally, why had only Harding been selected and not Denning? The answer to that was as unsavoury as it was obvious – Harding was the only one on the police computer.

It comes back to it being a copper. Shit and corruption! she thought as she pulled onto the drive. She now had a dilemma: if it was a police officer responsible then she could trust no one, not even her own team. So then who could she rely on to carry out the investigation other than herself?

You don't know it's a copper for sure yet. Worry about that when you do.

She climbed out the car, hoping Gordon hadn't thrown away what was left of the Chinese.

Chapter Fourteen

David was awakened by Louise putting a cup of coffee on the bedside table and turning the lamp on. He stirred groggily and looked up at her. She looked awkwardly sexy in one of his T-shirts. He glanced at the alarm clock and was dismayed to see it was only six thirty.

'It's a bit early,' he grumbled, his mouth feeling gummy and his lips stuck together.

'I was up anyway,' she said, sounding far more awake. 'Lucky I was – Rose called. She wants me in early to get the names and addresses of the boys involved in the abuse allegations and to interview them about Souček. And the parents too. I suggested that you help me and she agreed.'

'Oh,' was all he could think to say in reply. He reached for his mobile perched on the side of the table.

'Don't worry, I said I would call you.' Louise smiled and turned to leave the bedroom.

David watched her long and shapely legs as she walked out the door, feeling downhearted that a hoped-for morning romp was no longer on the cards. Sighing, he sat up and took a swig of coffee. He preferred tea but didn't have the heart to complain. Swinging his legs out of bed, he stumbled into a pair of jogging bottoms and pulled on a T-shirt then followed her into the living room of his flat.

He had bought the place a few years ago with the intention of accruing some equity and then selling up and buying a house, but had never got around to doing anything about it. It was a comfortable, if small, flat and since there had only ever been him on his own he hadn't yet found the motivation to move.

'What the hell is Rose doing calling you at six in the morning?' he asked after taking another sip of coffee.

'She said she wanted us on it as soon as possible. Apparently there's loads of other work now needing to be done and she wants us back at the office as soon as so we can pitch in.'

David grunted then said, 'Sounds like something new's come in.'

'So, you lazy bugger, get showered and get dressed, asap. We're going to need to get to my place so I can change and then get into the office by around half seven. Chop, chop,' Louise said, clapping her hands towards him.

'I haven't finished my coffee yet,' he grumbled but was already moving towards the bathroom. Just before he went in, he looked back at her. 'I prefer tea by the way, just so you know the next time you wake me at an ungodly hour.'

She made a face at him. 'Keep that up and there may not be a next time. Now get your fucking arse moving.'

They were in the office by seven fifteen, after a very brief stop at Louise's place. David had been amazed at how quickly she had showered and changed. Louise fired up her computer and announced she would get the details of the boys and their parents and that it was his turn to get the coffee. He didn't moan – his eyes were still feeling gritty from waking so early so he hadn't really wanted to sit looking at a screen anyway. He made himself tea rather than coffee, hoping his usual morning drink would wake him up properly.

Louise had the details noted down in short order. He had to gulp his tea down to follow her out the office. He hurried to catch up as she strode down the corridor.

'You're on one this morning,' he said, a touch breathlessly.

'Always, David. Always,' she said as she led the way out to the car park.

He had driven them in and so they only had his car.

'What's the first address?' he asked, doing up his seat belt.

'It's in Fenny – hopefully they're in. Name's Joshua Yakubu, parents Eileen and Joseph. He's an accountant and she's a nurse. Joshua is heading for uni in September, so unless he's got a summer job, he's likely to be dossing about.'

Fenny Stratford was not too far away and, like all of Milton Keynes, the roads were generally free moving so the drive would usually only take around ten minutes. The town was a driver's paradise with its American-style grid layout and clear, fast thoroughfares. David had been amazed to learn that many of the roads had been built before any other structures had been put into place. Louise had told him that on their first date. She had lived in the area most of her life, her parents moving up from London when she was just a baby. He had moved from Watford when he had secured his transfer to the Thames Valley force.

They were both pleased and a little surprised to find the whole family still in when they arrived. Mrs Yakubu had let them into the fairly large, new build house and called to the other two as she showed the officers into the living room. She had seemed worried when Louise had said they were calling in connection to Joshua's abusers, concerned that there was a problem with their convictions. Louise had reassured her and said that they only had a few questions regarding Evžen Souček.

Mrs Yakubu gestured to them to sit down and stood opposite, wringing her hands.

'Don't tell me it turned out he was involved all along?' she said, looking strained and worried. 'I'm not sure Josh or us could go through another trial.'

'No, Mrs Yakubu, it's nothing like that,' Louise reassured her.

Mr Yakubu and Joshua entered from a separate door to the one Louise and David had entered by. Mr Yakubu was tall and broad; his skin was very dark in stark contrast to his small and pale wife. Joshua looked like a slightly shorter version of his father. Mr Yakubu moved to stand beside his wife while Joshua slumped in a nearby armchair.

'So, what can we do for you, officers?' Mr Yakubu asked forthrightly.

Louise explained again why they were there.

'That bastard,' Mr Yakubu spat, 'I knew he was more involved than he let on.'

'We don't believe he was, Mr Yakubu. The thing is, Mr Souček was found dead a few days ago. We are just following up on all the leads we can. Did you have any contact with Mr Souček after the trial?'

'Dead, you say?' Mr Yakubu said almost thoughtfully.

'Yes,' Louise said evenly, 'he was murdered. So, you see the relevance of my question.'

'Murdered?' Mr Yakubu said, his eyes widening. 'And you think we had something to do with it?'

'No, Mr Yakubu,' Louise kept her voice low, 'as I said, we are just following up with anyone who may have had contact with Mr Souček.'

'Well, I haven't had anything to do with that son of a bitch since the trial,' Mr Yakubu stated firmly.

'And you, Joshua?' David asked, looking over at the young man.

'No none,' Joshua said a little sullenly.

'Why would he want anything to do with that man?' Mrs Yakubu asked. 'He let those horrible things happen to Josh and said nothing. We just want to be left alone to try and rebuild our lives. Josh is going to university – he just wants to get on and put it all behind him, don't you, Josh?'

Josh just raised his chin and then looked away.

'Do any of you know a Seamus Harding?' Louise asked, looking around at the three of them.

All three shook their heads.

'Why?' Mrs Yakubu asked.

'It's just something we are following up,' Louise said non-committedly.

'Josh, have you seen the other two boys recently?' David asked.

'No,' was all Joshua said.

David noted he avoided eye contact when answering.

'Is there anything else?' Mr Yakubu asked, glancing at his watch. 'Only Eileen and I have to get to work.'

Louise and David looked at each other, both raising eyebrows.

'No, I don't think so,' Louise said rising and offering her hand. 'Thanks for your time.'

She shook hands with all three of them, with David simply nodding in their direction. Both began to move toward the living room door. Just before they left the room David stopped and turned.

'Oh, one thing, Mr Yakubu,' he said quickly. 'Do you own a gun of any description?'

'What? No, of course not,' he answered firmly.

'Thanks,' David said nodding again.

Once they were back in the car Louise sighed. 'This is going to be a waste of time. It's a complete dead end.'

'We've still got the other two to check out,' David said, mildly. 'Besides, what else can we do, we have to follow up on each and every lead.'

'They're not leads – we're clutching at straws. We're no nearer anything solid. The boss is just flailing about, grasping at anything she can think of.'

'It's a fair line of enquiry,' David said, keeping his voice soft and reasonable. 'What else can we do? What would you do that's different?'

Louise shook her head. 'I have no idea.' She opened her notepad. 'Next, Simon Caulder. He's in Newport Pagnell. Or Nathaniel Bold who's in Willen.'

'Willen's on the way to Newport Pagnell,' David said turning the key. 'Nathaniel first and then Simon.'

'I'll call ahead, make sure they're going to be there,' Louise said reaching for her mobile.

Nathaniel Bold gave much the same answers as Joshua: no, he hadn't seen Mr Souček since the trial and no, he hadn't seen the other boys. His parents were already out at work but he gave Louise and David their work numbers. They too had had nothing to do with Souček since the trial and seemed shocked and disturbed by his murder.

Louise hung up and turned to David with a 'told you so' look on her face. David shrugged and turned the key in the ignition.

'Sunny Newport Pagnell, here we come,' he said, pulling out into the increasingly busy morning traffic.

Newport Pagnell was a small town lying a short distance to the north east of Milton Keynes. Although considered separate towns, there was a barely discernible gap between the two. The drive only took around fifteen minutes.

They found the Caulder household in a quiet cul-de-sac in a neat and prosperous-looking estate.

'Not one car on these drives is worth below twenty grand, I reckon,' David said as they climbed out the car for a third time that morning.

Louise rang the doorbell and they both waited patiently for an answer. She had to ring a second time before the door was eventually opened by a sleepy-looking youth. Simon Caulder was slimmer than Joshua Yakubu but still had an athletic build. His tawny hair was dishevelled and spiked to one side where he had likely slept with hair gel still in his hair. He looked blankly at the two detectives. Louise produced ID and introduced them both. Giving a shrug and a grunt he invited them in.

He showed them into an immaculate living room and promptly slumped into a comfy-looking armchair. They took up the seats on a sofa opposite despite not being invited to sit.

'Are your parents in?' David asked.

'Nah, at work.' Simon's mumbled and sleepy reply was barely audible.

'We have a few questions about Mr Souček,' Louise said. 'Are you OK to answer without them here? We can come back later if you'd prefer.'

'That old perv?' Simon's voice rose to more normal levels. 'What about him?'

'He was found murdered a few days ago. We need to know if you had any contact with him in recent weeks?'

'Nuh!' The boy made a face that was unreadable to the detectives. 'Wouldn't want to go anywhere near the bugg… uh, man.'

'You called him a perv just now,' David put in, 'but at the trial and during all your witness statements you didn't implicate him at all. You simply said you thought he knew something and didn't say anything. Was he actually involved?'

The boy blushed and looked away. 'I don't want to talk about that,' he said, looking down at his feet.

'I appreciate that it's very difficult to go through this again but it might be helpful for us to catch whoever killed Mr Souček – if you do have more information that didn't come out at the trial.' Louise kept her voice soft and reassuring. 'What you tell us here and now won't go any further. We're just looking for background information. Was he more involved than you said before?'

Simon continued to look at his feet and mumbled something neither of them understood.

'What was that, Simon?' Louise asked quietly.

Simon looked up at them, a defiant look on his face. 'I said I wouldn't be surprised if he was. The old git kept quiet and he knew. Why else would he say nothing?'

'Was he...' David paused, looking for the right words. 'Did he...? Was he involved with you?' He managed to stammer out the question. He had never worked sex crimes and felt extremely uncomfortable asking this young man about them.

'No. But that doesn't mean he wasn't involved with the others,' Simon said, this time quite forcefully.

'They didn't implicate him either Simon,' Louise said, relieving David from the awkward line of questioning.

'No, well...' Simon trailed off and looked back down at his feet.

'So, you don't think he was involved but you feel angry at him for saying nothing? Is that right?' Louise was still keeping her voice soft and even.

'Maybe,' Simon said with a shrug.

'Last question, Simon, and we'll leave you in peace,' David said. 'Have you seen any of the other boys in recent weeks?'

'Not since we met...' There was a short pause but both officers caught it. 'Not since the trial,' Simon finished. A slight blush appeared on his pale cheeks.

'Are you sure about that?' David pressed.

'Yeah, not since the trial,' Simon said more confidently.

David glanced at Louise who didn't return his look.

'OK Simon,' she said, maintaining eye contact with the boy. 'Thank you for answering our questions. We also need to speak to your mum and dad. Do you have their work numbers or mobile numbers?'

'Yeah, here...' Simon moved over to a coffee table where a phone sat charging. He unplugged it and moved over to the sofa. Swiping the screen, he held the mobile up so that Louise could see it.

'That's my dad's number,' and then after a couple more swipes, 'and my mum's.'

Louise jotted them down. 'Thanks Simon. We'll leave you to get on with your morning.'

Simon shrugged in acknowledgement and turned to replace his phone on the table. Louise and David rose simultaneously and made their way across the room and towards the front door. Simon followed just behind.

Louise thanked him again as they were leaving and again it was met by a shrug.

Back in the car, Louise turned to David. 'He was lying. Those boys have met up and recently I would guess. They all lied about it – why would that be?'

Before David could answer, Louise's phone began to ring. She mouthed 'the boss' to him and answered the call.

'Where are you?' Rose demanded immediately.

'We've just finished with the third boy from the school. I was about to call his parents – they're at work,' Louise said quickly.

'Well leave it. I need you in the office asap.' Rose pronounced ASAP as a word rather than an acronym.

'On our way,' Louise said and waited for a further explanation.

'I don't hear a car engine yet. Get a move on,' Rose said forcefully enough for David to hear, and he turned the ignition immediately.

'Ten to fifteen minutes, ma'am,' Louise said and hung up.

'What's going on?' David asked as he turned the car.

'No idea but it's got the boss wound up, that's for sure.'

David grunted and pulled the car back out onto the main road.

Chapter Fifteen

Anna and Christine were standing together at Anna's desk when David and Louise walked in. Louise gave them both a questioning look.

'There's been another one,' Anna said flatly. 'Gareth knows the details.' She nodded over to where Gareth was, sitting on the phone to someone.

'Typical,' Louise said with an upward nod of her head and a tut. 'I bet he's crowing about that.'

'No,' Christine replied, 'he's been pretty quiet and reasonable. Filled us in as soon as he had spoken to the boss.'

'So, how did he find out?' David asked.

'He got a call from Bedfordshire – he spoke to them the other day about Souček and of course told the DS he spoke to about the murders. Well, it turns out they've had one too, exactly the same with the notes and everything. Body was found this morning so he called Gareth back first thing.'

Bedfordshire was the neighbouring force; the two regions were closely linked and there was often crossover between the two forces.

'Where was the body found?' Louise asked.

'Near Woburn golf course. Same MO – shot and a note pinned to their chest,' Christine answered. 'Beds are sending over scene of crime photos as soon as they're available.'

'Where's the boss now?' David asked.

'She's with the Chief Super. They're ensuring that there's complete liaison and cooperation on the case. I'm pretty sure Beds will happily hand it over to us,' Anna said, before turning to answer her phone that had been ringing for a couple of seconds.

'She's on her way down,' Anna said as she hung up. 'Anyone for coffee?'

A few minutes later Rose strode into the office. 'Are we all here?' she said as soon as she was through the door.

'Rod and Sandra aren't,' Louise said.

'No, they're already on their way to the scene. I take it you've been filled in?'

'Only as far as we have another one,' Louise replied.

'Yes, we do. This time we have an apparent fraudster. He was found by two golfers looking for a lost ball at Woburn golf course. That's Bedfordshire's patch but they are now handing everything over to us. Gareth is now the liaison for the two forces – everything goes through him to be logged immediately.' Rose raised a finger to emphasise her point.

'I take it we have no ID on the victim?' Louise asked

'No, like the other two we have nothing to go on. The report I've had is he is potentially Afro-Caribbean, mid-thirties, medium build, no identifying marks or tattoos. That's your first task. Louise, you and Anna get onto that as soon as we have photos over from Beds SOCO. Any missing persons from here to the Bedfordshire–Hertfordshire border. We have no idea where this victim is from so there's a lot of ground to cover to find him. And we have to consider that our killer might be from outside Milton Keynes, but then Woburn isn't that far away so it's still likely that he's local.'

'Same MO as before, ma'am?' David asked.

'As far as I know. We'll get a full report from the scene in a short while. That's partly why I've sent Rod and Sandra to the scene – they know what they're looking for.'

'What do you want the rest of us to do?' David asked.

'You and Christine are on CCTV and traffic cameras. Maybe we can pick out something there. Go over to Woburn first and see what you can see in the way of cameras in and around the town. Maybe we can spot a suspicious car or at least log all the cars that are heading around the golf course.'

Rose spotted David about to protest. 'I know it's unlikely we'll get anything from it just now but it's got to be worth a shot,' she shrugged. There really wasn't much else they could do at this stage.

'How far back do we look?' Christine asked.

'The last two days, maybe three. This one's probably after Harding and definitely after Souček. Again, we'll know more in a couple of hours but we should try and get ahead of the game. Right, get on with it,' Rose said clapping her hands once.

Her officers moved immediately to get on with their assigned tasks so Rose headed into her office without saying anything further. She shut the door and then slumped into her seat. Her head pounded. She had received something of a dressing down from the Chief Superintendent when she had been unable to answer many of his questions. She had no leads and nothing to really go on and could not dress that up in any way that came across better than it actually was, which was very poor indeed. The Chief Super did not want to face the public with the news a vigilante was stalking victims – victims that appeared to be innocent of the crimes the killer accused them of – without also having something to say about how the investigation was going. As a result, he wanted a complete news blackout until there was more to go on. He could not hold the press off forever, though, so he wanted results and he wanted them yesterday.

Rose rubbed her eyes and sighed. She understood the Chief Super's need for quick results but she had no idea where to look for them. It hurt her pride that she couldn't bring a better progress report to her superior; she was normally right on top of any case that came her way. She would have a list of suspects within days and usually wrapped the case up in no more than a month. Her success rate was excellent and so she had risen to DCI relatively quickly. She had been promoted when she was thirty-five and now, eight years later, she was highly regarded and respected among all of her contemporaries. She had never faced the misogyny the police were infamous for, such were her abilities and professionalism. And she was not about to let her reputation slip on this case.

She realised her phone was ringing. She picked it up wearily.

'DCI McPhail.'

'Ah, my favourite Detective Inspector,' a familiar voice said on the other end of the line.

Rose raised her eyes to the ceiling – great!

'What can I do for you Scott? And it's Detective Chief Inspector.'

'I hear tell you have yet another murder on your hands.' Scott sounded far too cheerful to be talking about another murder.

'How the hell did you hear that, Ellis? Who the fuck is it that slips you this information?' Rose felt her cheeks redden as her anger rose.

'So, there has been one? Do tell.'

'No, none whatsoever, Scott,' Rose said flatly. 'I will call you when I want to talk to you. Goodbye.'

As Rose hung up, she heard Scott say something else but couldn't hear what it was and had no inclination to find out. Rubbing her forehead, she got up and moved back out to the main office.

'What have we got?' she asked the room in general.

'Photos should be with us in five minutes,' Gareth said, looking up from his screen. 'I've organised for the PM to take place here and not in Bedfordshire. Rod called ... he's on site and organising things down there. He'll let us know if SOCO find anything we can use and once they've fingerprinted our victim in case we have him on record. Sandra is organising and supervising door to door with Bed's uniform.'

'Good work Gareth. Louise, Anna? Anything?'

Louise peered round her screen. 'We've five missing persons reports so far – that's just from the Thames Valley region. Working on the others now. Those photos would be helpful, Gareth.'

'I just said five minutes,' Gareth replied testily.

'Right, Anna, get on to looking into any reports of fraud or the like, again from the whole search area, Bedfordshire and Buckinghamshire. Start recently and go back maybe a couple of years.'

'Will do,' Anna replied then turned her attention back to her screen and started typing.

Knowing that all she could do was go back to her office to fill out reports and log work being done, the one question that kept repeating itself in Rose's mind was ... *how is he finding them?*

Chapter Sixteen

They were tripping over themselves and Rose knew it. They hadn't moved the investigation of Harding or Souček any further forward and now they had a third victim. She suspected they would find his identity relatively quickly if the pattern of victims continued, and she had no reason to believe that it wouldn't. But what then? Where did that leave them? The obvious answer was nowhere – no further forward and still no clue as to where to look or who to target their investigation at.

And they still had work to do on the charges brought against Denning. She realised that that would have to be handed over to another team and hated the idea. But she and her team were stretched enough. If the other team came up with anything relevant to the murders then they would report it to her and then they could act on it. Right now, as with the other loose ends, Denning would have to wait.

There is still one place we haven't looked – this was the thought she had been avoiding that now came into her mind. If this latest victim followed the same pattern and had a note on the PNC for some minor infringement that was related to fraud, then the pattern said nothing else other than the offender was a serving police officer with access to the police's database. No one else would be able to get that information and it certainly wouldn't be in the public domain. She was sure that some if not all of her team had also had a similar thought and that would mean it would be openly raised by them at some point. And then she would have no choice but to pursue that line of enquiry.

Not for the first time she tried to argue herself out of that corner. Some of that information would be in the public domain. Souček could well have been named in the news reports of the scandal at the school. Was it possible that there was mention of Harding somewhere tucked away? And the latest victim, if he had committed an offence like fraud, wasn't it likely that it would have made a newspaper somewhere? That was definitely worth checking and would take them away from the horrendous idea that it might be a serving officer.

A knock at the door brought her out of her musings. She looked up to see Gareth standing at the door. She waved for him to come in.

'We have an ID,' Gareth said as soon as he walked through the door.

'He's on the system?' Rose asked, knowing the answer before he said anything.

'Yep,' Gareth said, looking pleased with himself. 'One Dion Myers. We had his fingerprints on record. A company he ran was suspected of fraudulent dealing, selling land as an investment, land that didn't belong to him. He was brought in and eventually charged with fraud. This was in Northampton. He was convicted but only given a suspended sentence and barred from being a company director for ten years. All of this was five years ago.'

'So, there's a slight change in the pattern,' Rose said quietly. 'Our man has actually been convicted of something. And that would very likely be in the public domain.'

'Sorry ma'am? What do you mean, public domain?' Gareth asked.

'What? Oh, nothing. I was thinking out loud really. Good work Gareth. Right, let's see what we can find out about Mr Myers' recent activity. Pass the information on to the others and all of you get to work on it.'

'Will do,' Gareth said and walked quickly out of the office.

Round three, she thought as she watched Gareth's retreating back. Right, first things first.

She picked up the phone and dialled the internal number for her colleague who ran the other serious crime team.

John Reid wouldn't be too happy at being handed work by her. Strictly speaking, it should go through the Chief Superintendent but she wanted movement on the Denning angle and they were against the clock in terms of holding him. She would square things away with the boss after she had handed it over.

Reid's deep voice answered the phone.

'John, I need you to take on an investigation for me. We've got a third victim and are now up to our eyes.' She said this in a rush, not wanting him to get a word of complaint in.

'Bloody hell,' Reid said, 'quite a collection you're starting. OK, what have you got?'

Rose had been ready for an objection so was surprised – pleasantly so – when he agreed so readily. She filled him in on the Denning case and made sure he understood that anything he had that might be useful to her should be passed straight back.

'Right you are,' he said. 'Where are the files?'

'I'll have Gareth run them over to you, and thanks John,' Rose said before hanging up.

She was about to start planning everything that needed to be done when there was another knock at her door. This time it was David.

'What can I do for you David?' she asked after signalling him in.

'It's the three boys from the school. Louise and I think they're lying about something. The first two said they hadn't seen each other since the trial but the third boy, Simon Caulder, let slip that they had and then immediately backtracked. I just thought that might be worth following up.'

'Everything is worth following up right now, David,' Rose said a little wearily. 'But let's get the run-down on our latest victim and then we can plan what needs to be done on the investigation as a whole.'

'Yes, ma'am. I just thought you should know.' David looked a little bashful as though he had stepped out of line somehow.

'I did need to know and thank you for telling me. We'll look at it again as soon as we have what we need about Dion Myers,' Rose said with a smile.

David smiled back, 'Yes ma'am.'

While the team were working on the background for Dion Myers, Rose decided that she should go see the scene for herself. She gave Rod a quick call to make sure the body hadn't been moved – which it hadn't – and told him she would be along as soon as possible. The drive would take twenty to thirty minutes and she needed some time to think and try to get an angle that could be worked.

Walking through the main office, she stopped at Anna's desk.

'Anna, start seeing if you can't dig out any newspaper articles, online stories – that kind of thing – on our three victims. It might be that that's how our killer is finding them.'

'Yes, ma'am,' Anna replied immediately and called up her web browser to begin the searches.

127

'I'll be at the scene if anyone needs me. Mobile will be on,' Rose said and left the office.

***

As she drove, thought after thought kept piling on top of each other and getting in each other's way. She couldn't grasp any of them long enough to get a handle on it and then another question would arrive or a new angle would occur. She decided it would be better if she cleared her head completely and thought of nothing for the rest of the way. She might have a chance of formulating a coherent thought when she reached the scene. She had more or less managed it by the time she arrived at Woburn Golf Club.

She followed Rod's instructions to the scene, a walk that took the best part of ten minutes, and picked her way through the woods to where the body had been found. The walk through the trees was eerily similar to the one she had taken at the site of Seamus Harding's murder, only this time it was in daylight and there was no rain.

The scene itself was also very reminiscent of the site where Harding had been found: a small clearing in a wooded area, surrounded by trees and bushes. She ducked under the police tape and looked around. A forensic tent had been erected over the body so she made her way over there.

There was only the body and Dr Matheson in the tent. The doctor was just rising from the body and nodded over to her. Rose moved over to the body. He lay propped up against a tree, with a neat circular wound in his forehead, just above the right eye, and the by-now familiar note pinned to his chest. There was blood on his chest where the large pin entered and left. His jaw hung slackly giving his face a pseudo-comic look of surprise.

'What can you tell me?' Rose asked quietly.

'He died twenty-four to forty-eight hours ago. I might be able to pin that down once he's back at the mortuary. Otherwise, it's depressingly similar to the other two: killed with a single gunshot, this time to the head, note pinned to his chest peri mortem. The position he's in would suggest he was already sitting against the tree when he was shot. There's no exit wound so I suspect we'll find a .22 calibre bullet somewhere in his skull.'

Rose nodded – the doctor was right. It was all too depressingly similar. The only difference was that they already knew who this was and the fraudster tag was at least in some way correct. She sighed and turned away. There was nothing to be learned standing looking at him.

'Where's Rod?' she asked.

'He's supervising the area search. I think he's over that way.' The doctor pointed out the direction she thought Rod would be found.

'Thanks, Stephanie,' Rose said, giving the doctor a tight-lipped smile. 'Let me know as soon as you have the PM results.'

The doctor nodded at Rose's back as she walked out of the tent. Rose picked her way across the small clearing towards where Dr Matheson had indicated. There were a few numbered, yellow forensic markers dotted around the clearing but Rose knew from experience that there were too few to mean there was any real evidence to be had there.

She found Rod a short way into the woods. He was crouched over alongside a uniformed officer and a SOCO, examining something on the ground.

'What have you got, Rod?' Rose asked as she neared the trio.

Rod looked up. 'Possible footprint. Might or might not be from the perpetrator or could be just a dog walker. It's not likely to be a golfer – no spike marks. We'll get a cast and have it compared to the print found at the site of Harding's murder.'

'OK, well found.' She looked over at the white overall-covered SOCO. 'Anything you can tell me?'

'I would guess at a size seven or eight, maybe nine at most – so, small for a man, on the large side for a woman,' she said, indicating the length of the print with a pen. 'We'll know more when I've photographed it and taken a cast but I would say it's a Doc Marten or similar.'

'So, if it's a man, we're looking at someone fairly short, would you say?' Rose asked.

The SOCO shrugged. 'Most men are on average size eight and above but that's not to say there aren't plenty with smaller feet. But, if I were to guess, then yes – it would likely be quite a short man.'

'The report on Harding's murder said there was a possibility that the killer was of short stature,' Rose said, directing this to Rod.

'It did,' Rod replied cautiously, 'but it was speculation really. We don't have a clear indication where the killer was standing when they shot Harding or exactly what position they were in. And this print could easily be a woman or a complete dead end, or both. It's quite a way from the body so it'll be difficult to prove it was whoever shot our man over there.'

'Yeah, all too true,' Rose said. 'Still, it's more than we've had from the other sites. Might prove useful if we get someone in for this.'

Rod nodded; he had wanted to say 'that's a big if,' but decided against it.

Rose looked about and then back to Rod. 'Anything else?' she asked.

Rod shook his head. 'Nothing else. Like the last two, the sites are well chosen, evidence is difficult to find and can be easily lost to the elements. And there's precious few people to witness anything, especially if we're assuming the killings happened at night.'

'I think we have to assume they're being carried out at night,' Rose agreed. 'This killer clearly plans well in advance and, like you say, picks their sites well. I can't see them risking anything in broad daylight.'

She looked around again and realised there was very little she could do here.

'Right, thanks Rod,' she said and nodded to the other two. 'I'll head back to the office and see what we've got there on the victim. Let me know if anything else crops up and then head back yourself.'

'Will do,' he said and turned his attention back to the footprint.

As she got back to her car, she spotted two people climbing into their car across the car park. She recognised them both. It was Scott Ellis and Bill Turner, a photographer that Ellis often worked with.

Bastards, she thought, and starting making her way towards them, hoping to intercept their car before it pulled out of the car park. She was just too late. The car was pulling away and Ellis gave her a little wave from the passenger seat.

Where the hell does he get his information?

She walked back to her own car and thumped the roof before climbing in, then thumped the steering wheel once she was inside. The frustrations of the last week were beginning to boil over. She leant her forehead against the wheel and drew in a long deep breath.

What the fuck am I going to do?

Chapter Seventeen

Rose left the team to it for the best part of the rest of the day and spent the time brooding in her office. She had managed to file the reports that needed doing but other than that she hadn't been able to summon the will to do much else. Instead, she sat with an open notebook and fretted over every last detail of the case. Her notes only told her what she didn't know, which came as no surprise.

She glanced at the wall clock and realised it was nearing six. She had called a team meeting for six in order that they could go over every last detail and make a new and concerted plan for the investigation. She figured that by hearing everyone's views and reports something might become clear. That was the hope anyway; the reality could well be as maddening as the case had already proved to be.

She got up and walked into the main office. As soon as she was out of her door, Anna called over to her.

'You're going to want to see this, ma'am,' she said, gesturing towards her screen.

Rose walked over, hoping that maybe they had something at last.

'You're not going to like it,' Anna said glumly.

What a surprise, hopes dashed again – Rose thought as she moved behind Anna to see what she had. It was the local newspaper's website and the main story, emblazoned with a huge headline, made Rose's heart sink even further.

Triple Murder in Milton Keynes, Police Clueless.

Three Men Slain in One Week.

Is there a vigilante killer on the loose?

'Bastard!' Rose spat. 'That little shit.'

She was about to read further when Gareth called over.

'I'm busy, Gareth,' Rose said forcefully.

'It's the Chief Superintendent, ma'am. He wants to talk to you immediately.'

'I bet he does,' Rose said quietly, 'and I now know why.' Then louder, she said: 'Tell him I'll be up in five minutes.'

Gareth nodded and put his phone back to his ear.

'Thanks, Anna,' Rose said, sounding anything but grateful.

'No problem, ma'am. At times like these I'm thankful for only being a DC. I would not want to be in your shoes right now.'

'I don't want to be in my shoes right now, Anna,' Rose replied with feeling.

***

Detective Chief Superintendent Abdighani was not known as a man who took fools gladly and especially when the said fool also painted him with the same brush. Rose knew he would be furious that the press had not only got wind of the case but appeared to have as much idea of what was going on as the police did. Any arguments saying that they would have found out sooner or later – or that it was about time they went public with the case – would fall on deaf ears.

Rose took a deep breath and knocked on the door.

'Come,' the Chief's deep voice resonated through the door.

Rose entered and stood beside the chair on the far side of the desk from Abdighani. He motioned for her to sit while he flicked through some paperwork. Rose knew this was always a prelude to a dressing down. He always made you wait, knowing you would be sweating on what was to come. Eventually, he looked up from the papers and looked at Rose for some time. Rose tried not to squirm like a naughty schoolgirl.

'What on Earth is going on, Detective Chief Inspector?' Abdighani said slowly and deliberately.

'Sir?' Rose said and immediately regretted it; playing innocent and unknowing would only make matters worse.

'Don't treat me like an idiot, Chief Inspector.' Abdighani kept his voice slow and carefully pitched, another bad sign. 'I am fairly sure one of your team will already have shown you the report in the Herald. What I want to know is how it got there and in so much detail.'

'I don't know how Scott Ellis gets his information, sir. As for the detail, he is a shrewd operator and I think he has probably just put two and two together.'

'Rubbish,' Abdighani said, emotion reaching his voice for the first time. 'He has far too many details for it to be guess work. He must have known the victims were –' he waved his hand trying to find the right word – 'labelled as criminals to get the vigilante angle. That has to have come from within.'

'Yes, sir, as I say I have no idea where he gets his information.'

'It has to be someone in your team, Chief Inspector. Don't you agree?'

'No, sir, I don't agree. Most of the station knows about the murders – it could have been anyone.'

Abdighani appeared to consider this for a second and then dismiss it. 'I am going to have to make a statement,' he said, changing tack.

'Yes sir,' Rose replied, voice neutral.

'And I have nothing to tell them, do I Chief Inspector?'

'No, sir.'

'And that is also your bloody fault.' Abdighani thumped his desk.

'Yes sir,' was all Rose could say.

The Chief Superintendent looked at her angrily for a second then his face relaxed.

'It's probably for the best,' he said, his tones more normal. 'We probably should be appealing for public information given we have precious little else to go on.'

'Yes, sir.' Rose did not feel able to proffer an opinion; it was safest to simply agree.

'Right, I want the most up-to-date brief you have and any further information you think relevant, and I want it in fifteen minutes, understood?' He gave her another hard stare.

'Yes, sir.'

'That'll be all then, Chief Inspector.' Abdighani waved a hand towards the door.

As Rose reached for the door handle, he spoke again. 'And Rose?'

Rose was surprised by the use of her first name; it meant the heat was off a little. 'Yes, sir?' she said, trying to hide her surprise.

'I have faith in you. I'm sure you'll get there. Just don't make it too long, eh?' He smiled thinly. This was as close as he ever came to a compliment.

Rose returned the smile. 'Thank you, sir,' she said and left the office, before he could think of anything else to get wound up about.

She went straight into her office as soon as she got downstairs, informing the team that the meeting was delayed and to carry on with what they were doing. She then set about creating the most comprehensive briefing she could. She did not want the Chief Super complaining about that too. She felt a little guilty that she had not laid some of the blame for the leak on her own shoulders. She had after all told Scott Ellis most of the details in his report. But, she reasoned, she hadn't told him in the first place and certainly hadn't informed him about the most recent murder. She was as determined as the Chief Super to find out which little rat that was.

Briefing written, it was time to pull the team together and try to forge a way ahead.

She was about to shut her office door when she heard the phone ring. Moving quickly, she reached over her desk and grabbed the receiver.

'McPhail?'

'Chief Inspector, it's PC Carmichael here – we've found a phone at the Seamus Harding site,' a young and breathless voice said at the other end of the line. 'It's been smashed and looks to be dead, but it could be his phone.'

'Brilliant,' Rose said, a smile spreading across her face. 'Well done Constable, get it straight over to the tech lab and have them relay the results to DCI Reid's team.'

'Yes, ma'am,' Carmichael replied, 'straight away.'

Rose put the phone down and smiled again. Maybe we're getting somewhere now – she allowed this optimistic thought to dwindle in her mind as she left her office.

They convened in a meeting room just down the hall from the office. Everyone had been pulled in. The front desk would take messages should anything happen whilst they were in their meeting.

Rose sat at the head of the long table and let the team settle in their seats. When they were all seated, she brought the room to order.

'Right, everyone, it's time we went through everything and see where it gets us. We need to get on top of this pronto. I'm sure you've all already reached the conclusion that our murderer is not going to stop of their own volition and is very likely to kill again sometime in the near future. So, let's look at what we have from every possible angle.' She looked around the room – it was full of nodding agreement.

'Have we got anything on any connections between the victims?' she asked the room in general.

There was a series of head shakes until Christine spoke up. 'None that we can find. There are no mutual friends or family, work places were totally different as were hobbies and past times, again as far as we can tell.'

'Apart from that they have all come into contact with the police,' Louise put in.

'Yes, apart from that,' Rose agreed. 'We'll come to that. First, what about the families of the people involved with each victim's situation? Has someone got a grudge against all three or perhaps had a go at Mr Souček and then somehow got the details for the others and decided to become a marauding vigilante?'

'Not that we can see,' Louise said. 'David and I interviewed the families involved in the scandal at the school and apart from a potential lie from the boys about meeting each other, none of the family appear to have wanted anything to do with him – never mind kill him. And I can't see how they would know anything about the others.'

'Which brings me to my next point. Anna, did you find any press reports about our victims?' Rose knew where Louise was driving and wanted to hold off the obvious conclusion until they had explored all other options.

'There is a small piece on Dion Myers from the Northampton Chronicle and Echo, which mentions he had been banned from being a company director as a result of shady dealings. And Evžen Souček is mentioned in the reports about the school but only briefly in a couple of them. There is a report about young men making a nuisance of themselves trying to film through people's windows but it mentions no one by name. Could be Seamus Harding but anyone reading it wouldn't know that.' Anna looked over at Louise; she was clearly drawing the same conclusions.

'And our killer wouldn't have got any details about where they lived or any other details that might have helped them,' Louise said, taking her cue from Anna.

'Yeah, I know where you're going, you two, and I'm pretty sure the rest of the room is thinking something similar but first let's just look at what we know, not speculate on who or what it might be. Now, weapon, what do we know?'

'Ballistics are still checking the most recent bullet,' Gareth said, 'but they are pretty sure it's the same weapon in all three cases – same calibre definitely and definitely the same weapon in the first two cases. No reason to think it will be different in the third.'

'Access to guns is still thankfully rare in Milton Keynes, so we must be able to do something with that,' Rod said.

'Not if it's illegally owned, which in every likelihood it is. We can't track them down until we find a suspect,' David said and Rod nodded in contemplative agreement.

'What about the potential victims of Denning and Harding?' Rod asked. 'Any joy in identifying any of the women in the videos?'

'DCI Reid's team are on that case now and they'll keep me appraised as they go.'

'I still can't see how someone involved in that would find out about the other two and have the information to track them down and kill them,' Christine said.

'All right, all right,' Rose said holding her hands up. 'Let's get it out in the open. I'm sure we're all thinking it.' She didn't say any more but looked around the room.

'It's possible we're looking at a copper. They would have access to the information they needed to select, track down and kill all three,' Rod said for the room.

Rose nodded, 'Yes, it is looking quite likely. And I agree we have to keep an open mind. But until we have something concrete, I don't want that getting in the way of the investigation. Now what else have we got?'

'Dion Myers was reported missing two days ago by his wife,' Gareth said. 'He didn't come home from work, and apparently he was always home by seven at the latest. She reported it when he wasn't home by nine. His office – which we think he was operating another dodgy sales outfit from – is in central MK. I've started pulling all the CCTV we can find. There may be something on there – the area is really well covered and we're bound to be able to follow him and see if there's anyone else following him or whatever.'

'Excellent, Gareth, when will you have the footage?' Rose said, relieved there was at last something solid.

'Tomorrow,' Gareth said and looked smugly around the room.

'Good. Speaking of Mr Myers' business, that needs checking out thoroughly. Maybe there's a disgruntled client out there that wished him harm. Rod, you get on that in the morning, then you and I will go pay the office a visit in the afternoon.'

'Yep, will do,' Rod said.

'Anything else?' Rose asked, looking around the room.

'Oh, yes,' Gareth said, sifting through some paperwork. 'Lab result back on the shoe print found at the Myers scene. It's a match to the one we found where Harding was killed.'

'Right, good. So, we can be relatively positive that it's our killer's print. If – when we find them that'll be some good physical evidence. Anyone else got anything to add?' Rose looked around the room again.

No one had anything further. Rose brought the meeting to a close and told them all to go home and get some rest. Rose stayed in her seat while they all left. She realised that everything now rested on the CCTV. They had very little else.

Please God let there be something on there, she thought as she got up to leave.

Chapter Eighteen

Rose slumped onto the couch and grabbed the TV remote. Chief Superintendent Abdighani had made his statement to the press and would be on the local news channel at nine thirty. She felt obliged to watch even though she pretty much knew what he would say.

Gordon came in from the kitchen bearing a glass of wine in each hand with the bottle tucked under one arm. He handed Rose a glass, slipped the bottle out from its precarious position and set it on the coffee table, finally settling down on the couch next to her.

'You don't normally watch the news,' Gordon said, as he sat down.

'Chief Super's on,' Rose said absently.

'Ah, we're still on the case, are we?' Gordon's voice was half jocular and half chiding.

'Afraid so, love,' Rose said, turning the volume up slightly.

Neither of them discussed their work with the other – it was the general unsaid rule between them. Their work was all too often grisly and very unpleasant; both of them dealt with human trauma and tragedy on an almost daily basis and neither really wanted to relive their day all over again. It was also accepted that in some way they would burden the other with their own demons and both had enough of those to last a lifetime. But that evening Rose had been so frustrated with the whole case, and knowing it would be on the news she had chatted briefly with Gordon about it. She had avoided a lot of the detail and really it was just a rant about a bad day, but he had listened patiently and offered consolation where he could.

'You'll get there,' he said as the Chief Superintendent's face appeared on the screen and the press conference began. 'You always do in the end.'

'Not always,' Rose said, a sadness in her voice.

'The three victims appear to be entirely unconnected…' the Chief's clear, confident voice was saying from the TV.

'Well, OK, most of them,' Gordon said, sipping his wine.

'We are working on several lines of enquiry and hope for an arrest soon…'

'Bollocks,' Rose said with feeling, then turned to Gordon. 'Most of them have things like evidence and clues and leads to follow. Many of them are straightforward with one prime suspect and an obvious motive. This one has none of those things.'

'They'll turn up. You never know what might come in from this,' Gordon said, indicating the television with his wine glass.

'Yeah, and we've got the CCTV that's coming in tomorrow,' Rose said unconvincingly.

'… reassure the public…'

Gordon nodded, 'There you go then.'

'I'm not convinced. Our killer is very clever and extremely aware of how we work, a bit too aware. I doubt they've been daft enough to be captured on CCTV for us all to see.' Rose took a long drink of wine and then set the glass down. She couldn't drink too much; she needed to be fresh and ready to go straight from the traps the next morning.

'A bit too aware?' Gordon asked, a slight frown on his face.

On the TV, Chief Superintendent Abdighani had opened the room for questions. Rose noticed but was unsurprised when Scott Ellis' hand was the first in the air.

'How do you think the victims are being selected?' he asked.

'As yet we don't know but rest assured that is a major part of the enquiry,' Abdighani replied, stone-faced.

'That's not quite the case,' Rose said, pointing at the TV. 'We think that it might be a copper. All the victims were on the PNC for minor offences. It's possible a member of the public would have spotted small press pieces about the victims but there's very little chance they would be able to find enough information to track them down. That information would only be available to…' She trailed off.

Gordon nodded. 'A police officer,' he finished for her.

Rose picked her glass back up – *stuff it, this wine is getting drunk*, she thought.

'Yep, a police officer,' she said after another deep drink. 'Thing is they must have spent ages trawling through the PNC to find them. There are far more obvious targets on there, those already convicted of actual crimes. Why go for these people with minor offences or nothing at all against their names? That's what I don't get. If you're a vigilante, surely you go for the obvious targets – the known housebreakers and drug dealers, the convicted paedophile. Not three obscure and relatively innocent individuals.'

'Maybe the killer knew them all?' Gordon said, trying to be helpful but knowing he really wasn't giving much assistance.

'Thought of that,' Rose said, draining her glass. 'We can't find any common threads between the three, other than they've been involved with the police in a comparatively minor way. I just can't see how they're being selected, and as a result we can't even determine who or what type of person might be next.'

'You think there will be more?' Gordon asked, refilling her glass.

'Oh yes,' Rose replied, nodding her thanks. 'This one is highly unlikely to stop.'

The press conference was drawing to a close, with Chief Superintendent Abdighani refusing to answer any more questions or give any further details.

'I would ask if any member of the public has any information, no matter how small or trivial it may seem, about the three victims or who may be responsible, to do the right thing and come forward,' he said in closing.

As the Chief was turning to go, Scott Ellis' voice was heard calling, 'Don't you think the public will actually be behind a vigilante? After all they're keeping the streets a safer place.'

Abdighani turned and gave Ellis a hard stare.

'I have no comment to make as to whether this is a vigilante or not. The fact is the perpetrator of these crimes is a murderer and nothing more. Now that really is all, thank you ladies and gentlemen. Good night.'

'Well,' Rose said, turning the TV off, 'that wasn't a total disaster, I suppose.'

Gordon shrugged and said nothing.

'I wish I knew where that Scott Ellis gets his information from,' Rose said after a pause. 'He seemed to know where the third victim was almost before we did. Someone is tipping him off.'

'Maybe he's your killer?' Gordon said with a chuckle.

Rose gave a short snort of a laugh, 'I hadn't thought of that. Maybe he is.' She laughed again. 'I can't really see it though – it'd be a bit Agatha Christie.'

'Or, Conan Doyle,' Gordon put in. 'What was Holmes' thing? When you've eliminated the possible? Or something like that?'

'Something like that,' Rose agreed with a smile.

'Well,' Gordon said, patting her knee, 'as much as I'd like to sit here playing detective, I have a six o'clock shift tomorrow. Off to bed for me.'

He kissed her and rose from the couch.

'I think I'll stop up for a bit,' Rose said. 'Night.'

After Gordon had left, she continued to plough her way through the bottle of wine and resumed her brooding from earlier that day.

Chapter Nineteen

David woke to the sounds of clunking and banging and cupboards being opened and closed. He looked across to his alarm clock – six forty. He grunted and heaved himself out of bed. It had been another late and energetic night. As a result, he felt both exhausted and elated at the same time.

He found Louise in the kitchen, opening and closing cupboards and pulling out bowls and mugs. The kettle was just boiling.

'Morning,' he said and moved over to stand behind her. Placing his hands on her hips, he kissed her neck, took a deep breath and inhaled the pleasant aroma of her hair and T-shirted body. He ran his hands a little further up over her ribs and started to move them around to cup her breasts.

She slapped his hand away. 'There was enough of that last night,' she said, 'and we have to get to work.'

He sighed in mock indignation and moved his hands.

'Tea,' she said and handed him a mug.

He smiled, 'Well remembered.'

'Right, I'm off for a shower and to get dressed. Drink that and follow suit.' She moved past him and left the kitchen.

He watched her go for a bit and then wandered into the living room and flopped onto the couch with his tea, taking small sips the whole while. He had only drunk about half the tea when Louise came out of the bathroom and made her way across the hall to the bedroom, wrapped in a towel. He became semi-aroused at the thought of striding through and whipping the towel off her but then looked at the time and realised she would just slap him away again. He finished his tea and made his way to the bathroom.

He showered and shaved then walked out of the bathroom. As he was moving through the hall, he caught sight of Louise sitting in the living room hunched over the coffee table, arms resting on her legs. Her hand moved and appeared to turn a page. There was only one thing she could be reading – his diary which he always left on the table ready to be filled in each evening.

He wasn't entirely sure why he kept one. Most of the time the entries consisted of 'work' and the occasional 'Watford playing – showing on Sky' and very rarely he would excitedly write 'date'. He moved over to where Louise was sitting.

'What are you doing?' he asked, a hint of anger in his voice.

She jumped and looked round at him guiltily. 'Sorry,' she said quickly. 'I couldn't help myself. It's the job, you know? Constantly curious and all that.' She quickly shut the diary.

'Hmm, well don't do it again. That's well and truly off limits,' he said and turned to go into the bedroom.

'Hiding all your other girlfriends in there, are you?' Louise chided his retreating back.

He looked over his shoulder. 'Ha, chance would be a fine thing.'

She stuck her tongue out and he retreated into the bedroom. That was the first time she had called herself his girlfriend and he felt a sharp tingle of pleasure run along his spine.

Louise waited until he had definitely left the room and there was little sign he would come back out again and quickly moved back to the diary. She flicked back to the pages she had been looking at and then turned a couple more, scanning the pages as fast as she could. Then she sat back and looked thoughtfully at the ceiling.

'And what do I do with that information?' she said quietly to herself.

Kiss me quick

'It all got a bit too easy, o'course. See once you've done it more 'n once and used a variety of stuff, garrotte, knife and even yer bare 'ands, it gets a bit samey, y'know wot I mean? It's like goin' on a fair ride or summink, y'know, like you've been on it, like, a couple of times an' then it gets kinda boring. I ain't saying it got any less satisfying just all a bit similar, y'know?

So, I needed to spice it up a bit. Make it all a bit more on the risky side, sorta fing. So, then I decided it would be in people's 'omes. Inside, like. So, I set about learnin' how to break in to 'ouses. Got most of that offa the internet an' all. Well, that and talking to a couple of old mates o' mine that I knew 'ad done time. For 'ouse breaking, y'know?

They weren't too interested in telling me at first. Suppose they fought I was gonna get on their patch and start up on me own. I said to them, "Nah, don't be fuckin' daft! I got kiddies an' a missus at 'ome. I just wanna know how to protect meself, y'know, like prevention is better than cure an' all that?"

So, they give me a bit of gen an' I worked the rest out for meself.

Charlie, 'e was one o' them. 'E was a right character 'e was. In an' out of nick all the time. Funny thing was, every time 'e came out 'e seemed to 'ave another bird on the go. 'E used to say it was the smell of the jail, they loved it, 'e reckoned. No idea how he did it. Wasn't like 'e was a 'andsome cunt or nothin'. An' 'ow 'is missus never found out

I'll never know. Mind you, yer mum never knew what I got up to on me 'olidays. Or she didn't care.

Anyway, back to the 'ouse breaking. See, I knew by then I wasn't likely to get caught any time soon, if ever. I'd done for, oh I dunno, 'alf a dozen, maybe as much as ten by then? An' not a single knock at the door. See, I figured that it's only once every four years an' all over the country. Coppers 'ad no clue, did they? An' like I say, I was getting a bit bored of the usual killin' strangers in out of the way places. Funny really, in't it? Y'd fink it would be more of a thrill bein' out in the open an' all that. But, like I said, it all gets a bit samey after a while. I'd perfected my technique by then. Get in quick when the time was right an' take 'em out fast. I 'ad it dahn to a fine art. But after a while it just weren't cuttin' the mustard. No spark an' less fun.

I fink it was the unknown that made me do it, in 'ouses I mean. See, you 'ad no idea 'oo might be in there an' no clue where they'd be. An' I knew that there was a greater risk of leavin' evidence about. It's much 'arder to clear up after yerself in a 'ouse. But after a bit I couldn't 'elp meself.

First one was a bit of a disaster. I made a right fuckin' mess of the door. Made far too much noise and still couldn't get the fucker open. Lights come on dahnstairs an' I panicked an' run. I was smart enough not to try that again for a few days an' then try well away from the first attempt.

This was dahn in Somerset. Lovely tench lake and some ornamental lakes an' that kinda fing. Loved the fishin' down there, I did. Any road, fing was round there that there's plenty places well out of the way. So you can 'ave a go at one an' if ya' fucked it up you could go for a long drive an' find another place as far away as possible from the first. Cor, there's some cracking places round there an' like plenty of farm 'ouses an' isolated cottages, all that kind of fing.

So, anyway, second attempt went much better. Got into this little cottage an' it's just this old gal. On 'er own she was. Bloody shame I fought, leavin' an old gal like that all on 'er own. Where's 'er family, I fought? Y'know whos looking after 'er? So, best fing I could do was put 'er out of 'er misery, weren't it? It was all fairly easy once I was in, except the dog, fuckin' collie, y'know, sheep dog? It was as old as the old gal, mind, but it din't half kick up a stink when I got in. Lucky I was in the kitchen an' I just grabbed a knife an' stuck it right between the ribs. That sorted that out. The old gal 'ad come dahnstairs by then, o'course.

She weren't up to much, in the physical sense, like. Pretty frail an' easy to overcome. I got 'er to the floor in the front room an' pinned 'er down. I 'ad a length of chord with me, not a proper garrotte, just something to throttle 'er with. See I cased this place, unlike the first one. Kicked meself about that, Charlie 'ad said 'e always watched a place for a evening before 'e went in. So, I done that this time. I'd watched an' I knew it was just the old dear. So, I just 'ad this bit o' chord wiv me, din' I? Fought it would be enough.

Fing was, the old gal, she might not 'ave 'ad much fight in 'er when it came to fending me off, but Jeesus, she din't 'alf 'ave plenty of life in 'er when I tried to snuff 'er. She clung on for fuckin' ages. Felt like 'alf an hour but was probably only ten minutes. It's pretty fuckin' 'ard 'olding a rope round someone's neck that long I can tell ya'. Should've made up a garrotte, I 'spose, but there you go, that's me all over, always looking for the next thrill. Make it 'ard on meself, like. Still a new challenge every once in a while, does ya' good I say.

Anyway, that's 'ow I got into killing people in their own 'omes. Kept that up on the next 'oliday an' all. Then it all stopped o'course. I was too old by then, anyway. Worried some cunt'd stick me back or summin'.'

Chapter Twenty

They had something. It wasn't much but the CCTV had come through and there was something they could follow. Gareth and Christine had spent hours checking footage until they had picked out Dion Myers, shortly after he'd left his office. They could follow him along his route to a dark and quiet car park where, unfortunately, they couldn't track him any further; the cameras were too far apart and didn't cover where he had walked. The more interesting thing was that about ten or twenty yards back from Dion someone appeared to be following him. The footage was poor and the figure kept tight into the buildings meaning their features and anything particularly distinctive was hard to pick out in the low light conditions. But there was definitely someone and they certainly looked to be following Myers.

Rose watched as Gareth and Christine took her through the footage with a growing sense that this might at least be something of a break. They had taken longer to trace Myers because he had left his office later than usual; that was something else to check out. There were quite a few other people in the footage heading in approximately the same direction but there was something deliberate in the movements and pacing of the shady individual that suggested to the officers that someone was trying to follow Myers at a discreet distance.

Rod joined them and stood behind Rose, looking over her shoulder.

'Is it just me or do they look on the short side?' he asked, after a few minutes of watching.

'Could be,' Gareth said, 'but the angle of the camera and the low light can be deceptive. I would say they're shorter than Myers.'

'How tall was Myers?' Rose asked, as she watched the two figures – still ten metres or so apart – enter the dark area of car park that wasn't well covered by cameras.

Rod moved over to his desk and looked for the information in a file. 'Five foot eleven,' he called over to Rose.

'I would guess then that this individual,' she said, tapping the screen with a pen, 'is no more than, what, five eight maybe nine?'

'I would say that's about right,' Christine agreed.

'So, after they enter the car park we lose them for about ten minutes. The exit camera then picks up what looks like a black or at least dark-coloured car leaving. This could be a VW Golf – it's hard to be sure as the headlights obscure the number plate and it's pretty indistinct anyway. Myers' car was found in the car park yesterday afternoon. It had picked up a number of tickets … luckily an eagle-eyed uniform recognised the number plate. I think we can assume he was abducted in that car park between eight and ten past and that he was in that dark-coloured car.'

'I agree,' Rose said, straightening up from where she had been bent over the monitor to get a better view. 'So, does that mean our killer already knew exactly where his car would be and realised that the area was only partially covered by cameras, giving them the perfect opportunity to snatch him? Or were they simply following on the off-chance?'

'I would say that they've been very careful up until now – no CCTV, very little in the way of forensic evidence, and the killings look organised and well planned. I doubt our man would leave very much to chance,' Rod said, walking back over to join them.

'I think you're right Rod,' Rose said. 'Our man does not leave anything to chance – in which case, maybe we can pick them out earlier in the day scoping out Mr Myers' parking space. Gareth, you and Christine start going back to first thing that morning and see what you can find.'

Gareth gave Christine a look. They were in for several eye-reddening hours of scrolling through footage from several cameras. Knowing the all-important area wasn't covered they would also have to pay particular attention to who was walking by and cross-reference with the footage they had from the evening to try and spot their man. Rose patted Gareth on the shoulder, knowing what she was asking.

She turned to Rod, 'Get Anna and Sandra on to pulling all the CCTV footage from Woburn and for a five-mile radius around the other sites. Let's see if we can't find the same vehicle on those. Let's go back two days from each murder.'

'I thought we'd already checked that?' Rod asked.

'We have, but now we know what we're looking for,' Rose said and moved off towards where David was sitting.

'David?' she said, and the young man looked up. 'You and Louise have another go at the kids from the school – follow up on them meeting up.'

'Yes, ma'am,' David said and pulled his coat from the back of his chair. Louise had heard and was following suit.

'Rod,' Rose called over the office, 'you're with me. Let's see what kept Mr Myers late at his office.'

Dion Myers' office was in a high, glass-fronted block of offices a stone's throw from central Milton Keynes. It looked extremely impressive both outside and in. The main reception hall was floored in what looked like marble with a large wood-covered reception desk. The desk was staffed by two women with head pieces affixed over opposite ears, eyes fixed on the screens in front of them.

Rose and Rod had to wait a few minutes before one of the women looked up from the call she was fielding. She gave them a 'one second' hand gesture and returned to looking at her screen.

Rod looked around the reception hall. 'Posh place.'

As soon as the call was finished, she looked back up at Rose.

'Detective Chief Inspector Rose McPhail and this is Detective Sergeant Laing. Where can we find the offices for The Land Investment Group, please?' Rose said, showing her ID to the receptionist.

'They're on the third floor, office eighteen,' she replied. 'Shall I call up and let them know you're on your way?'

'No, thanks,' Rose said, 'we'll just head on up.' She looked around deliberately.

'Lifts are just over there,' the woman said, pointing to a bank of four lifts.

'Thanks,' Rose said and moved off in the direction of the lifts.

'Just a tick,' Rod said as they walked across the reception hall.

He turned back to the desk and approached the two women again, waiting patiently while they dealt with another call each. The woman they hadn't spoken to finished first but Rod indicated that he wanted to speak to 'his' receptionist.

She finished her call and looked up at Rod, a slight crease on her face.

'Was there something else?' she asked.

'I was just wondering,' Rod said, 'you didn't seem overly concerned that the police were calling on The Land Investment Group. Have we been in before?'

'Yes,' the woman replied, 'a couple of days ago. Two uniformed officers came to visit.'

'Ah, yes of course,' Rod said, nodding his thanks and turning to leave. There would have been some questions asked when Myers had been reported missing and hadn't turned up by the following morning.

'It's a shame what happened to Mr Myers,' she said as he began to walk away.

'You knew him?' Rod asked, turning back.

'Only by sight and from passing messages of course. Plenty of them,' she said, shaking her head.

'He had a lot of messages then?' Rod asked casually.

'Loads … all angry people demanding to speak to him or whoever was in charge up there. Sometimes we'd get the same person four or five times a day. I don't think he ever called them back. Gave me the impression they were a bit dodgy. Still, you wouldn't wish that on him, no matter what.'

'No, you wouldn't,' Rod said. The receptionist had clearly watched the news the following evening. 'Thanks,' Rod added, tapping the desk in appreciation of the unasked-for information.

Rose gave him a questioning look as he approached her back at the lifts.

'Receptionist thinks they're dodgy,' he said as he moved to stand beside her and watch the lift display.

Rose nodded and said nothing. There was a ping from one of the lifts and the doors slid open smoothly. They entered the lift and Rod pressed for floor three.

They found the office they were looking for easily enough. Rose knocked on the closed door and then opened it without waiting for someone to answer. There was no obvious reception area in the small, open-plan office, just several desks aligned along each wall all occupied by young men. All of them sported headsets and appeared to be engaged in intense conversations. Rose looked around for someone to talk to. There was a desk at the far end that was sitting against the wall, and positioned in a way that it overlooked the others. A very young man – Rose guessed he was no more than twenty-three – was sitting at the desk, also engaged in a conversation via his headset but looking up and over the other workers. Assuming he was some kind of supervisor, she tried to catch his eye. Eventually, he noticed her and gave an upward nod of his chin in acknowledgement, a frown creasing his young, unlined brow. As soon as he had finished his call, he pulled his headset off and approached the two detectives.

'Can I help you?' he said, when he was still several paces away, a defensive tone in his voice. Several of the other young men looked up with puzzled expressions. They were clearly not used to visitors and certainly not ones that appeared out of the blue in their office.

'DCI Rose McPhail,' Rose said and proffered her warrant card to the approaching young man. 'And this is DS Rod Laing. You are?'

'Er, Andrew Simpson,' the young man replied, his voice and expression wary. He didn't offer his hand, but instead shifted his feet nervously.

'We need to ask some questions about Dion Myers,' Rose said, keeping her voice authoritarian and brusque. It would do no harm to have this shifty-looking young man on his toes for now.

'Oh, er, yes right, of course,' he said, appearing to relax a little. 'Terrible. I saw the news last night ... couldn't believe it. When he went missing, that was strange enough. And worrying, naturally. But then to find out he had been murdered. Well...' Simpson rubbed his very cleanly shaven chin.

'We need to ask about the last time you saw him. Up to when he left the office the evening he disappeared,' Rose said.

'I told the other officers about that. It was just a regular day really,' Simpson said with a shrug.

'We believe he left the office later than usual?' Rod asked.

'Yes, that's right. He usually left at around half five, six, just after the others had left. He'd leave me to finish the day's figures – you know, tally up the sales performance charts and that kind of thing. But the day he, er, disappeared he said he would close up. He said he had a call to make, a potential client I think.'

'You don't know who the client was?' Rose asked.

'No, but I think it was a woman,' Simpson told her.

'Why do you think that?'

'I caught the front end of the conversation as I was leaving – well, just Dion's side obviously. He had a... a way of talking to women, I mean. You know? Like almost flirting? He was talking like that when I left.'

'I see. What time did you leave, Andrew?' Rose asked.

'About six, I think,' Simpson answered.

'We should get the phone records if we can,' Rose said to Rod who nodded.

'Which desk was Mr Myers'?' Rod asked, looking around the office and seeing only one spare desk in the middle of one of the rows.

'Oh, it's, er, was, that one,' Simpson pointed to the desk he had been sitting at.

'Right, so you're his what? Assistant? Deputy?' Rod asked.

'No, I suppose I'm the senior salesman. I fill in when Dion isn't here.' Simpson puffed his chest a little, clearly proud of his position in the business.

'Did you think it unusual when Mr Myers didn't come in the other day, without phoning or anything?' Rose smiled at Simpson – she couldn't help it. The thought of the young man being described as senior anything made her chuckle inside.

'Yeah, he was never off. Only for holidays occasionally, but he didn't take many of them. He was never sick, always here. So, him not coming in was really unusual.'

'Was it unusual for him to make a call to a client?' Rod asked.

'No, not especially. He liked to keep his hand in, as he put it.' Simpson laughed quietly. 'He used to say he was showing us what a real salesman looked like. We all knew he was way better than any of us.'

'But it was unusual that he made a call so late in the day?' Rod pressed.

'Yes, that was unusual,' Simpson answered. He looked around the room. 'Look I really ought to get back on.'

'Just a few more questions, Andrew,' Rose said evenly. 'How did Mr Myers seem in the days leading up to his disappearance?'

'Fine,' Simpson responded with a shrug.

'He didn't seem stressed or worried about something?'

'No, he was just the same as always.'

Rose nodded and looked to Rod. The late evening call to a client was of the most interest to her but she knew she would get little or no more information about that from Simpson.

'What'll happen to this place now?' Rod asked casually.

'Honestly, I don't know,' Simpson said with another shrug. 'The accountant wants us to keep going for now … he thinks someone might want to buy the business as a going concern.'

'The receptionist downstairs seemed to think you got a lot of calls from what sounded like disgruntled clients. Is that right? Do you get a lot of those calls?' Rod continued. Rose realised he was doing what he called 'riffing' – asking any question that came into his head and seeing if anything sparked a notable response. It was always worth a try.

'Not that many,' Simpson replied, defensively. 'There's a few. There's about five who call a lot, but most of our other clients are fine.'

'Were there any that Mr Myers seemed worried about, or that maybe threatened Mr Myers or one of you guys?'

'No, nothing like that,' Simpson responded, the crease in his brow indicated he was thinking about that one.

'Sure?' Rod pressed.

'Yeah, I'm sure. There was no one that threatened Dion or any of us.'

Rod looked to Rose with a slight shrug. He could think of nothing else to ask.

'Well, thanks for your time, Andrew,' she said, and offered her hand, which he took and shook, doing the same with Rod.

'No problem,' he said. 'I take it you know your way out?'

'Yeah, the way we came in, in reverse?' Rod said with a wink.

Simpson smiled. 'That'll be the one.'

'Thanks again for your time,' Rose said, and she and Rod filed out the door.

As they were walking back to the car, Rod looked across at Rose. 'Late evening caller could be interesting.'

'Yeah, though could be a coincidence that they happened to call the night he was abducted and murdered,' Rose said with a shrug.

'Could be,' Rod agreed. 'But I was never one for coincidences. Feels suss to me.'

'No, I'm not one for coincidences either, really,' Rose said, pursing her lips. 'As soon as we're back, see if you can get the phone records – he dialled out so we should be able to spot the number easily enough, at six-ish on the day he was abducted. It was probably the last call made that night. See if we can't find who the mystery woman is.'

'What do you think the connection is though?' Rod asked. 'An accomplice? Or the killer is a woman? What?'

'I don't know right now. And we won't know until we find her. Assuming it was a her, of course. We only have young Andrew's word for that.' She stopped walking for a second. 'Do we know exactly what they do there?'

'As far as I can tell, they sell small plots of land on green belt that might be developed at some point in the future. It's not illegal but on the grey scale, if you get what I mean. I'll get on to the fraud boys and see if they have any more on them.' Rod had kept going a couple of paces and then turned when he realised Rose had stopped. She resumed walking.

'We're still no closer to knowing how he's selecting them. How are they being found?' She was talking almost to herself, throwing the question open to the wind.

Rod stopped this time. 'I agree with the rest of the office,' he said quietly. 'I can't look beyond it being internal. Who else would get this information?'

Rose sighed; she had no choice but to agree. There was no getting away from it; the chances were looking more and more likely that it was someone inside the force, someone that could access the records – however small and inconsequential – of all three victims.

She nodded slowly. 'You're right, we have to start assuming it's someone inside the force. But we're going to have to play that very carefully.'

'Well, let's keep it very close to our chest for now,' Rod said. 'Maybe not even raise it again in front of the team. Let the evidence do the talking?'

'Ha, what evidence, Rod?' Rose shook her head angrily.

'It'll come,' Rod said. 'It always does in the end.'

'I hope you're right,' Rose said with feeling. 'I still can't get my head round why these people? I mean there's hundreds of people on that database and in the press with records as long as your arm. Why not them? If it's a copper they'd have their pick of thousands. And if it's not and it's a civilian taking the law into their own hands then they'd have dozens of targets just from watching or reading the news. I just can't see why they picked these three.'

'That points to a copper, for me. Those pieces in the press about our victims were too brief and easily missed and they gave no details. But as to why them and not actual criminals – I have no idea.' Rod fished in his inside jacket pocket and pulled out a packet of cigarettes, lit one and then as an afterthought offered one to Rose.

'I quit years ago, you know that,' she said, feeling sorely tempted. 'Let's get back and follow up that phone call.'

They began walking again.

'You know,' Rod said as they neared the car, 'the height thing? We could be looking for a woman. And now we have one in contact with one of the victims on the night they were killed.'

'We don't know for sure it was a woman,' Rose answered. 'And I just can't see it somehow. But maybe there's something in it. Jeez, that widens the bloody search doesn't it?'

'Yep,' was all Rod said.

'It feels like a man to me though,' Rose said, getting into the car.

'I wouldn't know what one feels like,' Rod said, deadpan.

'Shut up, Rod,' Rose said with a chuckle.

Chapter Twenty-One

As soon as Rose and Rod walked back into the office, Gareth all but leapt out of his chair.

'I might have something, ma'am. Well, two things actually,' he said from across the office.

Rose strode over to where he was standing. 'What is it, Gareth?' she asked, hope of a breakthrough showing in her voice.

'One of the ballistics guys has come up trumps. He must have spent hours trawling the database but he's found our gun.'

'Really?' Rose found it hard to keep the excitement out of her voice.

'Yeah, it might not be entirely useful but it is interesting,' he said, tapping his mouse to pull up the report.

Rose felt her early enthusiasm beginning to diminish. 'Define interesting,' she said dryly.

'It's interesting in that he's matched the bullet to ones found in two victims in a shooting in Dumfries in Scotland,' Gareth said, cocking an eyebrow.

'Dumfries?' Rose said incredulously. 'You're bloody right it's interesting, but how the hell are we dealing with a weapon that was used in Dumfries, for God's sake?'

Rod came over to where they were standing. 'Dumfries, I've heard of it, where is it again?'

'The south west of Scotland,' Rose answered. She had often holidayed in the area as a child. 'Thing is they don't get shootings there ... ever. Did they get anyone for the shooting?'

'No, ma'am,' Gareth said. 'Case is still open. It was two young guys so there was speculation it might have been drug related but they couldn't pin it on anyone and the gun was never found.'

'Until now,' Rod said. Gareth nodded.

'What the hell are we supposed to make of this?' Rose asked, flapping her arm.

Both men looked at each other and back to Rose and shrugged.

Rose shook her head. 'OK, well get a full report from our friends north of the border and let's see what, if anything, we can make of it. You said you had two things?'

'Yeah, the other is Jonathan Bold, father of Nathaniel Bold, one of the boys from the school.' Gareth pointed at his screen. 'I did a bit of digging in the case files and there's a connection between him, Dion Myers, Evžen Souček – which we knew about – and Seamus Harding.'

'Bloody hell,' Rose said, giving Gareth a grim smile. 'What are they?'

'Well, we know he knew Evžen Souček, but he is also an investor with The Land Investment Group and he made a complaint to trading standards about their practices, which they passed on to us, which made me check to see if there was anything that might have involved Seamus Harding.'

'And, is there?' Rose could feel her hopes rising with every word.

'Yep,' Gareth said a little triumphantly. 'Bold made a complaint about two months ago about someone hanging around his house. He says he thought they were casing the place out. We checked on it but by the time we got there, there was no one to be found. He made another complaint three weeks later, same kind of thing, except this time he claimed the person outside was filming or photographing with their phone. Now, it's still tenuous but that could well be Seamus Harding.'

'Yes, it bloody well could,' Rose said firmly. 'Right, get him in.'

'I took the liberty of calling him and asking him to come in. He's coming at four.'

'Excellent, Gareth you are a star,' Rose said, patting Gareth's shoulder.

'Makes you wonder why Louise and David didn't find any of that out,' Gareth said nonchalantly.

'Well, we didn't know about Myers at that point and I'm sure they would have asked about Harding,' Rose said, not rising to Gareth's bait.

'Hmmm,' was all Gareth said in reply.

Rose could hear her phone ringing in her office so moved away from Gareth and headed in that direction, turning as she walked, 'Rod, get on that phone number, will you?'

'Yes, ma'am,' he replied smartly.

She picked the phone up before sitting down.

'McPhail,' she said curtly.

'Rose, it's John.' DCI Reid's unmistakeable tones sounded in her earpiece.

'Hi John, what have you got for me?' Rose knew he wouldn't be calling for a social chat, he never did.

'They're still working on the phone – it's pretty bashed up – but we have identified one of the women in the other videos. Not the one from the canal unfortunately, a different but similar one. She reported it over six months ago – she'd spotted them filming and called it in straightaway. Anyway, we've been going through all and any reports of that nature and hit the jackpot with her.' His tone never changed even when imparting good news.

'Did you get her to ID Denning or Harding?' Rose asked, thinking that at least they would get a result on that case.

'Yes, she's fairly sure it was them,' Reid replied. 'But here's the main thing. Her husband works at Amazon. Might be worth you following up and seeing if he knew Harding and maybe any connections to your other victims.'

'Great, yes it certainly will be. What's his name?' Rose asked, scrabbling for her notepad and a pen.

'Donald Price, known as Donny. We've checked him out, nothing on the system.'

'Thanks, John, I owe you one.'

'What goes around, comes around,' Reid said and rang off.

God, she thought, no suspects whatsoever and now two crop up at once. Well, two half ones at this stage, I suppose.

There was half an hour until Jonathan Bold was due in so Rose buzzed through to Gareth.

'Can you dig out anything we have on Jonathan Bold and bring it through to me?' she asked.

'I've already checked him out, ma'am. There's nothing on the system, not even a parking ticket.'

'OK, thanks, Gareth,' she said and hung up.

She was about to go and see what Rod had on the phone call to Dion Myers' office when he knocked on the door. She waved him in.

Putting his head round the door, he said, 'I think I've found the number that called Myers the night he was killed – untraceable I'm afraid. Pay-as-you-go job.'

'Figures,' Rose replied. 'Thanks, Rod.'

Rod nodded and turned to go back into the office. 'Oh, one thing you can do, Rod,' Rose called after him, and he turned and stuck his head through the door. 'Can you go to Amazon and see what a Donald Price has to say about Harding and Denning, and if there are any connections with the other two victims?'

'Sure,' Rod said, 'how's his name come up?'

Rose explained, then said, 'Take Anna or Christine with you.'

'Will do,' Rod said and disappeared back into the office.

Rose spent the next twenty minutes gathering her thoughts before Jonathan Bold was due in. He could be the break they were looking for or it could be a complete coincidence. She didn't believe much in coincidences but this was such a significant one that she couldn't help but get her hopes up for the first time since they had found Harding's body. He may just be their man.

Her phone buzzed and the display said it was the front desk. The constable on the desk informed her that Jonathan Bold was downstairs.

'Show him to interview room two, please,' Rose said and got up from behind her desk.

She collected Gareth and the files on their three victims on the way down to the interview room. Jonathan Bold was waiting for them when they entered, a plastic beaker of tea or coffee in front of him. He looked a little stressed and worried.

'Mr Bold,' Rose said, 'thank you for coming in. I'm DCI McPhail and this is my colleague DC Exley.' She offered him her hand.

He stood, shook it and then spoke very quietly. 'No problem, what's this about?'

He was a small rotund man with a balding head and red cheeks. Short, Rose thought.

'Just some questions we need to ask about the murder enquiry we're working on,' Rose said, taking a seat opposite Bold. Gareth took the seat next to her. Bold sat back down and looked even more worried.

'I believe you spoke to one of my colleagues about Evžen Souček as part of our enquiry into his death?' Rose asked, pitching her voice to a similar volume as Bold's.

'Yes, that's right, terrible business,' he said, shaking his head and making his jowly cheeks wobble slightly.

'Mr Souček's murder or are you referring to the school?' Rose asked.

'Both, I suppose,' Bold said, looking between the two officers.

'Can I just confirm that you told my colleague, DC Louise Carney, that you hadn't seen Mr Souček since the court case. Is that right?' Rose was deliberately keeping the questions light and easily answered.

'Yes, that's right. I didn't really want to have anything to do with anyone from that place, not after what had happened. And whilst I bore Mr Souček no ill will, I had no need or inclination to see him again,' Bold said, looking puzzled.

'Right,' Rose said, then opened one of the files sitting in front of her. She pulled out a picture of Dion Myers and placed it in front of Bold. 'Do you know this man?' she asked.

'No,' Bold said immediately.

'You don't know him?' she asked again.

'No,' Bold answered a little more emphatically. 'Should I?'

'Well, you made a complaint about him,' Rose said, her eyebrows rising with the question.

'What do you mean?' Bold asked, looking very perplexed. 'How would I make a complaint about someone I haven't met?'

'This is Dion Myers. He runs The Land Investment Group. You were one of his clients I believe,' Rose said, pointing to the picture on the table.

'Oh, that charlatan. Is that what he looks like?' Bold said, anger creeping into his voice.

'Yes. Now you know who he is, are you certain you haven't seen him before?' Rose pressed.

'No, I never met him. I made the complaint to trading standards and left it with them.'

'What was the nature of your complaint?' Rose asked.

'I had paid him for a small plot of land that he said was due to be developed in the next ten years. He said the value would rise exponentially. I fell for it, like an idiot. After I had purchased the land and got a fancy-looking certificate, I decided to check it out. I don't know why I didn't before, but there you go. That shark could sell ice to the Eskimos. Anyway, when I checked the land out, it appeared to be already owned by a land developer. In reality what he had sold me was a piece of paper.'

'How much did you pay, Mr Myers?' Rose asked quietly.

'Three thousand pounds,' Bold said, lowering his gaze.

'That's a lot of money,' Rose said, raising her eyebrows. 'You must have been pretty angry when you found out you hadn't in fact purchased the land?'

'I was bloody furious,' Bold spat. His cheeks became redder for a second or two and then he visibly calmed down again.

'Did you get the money back?' Gareth asked. He had been taking notes but now looked up from his pad.

'No. Not a penny. Last I heard you lot were looking into it but that was months ago and I've heard nothing else since. I've pretty much written it off as a bad job gone worse.'

Rose nodded and then pulled a photo out of another file.

'How about this man. Do you know him?' she said, showing Bold a picture of Seamus Harding.

'Again no,' Bold said, looking puzzled.

'You made another complaint to us a little while ago regarding someone outside your house. You claimed they were taking photos or video. Do you remember?'

'Yes, of course,' Bold said, the frown still on his face.

'Did you get a good look at the person?' Rose asked. 'Could it have been the person in this picture?' Rose tapped the photo.

'Oh, I see,' Bold said. 'I'm not sure. I did get a fairly good look at him but I don't think this was him.'

'How about this person, could this have been who you saw?' Rose produced a photo of John Denning.

Bold stared at the photo for a little while, a moue forming on his lips. 'That could have been him, yes,' he said eventually. 'But I couldn't say for certain.'

'I see,' Rose said.

'I don't see what all this is about,' Bold said when Rose didn't say anything else. 'Have you brought me in here just to check on some complaints I've made to the police?'

'No, Mr Bold,' Rose said. 'You see, the two men in these pictures –' she pointed to Myers and Harding – 'along with Mr Souček, have also been found dead. Murdered. And we are certain that they were killed by the same person. And it just so happens that you are the first person we have come across that has a connection to all three.'

Bold's red cheeks became almost crimson. 'And you think that I'm involved?' he spluttered.

'Well, it is a bit of a coincidence, don't you think?' Rose asked.

'Yes, I can see that. But I've just told you I had never set eyes on Myers and I certainly haven't seen this man before,' he said, jabbing a finger on the photo of Seamus Harding. 'You can't possibly think I had anything to do with any of their deaths?'

'We don't know, Mr Bold. We're just trying to see if there actually is a connection. Where were you three nights ago?' Rose asked.

Bold seemed a bit taken aback by this change of tack. His eyes widened slightly and his brows creased. 'I, er, I was at home.'

'What time did you arrive home?' Gareth asked.

'About seven-ish, I would say,' Bold said.

'Can anyone verify that?' Gareth asked, making a note.

'Yes, my wife and son were already in when I arrived.'

'And you were in for the rest of the evening?' Gareth asked, making another note.

'Yes,' Bold said.

'What car do you drive?' Gareth asked next.

Bold shook his head; he was clearly having trouble working out the quick switches in questions.

'A BMW,' he eventually replied.

Gareth nodded and made another note on his pad.

'I'm going to ask outright, Mr Bold,' Rose said, pointing back to the photos. 'Did you have anything to do with the deaths of these three men?'

'No, I absolutely did not.' Bold sounded and looked angry. 'And I resent the fact you are even asking me that.'

Rose raised her hand, 'I understand that, Mr Bold, but I had to ask. You can see that, can't you?'

Bold calmed a little. 'Yes, yes, I suppose you must. But I will say again I had nothing to do with any murders.'

'OK, Mr Bold, thank you for coming in,' Rose said and got up from her seat, offering him her hand again.

'Well, I would say it was no trouble but it was. As long as that's everything.' He got up and shook Rose's hand.

'We may need to ask some more questions in the future. We'll let you know if we do,' Rose said. 'DC Exley will show you out.'

Gareth gestured to the door and Bold walked out of the interview room with a shake of his head. Rose waited for Gareth to return from the front desk.

'It's not him, is it?' she asked as he approached.

Gareth shook his head. 'Car's wrong and I bet his alibi stacks up. Height was about right though, wouldn't you say?'

'Yeah, the height was right but nothing else is. Oh well, back to the drawing board.'

Gareth shrugged and they walked back to the office in silence.

Chapter Twenty-Two

Rose walked straight back into her office, gesturing Rod to follow her in. She sat behind her desk and let out a long, exasperated sigh. Rod closed the door and took the seat opposite her.

'No-go with Bold?' he asked.

'No,' Rose said tiredly, 'doesn't look like it. Did you find out anything more about the call to Myers?'

'Yes and no. It was a pay as you go, like I said, but we have been able to find where it pinged a mast at the time the call was made. Whoever it was, was in a café not five hundred yards from Myers' office.' Rod pursed his lips and shook his head. 'Still doesn't give us much.'

Rose nodded. 'Didn't really expect anything from it but it was worth a look. Get one of the team to check the café out and see if they remember anyone – it's a real long shot but maybe our mystery woman was in there on her own or something.' She paused for a moment, looking down at her desk. When she looked back up, resignation was etched on her face. 'We've run out of all other options. It's time to look internally. The only way the victims can be connected is that they are being selected because of the minor footnotes we hold on them. It has to be someone on the inside.'

'I think you're right,' Rod said quietly. He didn't like the thought any more than Rose did. 'Where do we start, though?'

'We can access the records and see who has looked at our victims' files in, say, the last month, maybe two. If the same officer accessed all three files, it's possible that they're our man. There can be no reason I can see for one officer to have had reason to look at all three in that time scale.'

'Yeah, that would be a good start. We would need more than that though. To make any sort of move, I mean. Their Federation rep would never stand for that as reliable evidence and if there is a copper that has looked at all three files, they will already have a reason to justify it, I would think,' Rod said, thoughtfully.

'All very true, but it would give us a starting point, which is more than we've had so far. If we're going down this route then I need to let the Chief Super know, and I think we keep this between the two of us for now,' Rose said, reaching for her phone.

Rod nodded and rose from his seat, taking the hint that the conversation was over. 'I'll get on to the records straight away.'

Rose put the phone down before dialling. 'Let's not forget the phone call to Myers – I still have a sneaking suspicion that it's related, in which case we may need to assume it's two people, maybe both on the force or just one. And one of them is a woman.'

Rod turned his hand on the door handle. 'I don't see we can do much more with that at the moment, but I'll bear it in mind.'

'OK, let me know the second you have anything,' Rose said, picking up the phone again.

'Shouldn't take me too long,' he replied and left the office.

Rose dialled the internal number for the Chief Superintendent and prepared herself for a difficult conversation. Abdighani answered within two rings.

'I hope,' he said without a greeting, 'that you have something for me, Rose.'

'Maybe, sir, but it's not going to be easy listening,' Rose replied.

'Then you'd best come up. Five minutes?' Abdighani said, a note of caution in his voice.

'Five minutes it is, sir,' Rose replied and hung up.

She moved into the main office and walked over to Rod's desk. 'I'll be with the Chief Super,' she said quietly.

Rod nodded and quietly replied, 'I'll leave any log-in details on your desk and then I'm off to check Donny Price out at Amazon.'

'Good, I'll catch up with you at say, six. See what we have.'

The office was noisy. Ever since Abdighani's television appearance the team had been receiving calls from the public about suspicious activity. Most of the information was useless: people with a grudge against a neighbour, busy bodies who thought every movement on their street after eight o'clock was suspicious, and similar unrelated reports. Although time-consuming and tying up most of her team, Rose knew that there might just be a nugget in there somewhere.

The only two not on the phone were David and Louise who appeared to be in quiet conversation at the water cooler. Rose smiled; she had had her suspicions about those two for a couple of weeks and wondered if they weren't organising to get together after work. Well, good luck to them.

Chief Superintendent Abdighani called for her to enter as soon as she knocked. He gestured to her to sit when she walked in and played his usual trick of studying paperwork for a minute or so.

Eventually, he looked up. 'So, what have you got that's so unsettling?'

'Well, sir, I'm afraid to say that I now have a strong suspicion that we may be looking at a serving police officer in connection with the murders.'

Abdighani's eyes narrowed. 'A serving officer? How do you come to that conclusion?'

'The only connection we can find between all three victims is that they are on our system for minor offences or as a footnote to a larger investigation. The likelihood of their details being in the public domain with enough detail for them to be tracked down is slim. The only people with enough access to that information are internal.' Rose stopped for a second but Abdighani didn't say anything, so she continued. 'It may not be that an officer has actually committed the murders but has perhaps passed on information to someone else that led to the killings.'

'So, you think there's two of them? That's another new twist,' Abdighani said, raising his eyebrows.

'I'm keeping an open mind on that, sir. But it's a possibility.'

'OK then, follow that line of enquiry, and keep me informed at all times. If it is a serving officer it could turn into a real shit storm.'

'Yes sir,' Rose said and waited to see if her boss had anything else to say.

'Well get on with it, Detective Chief Inspector,' Abdighani said and waved a hand towards the door.

'Yes sir,' Rose responded and got up from her seat.

Abdighani returned to his paperwork but Rose could see he was rattled by the turn the investigation was taking.

***

Rod walked out of the Amazon building for the second time in a week. He still marvelled at the sheer size of the place and the number of people it employed. Donald Price had been a no-go from the start. He was at least six foot two and wiry in build, nothing like the person following Myers in the CCTV footage. And he had a stone cast alibi for the day that Harding had been murdered: he had been doing a double shift, which his supervisor confirmed, and had been given a lift home by another co-worker. He knew of Denning and had, understandably, a high level of animosity towards him.

'I'll kill the pervy bastard if I see him again,' he had said, completely oblivious to the fact he was talking to a police officer.

Rod had wound things up as quickly as possible. He had no desire to be hanging around there for any longer than necessary. There was something downtrodden and depressing about the people working there. He figured it was something to do with the nature of the work – relentless and monotonous at the same time. He was also conscious of the time. The sooner he was out the longer he would have for a pint or two before going back to the office to meet Rose. He glanced at his watch; it was four thirty, time enough for an hour down at the King's Arms.

He arrived in the pub car park ten minutes later. He knew many, if not all of the pubs and bars in the area and could unerringly pick the closest one to his location. There were plenty of places to choose from which meant he was never more than half an hour away from a bar and friendly bar staff to serve him his beer.

Walking in, he had a quick glance around but didn't spot anyone he recognised. Having breathed a sigh of relief that he wouldn't have any awkward conversations about drinking on duty, he strolled to the bar and ordered a beer.

Choosing a table in the corner he sat down and pulled a folded newspaper out of his inside jacket pocket. Smoothing it out on the table, he took a sip of beer and turned to the sports pages at the back of the paper.

He was swallowing the last few drops of his pint when a figure appeared in the corner of his eye, approaching his table. He swore under his breath and clucked his glass down on the table. Scott Ellis placed a pint and what looked like a mineral water down on the table and pulled out the seat opposite Rod.

'Afternoon, Rod,' he said with a smile that was half genuine and half predatory.

'Scott,' Rod said in greeting and pulled the pint over.

'What's happening with the case? It's all gone a bit quiet over at the station,' Ellis asked, still smiling.

'There's nothing I can tell you,' Rod said, avoiding eye contact with the reporter.

'Oh, come on, Rod. Give a dog a bone.' Ellis spread his arms wide, his smile widening into a wolfish grin.

'I'm telling you, there's nothing I can say right now,' Rod said firmly.

'I'm not sure I believe that. Besides, you still owe me big time. Are you sure there's not a little nugget you can give me?' The smile had dropped from Ellis' mouth and he leaned in closer, studying Rod's face carefully.

Rod frowned and shook his head. A few months past he had been leaving a pub late at night, having had a fair few to drink, and had stupidly climbed into his car to drive home. He had thought nothing of it until the following morning when his phone had pinged and he opened a text showing a couple of photos: one of him at the bar and another showing him in the car about to pull out of the car park. The text had come from Scott Ellis; he must have been in the same pub, and Ellis being the man he was had made hay while the sun shone. The pictures were not in themselves particularly incriminating – Rod could always say he had been on orange juice – but the message was clear enough: I have more than this and I will use it. Ellis had called him later that day and quietly pointed out that he could take his information to Rod's superiors or he and Rod could come to what he called 'an arrangement'.

Faced with disciplinary action and at the very least a reprimand, if his superiors believed the reporter's story, and also wracked by guilt at having done such a stupid thing, Rod had agreed to drop certain pertinent pieces of information in the reporter's direction. He cursed now that he hadn't enforced a timescale on the deal at the outset, and was now in too deep to back out. Ellis had the 'drink drive' accusation and he now had the fact that Rod had been passing him sensitive information for months. If he didn't keep Scott Ellis sweet, Rod knew he was in very deep water.

'Listen,' Rod said quietly. 'There really isn't very much I can tell you right now. To be honest, we haven't got any further along, but there is something in the offing that might be big. It'll give you the shock value you crave so bloody much.' Rod sneered the last few words.

'Oooh, sounds juicy,' Ellis said, a laugh in his voice.

'Might be,' Rod said, taking a swig, 'but right now there is no way I can tell you anything, OK?'

Ellis held his hands up in surrender. 'I hear you. Just make sure you give me plenty of heads-up when the time comes. Right, I'll leave you to the last of your beer, or is this you for the evening?' He tapped the table as he stood up.

'None of your business,' Rod growled.

Ellis turned away and gave Rod a little wave from behind his back.

'Wanker,' Rod said and turned his attention back to the newspaper.

***

Rose sat thinking in her office, waiting for Rod to get back from Amazon. He had left a note on her desk to say no one had looked at the entries for any of their victims in the last three months. He had gone further back and found one log from six months back. A uniformed PC had looked at the entry for Evžen Souček. The PC hadn't added a note as to why he had looked at the file – as was the usual procedure – but then Souček could have come up in some random search and the officer could just have clicked on the file out of interest. Whatever the reason, it would have to be followed up.

She felt frustrated that nothing more concrete had come of the search but at the same time she wasn't overly surprised. They appeared to be hitting dead ends wherever they turned. They would have to extend their search further back and see what that turned up. If that was fruitless then she had no idea where to go from there.

She turned her attention out to the main office. The phones were still ringing and most of the team had agreed to stay on for a while into the evening to take the calls. There was still a slim chance that something might come of it and everyone seemed keen to be doing something – all except Louise who had apologised, saying she couldn't stay that evening as she was meeting family. Rose hadn't begrudged her the evening off; she worked hard and rarely if ever skipped out of doing extra hours. Rose had watched with mild amusement as David made a forlorn face at Louise's back as she had walked out the office. *No sneaky shag for you tonight, young man,* Rose smiled to herself.

Rod walked in at around half six. Rose hadn't been bothered that he was later back than agreed, after all he could easily have been delayed at Amazon, but she became annoyed when the smell of alcohol drifted over to her from his direction. He sat down opposite her with a weary sigh. She looked at him for a moment or two before speaking.

'Kept at Amazon, were you?' she asked shortly.

'Yeah, they took a while to find him,' Rod said, blank-faced.

Rose pursed her lips and then decided to leave it. It would do no good having a go at him and right now she needed her sergeant on her side.

'And?' she asked instead.

'Oh, no, he's a non-starter. Cast-iron alibi for Harding and he's six two if he's an inch,' Rod said, waving a hand in dismissal.

'Right, so all we have now is this PC looking at Souček. I've checked the roster and he's on at eight tomorrow. You and I will have to catch him before he leaves on patrol.' Rose tapped the table for a moment, thinking. 'We need to go further back. There's still a chance our man has been daft enough to leave a trail. After we've seen PC Williams tomorrow morning, get on to looking back say a year and then if necessary two years. There must be a link we can find.'

'OK. And if there isn't anything?' Rod asked.

'Then we're back to square fucking one,' Rose said with feeling.

Rod pursed his lips. 'Well let's see what the morning brings. Er, if there's nothing else you want me for this evening?'

'No, that's fine, Rod. You get yourself home,' Rose said, thinking that he was unlikely to see home for some time yet this evening.

'Thanks. See you in the morning.' He got up, nodded, looked around her office for a moment as though he'd lost something and then nodded again and left.

Rose stayed on with the rest of the team until after eight and then called it an evening for everyone. The duty team could take any further calls that came in. Everyone filed out, tired and a little downcast.

As she was heading for her car, she overheard David on the phone.

'… I could see you after...' she caught him saying. There was almost a pleading whine in his voice.

Poor sod, he's got it bad – she thought, smiling to herself as she climbed into her car.

Chapter Twenty-Three

PC Alexander Williams, known to his colleagues as Big Al, for good reason, was pulling on his stab vest readying for a day out in one of the patrol cars. His partner was also in the changing room, fully kitted up and ready to go. As Rose walked in both men's heads swung up and round like a pair of Meerkats sensing danger. Rose smiled at them both.

'PC Williams? Can I have a word please?' she asked smoothly.

'Yes ma'am, what can I do for you?' Williams answered, glancing at his colleague.

'It's about a search you did on the PNC about six months back,' Rose said, catching the glance and wondering if Williams' colleague would excuse himself or stay and be nosy. He didn't move. Nosy it is then.

'OK, what was it for?' Williams asked.

'I'm not sure, I was hoping you could tell me that. It was for an Evžen Souček – name ring any bells?' Rose wasn't the tallest of women and she felt tiny in the presence of such a large man, but she carried real authority in the station and not just because of her rank. PC Williams was no different to any other officer when being questioned by Rose.

'No, sorry, ma'am. I can't say it does. What is that? A Polish name?' Williams asked.

'No, it's Czech. You're sure it doesn't mean anything to you? This would be about six months back.' Rose had watched the man carefully when she had said the name and there had been no sign of recognition at all.

'Right, um, no – still doesn't mean anything to me. It certainly can't have been particularly important. I normally remember things like that. Mind you we do get a number of people through with Polish names. It might be that I was looking for someone with a similar name and just happened to hit on that one as part of the search. What's he done anyway?' Williams scratched his chin as he asked.

'He was murdered last week,' Rose said, studying his reaction. There was nothing but surprise.

'Oh, I see,' Williams said, shaking his head. 'What was he on the PNC for? It might jog my mind.'

'Nothing ... he was a minor witness to the trouble at Cedars School. You know, the abuse? He drew a little suspicion from the investigating team but nothing more than that. Does that help?' Rose already knew that Williams had no idea who Evžen Souček was, or that he had for some reason called up the man's records, but needed to ask anyway.

Williams shook his head slowly, 'No, I'm really sorry ma'am but it doesn't. Were there any notes I left or a log or anything?'

'No, it's just the search log, which says you opened Evžen Souček's entry. There's no notes as to why.'

'Well, if he wasn't who I happened to be looking for at the time, I would just have come back out and got on with my search. I wish I could help some more but I really can't tell you anything,' Williams shrugged.

'No, that's fine Al. It was something of a long shot. Thanks for answering my questions.' Rose smiled at both men and left the room.

She believed PC Williams; he really didn't seem to have a clue who Evžen Souček was or have any recollection of looking him up.

Superintendent Abdighani was walking in the opposite direction along the corridor that led to her office. Rose stopped and hoped he hadn't been looking for her.

'Sir,' she said as he approached.

'DCI McPhail,' Abdighani acknowledged her greeting with a nod. 'How's things going? Any progress?'

'No, sir, not as yet. We're looking into anyone who might have accessed the records of our three victims, but so far we don't have anything. DS Laing is going further back this morning – he might already have some information if you'd like to come and join us?'

'No, no, you get on. I have a meeting to attend,' Abdighani said, smiling ruefully. 'Never out of the damn things.'

Rose returned the smile. 'I can sympathise, sir. I'll let you know if we get anything.'

'Yes, as soon as you have it, I want to know. I hope you're keeping things discreet?' Abdighani said, leaning in a little and lowering his voice.

'Yes sir, it's just me and DS Laing working this angle at the moment. I have the others following any leads that have come up from the press conference. They have already expressed their suspicion that it may be someone on the force, but so far I haven't let them know we are actually working that angle. They will have to be told if we get anywhere, of course.'

'Yes, best keep it tight for now. Right, I'll leave you to it. I want to hear the second you have anything.' Abdighani raised his finger to emphasise his point and then moved to go past Rose.

'Yes, you'll be told immediately, sir,' Rose said as he moved off.

The phones in the office were quieter than they had been for the last couple of days and much of the team were still to get in so the office was almost peaceful. Anna was at her desk catching up on paperwork from other cases, a large stack of folders balanced on the corner of her desk. Rod was at his desk, completing his checks on the entry logs. And Gareth was boiling the kettle in the corner of the office.

'Tea please, Gareth,' Rose called over.

Gareth waved a mug and clinked a teaspoon against the side. 'Coming right up.'

She moved over to where Rod was sitting. 'Anything?' she asked quietly.

Rod's expression was thoughtful but didn't contain any hint of hopeful or encouraged. 'Yes and no really. There are entries against all three victims, but not from the same person. I've discounted where it's clearly been an investigating officer that's left a note and that leaves me with three officers – two detectives and one from uniform. They all appear to have looked at the entry for one of the victims but left no log note. But that's about it,' Rod shrugged.

Rose shook her head in annoyance. 'So we still haven't got a single lead.'

'Afraid not,' Rod said, glancing back at his screen – perhaps in the hope that the information he had gleaned would change and they would miraculously have a prime suspect.

'How far back have you gone?' Rose asked.

'A year. Myers hadn't long come on the system then, same for Harding. Souček has been on here a little longer, of course.'

'The selection of the victims still bothers me,' Rose said. 'If the killer was looking on here –' she pointed to Rod's screen – 'they would have a list as long as their arm of genuine villains. It just makes no sense that they would select these people.'

'No, it doesn't,' Rod agreed. 'And now it looks like no one individual has looked them up anyway.'

'God,' Rose said through clenched teeth, 'this is ridiculous.' She pulled her hand through her hair and sighed deeply.

'Looks like we're back to it being a member of the public, then, doesn't it?' Rod said.

'Yes, it does.' Rose shook her head. 'But how are they selecting them? This is what I can't get my head around. How did they find them and pick them out as criminals? There's so little information out there on any of them in the media. And two of them haven't been convicted of anything so there wouldn't be any public record, aside from a tiny mention of Evžen Souček in the press and Dion Myers' conviction which only made a small footnote in the Northampton paper. That's all there is. There's just no way a civilian could target them, that I can see.'

'I don't know any more than you do,' Rod said, mirroring Rose's head shake. 'But they must be, somehow.'

'Well, yes,' Rose said a little impatiently. She checked herself before continuing: 'We still need to speak to those three officers – they might know something or remember something.'

'I'll get on it now,' Rod said, picking up the phone. 'I know one of them. We worked CID together five years or so ago.'

'Do that. I need to think. I'll be out for about an hour or so – call me if you get anything. And keep the others busy,' Rose said and moved to her office to collect her bag.

She always found driving and music a good catalyst for thinking. If she drove somewhere that she knew like the back of her hand she could zone out and concentrate on whatever was troubling her. Normally after a drive of about an hour she would at least have the beginnings of a solution.

She exchanged waves with Louise who was entering the car park as she was leaving. Then she saw David on the road that led up to the station, quickly followed by Christine. Once she felt she was far enough away she slotted the CD into the car stereo. Motorhead began to play 'Ace of Spades'. She turned the car towards the motorway where she could put her foot down and turn the music up.

She accelerated on to the M1 and turned Lemmy and his band up to near full volume. The music blared through the speakers; Rose loved it and was immediately transported back to a Motorhead gig she had attended many years before. They had been so loud that the music had made her chest and stomach pound with every beat and her ears had rung for days afterwards. The memory managed to clear her mind of her current troubles. She simply drove and listened, tapping her hand on the steering wheel along to the pulsing, crashing rhythm.

Slowly she came back around to thinking about the case. The selection of the victims was a key part of the investigation that was missing. Well, that and no forensics, no information and no useful evidence, she told herself bitterly. But she came back to the victims and why the killer had chosen them. The assumption that it was a police officer didn't seem to stack up; she was unwilling to let that go completely but at that time there was simply nothing to make that case. If it was a member of the public then she had to assume they were using the media and whatever public records they could lay their hands on. It still didn't explain why these three obscure, unconvicted – aside from Myers – to all intents and purposes, innocent individuals had been targeted. And how would anyone be able to find out they had appeared on the police radar with no action taken? And whoever it was knew why they had appeared on the police's radar. If the killer's motive was vigilantism, then they would have picked obvious and known criminals – ones they could find a great deal of information about just from the press, and then some simple homework would lead them right to their target's door.

Then there were the locations. The victims must all have been driven there under gunpoint. The killer must have planned very carefully where and when the victims could be abducted in that fashion. That was not a daylight and in the centre of town operation. The victims must have been stalked and checked out for some time before they were abducted and murdered. That was something the team could check. They could find out everywhere the victims went and when, what routines they followed, if any, and then start going back as far as possible with CCTV. They might catch a glimpse of their killer. They might just spot the same person following the other two that had followed Dion Myers to the dark car park. That would at least give them something to go on.

Her thoughts turned back to the selection of the victims. It was likely the killer got at least some information from the media, no matter how little. She wondered if it wasn't possible for them to also use the media in some way, other than the obvious appeals for help. She began to wonder if Scott Ellis would be willing to put something together – a trap of sorts, that could lure the killer out where she and the team would be waiting. It could be a small article, maybe, about someone suspected of some wrongdoing or with a minor conviction that could be extrapolated into a much more serious one. That was something to consider but she didn't completely trust Ellis and so she filed it away under 'for later'.

She realised that she was almost at Northampton and would soon hit the almost inevitable snarl-up that tailed back from the junction with the M6. If she stayed on the motorway much longer she was in danger of it taking hours to get back off. The next junction was only a few miles further on so she decided to come off there and turn around.

Once back on the motorway heading south, the traffic was more sluggish. The morning rush hour had still to tail off and Rose knew that it would be stop–start most of the way back. Motorhead had finished so when the traffic had come to a complete standstill, she dug in her glove box for another CD. The first one she pulled out was Bon Jovi, *'Slippery When Wet'*, an old one from the eighties. She smiled … this would take her all the way back to her early teens. She had been in love with Jon Bon Jovi back then; a huge poster had adorned her bedroom wall and she had spent many evenings listening to their albums and staring at the poster. She laughed as she realised it had been cassettes and vinyl records back then; her kids wouldn't have a clue what to do with them. Then it occurred to her that her kids wouldn't know much, if anything, about CDs. You're getting old! – she thought, shaking her head.

As she neared Milton Keynes and was readying to pull off the motorway, she had her plan sorted out. It wasn't much of one but it was something at least. She would have the team scour CCTV for the victims from as far back as six months in the first instance. It would take the whole team some time to get through that amount of imagery but it was all they had. If they could find the same individual following each victim it would be a major breakthrough. They would have a suspect, albeit one with no identity, but still a suspect nonetheless. In the meantime, she would think on what she could do with Scott Ellis that might just help them along.

She felt better as she pulled back into the station. She would be doing something, actively investigating the crimes and not just sitting and waiting and wondering. She just hoped it would lead somewhere; if they hit another brick wall she might just crack under the pressure.

Chapter Twenty-Four

The car behind had been flashing its headlights at her for quite some time. It was really beginning to annoy and worry her. The road they were on was quiet and dark. There weren't many places to stop and even if she did, she was nervous of whoever might be in the car behind. At the same time, she was worried that there was something wrong with her car. It seemed to be OK but then she knew very little about cars aside from how to drive them.

In the end, the persistent flashing worried her enough to pull over into a small lay-by. The car followed her in and parked a little way back from her. She looked in her rear-view mirror apprehensively and was almost blinded by the full beam headlights reflected there. She tutted that whoever this was, was so inconsiderate that they hadn't even dipped their headlights when they had pulled in.

A barely distinguishable figure left the car behind and walked slowly over to her. She wound her window down and tried to adjust her eyes to the darkness after the blinding headlights.

'Can I help you?' she said, when the dark figure got to her door. She could hardly make them out; they were dressed head to toe in black and her night vision was still shot.

The figure raised their right arm and she made out the slightest hint of a metal tube. She opened her mouth in horror but no sound came out.

There was a dull thud and she slumped onto the steering wheel, searing pain wracking her right arm and shoulder. She moaned quietly for a second and then began to panic when her door was pulled open. She frantically tried to undo her seatbelt and screamed when the person grabbed her hair and pulled her head back. She saw something white flash towards her and then there was a sharp, intense pain as something pierced her jersey and was driven into her right breast. She screamed again.

Her hair was released and her attacker took a step back. The pain throbbed down her entire right-hand side. Her arm felt weak and she could feel blood running onto her hand and down her torso.

Then there was one final dull thud.

Roll up, roll up, win a prize every time!

'I knew when it was time for me last 'oliday. I was getting old an' slow. Knew it on the one before that, actually. See, there was this geezer in Norfolk. I was fishing the Broads mainly up there, the odd lake that I found was alright but they were all proper commercial, day tripper rubbish. You know? All stocked to the gunnels and all the fish manky from poor handlin' an' shit like that. Anyway, I liked the Broads ... I'd hired a little boat for the fortnight an' I would just potter along until I saw a likely spot. Then I'd just stop an' 'ave a few hours, y'know?

Anyway, I'd seen this bloke a few times go past me in 'is little boat, probly doin' much the same as me. 'E was on 'is own, an' all. And I fought, I'm gonna fuckin' 'ave you. I'd already done a woman in Diss – that's a small place, that, an' I was takin' a risk wiv 'er, y'know? Too many fuckers about to interfere – but this bloke an' me we were all alone in the middle of nowhere. So, I decided to 'ave him with me knife. The upshot was I was goin' to just sneak on to 'is boat an' do 'im in 'is bed, but 'e fuckin' woke up, din' 'e. I wound up chasing 'im all over the bloody shop – cunt nearly got away an' all. I just managed to grab 'im when 'e slipped on some wet grass, then 'e put up an almighty fuckin' scrap. Just wouldn't go dahn. I 'ad to stick 'im twenty times, I reckon, before 'e dropped. I fought to meself then that I was getting a bit past it. I fink that's when I really started noticing me arthritis, an' all.

But another four years went by ... you two were in your early twenties by then I reckon, so not that long ago. I thought to meself, this is probably the last chance I'll get. Like I say, I was already too old really an' I knew that, but y'know, one last hurrah an' all that shit. So, this time I went to Scotland. Fuck knows why, it took me fuckin' hours to get there. Mind, it was alright when I did. Did loads of fly fishin' ... brilliant catching big rainbow trout on a light rod. I used to watch this bloke on the telly did them fishin' programmes – John Wilson – an' 'e would sometimes do a bit of fly fishin' on there. I always liked the look of it, y'know? Looked a bit more active than sitting behind a couple of rods. Moving about an' picking your spot looked pretty good to me. So, I got meself a rod an' some gear, flies an' all that. Turned out I was alright at it as well.

Like Norfolk, I moved around a bit up there. I'd got a bit nervous over the years staying in one place ... might 'ave proved a bit obvious. Mind you, never a sniff from the old bill in all that time. But still, better safe than sorry, eh? So, I moved from place to place. I'd taken a tent so I could stop wherever more or less an' kip in that. The other major difference was I took a gun for the first – an' last – time. I learnt from chasing that fucker about the broads – wasn't gonna go through that malarkey again.

I got the gun from me mate – well I say a mate, 'e was what you might call an acquaintance. From the pub, y'know? 'E was a right wrong 'un in 'is day. Real fucking villain. Thing was, I got on wiv 'im just fine. I suppose I never really bovvered 'im so 'e never really bovvered me. So, one night we gets to talkin' an' 'e was sayin' all the usual villain bullshit, y'know, this job 'e'd done and this bloke 'e'd fuckin' stuck an' all that shit. But somefing 'e said stuck wiv me. 'E told me 'e still 'ad a piece 'e used to use to frighten folks with. 'E reckoned 'e 'ad never used it in anger, not proper fired it or nuffin'. An' that got me finking. See, if 'e'd never fired it an' no one knew about it, 'ow would the old bill have a clue 'ose gun it was or even know it existed? I knew I needed a new method – I couldn't keep goin' wiv the garrotte or knife an' that kind of fing. An' I couldn't go runnin' about after people no more. So, I said to 'im one night after that, that I would 'ave the fuckin' thing. Told 'im I wanted to for like a collector's piece or some crap like that. 'E wasn't really up for it at first. But I persuaded 'im that 'e was best shot of it – we 'ad a laugh at that, 'shot', y'see? So, in the end 'e agreed an' sold it to me for a song, really. A few quid for a fully workin' fuckin' gun! Even came with bullets and a fuckin' silencer. Proper fuckin' James Bond it was. Touch, I fought.

So, I 'ad me gun an' me trip to Scotland all sorted out. I wasn't sure about using the thing but I watched some videos on the internet an' it all seemed pretty straight forward – out wiv it an' pull the fuckin' trigger. All very interesting, y'know, the ballistics an' all that? I watched this fing, it showed exactly what 'appens to a bullet when it goes through a body. Fascinatin'.

All the gun stuff reminded me of this spy fing I used to watch as a nipper. Can't remember what it was called now – 'ad that right 'andsome bloke in it. Real smooth 'e was an' like all posh charm. 'E was a spy or something, got into adventures an' that sort of fing. Anyway, 'e always used a pistol wiv a silencer. For a bit there I fought I was 'im.

What was that bloody thing called? Oh, 'e was right famous an' all, the actor. Always wondered why 'e never got James Bond. Shoulda done. That Pierce Brosnan got it at the time but I thought this other bloke woulda been better. God, what was 'is name. Simon Templar, that might 'ave been it.

Anyway, there I was in Scotland wiv me fuckin' gun. No idea who or what I was gonna do with it but someone was gonna get a bullet in their noggin. Me first thought was Glasgow would be me best bet. It's big an' busy an' all that. But turned out it was too fuckin' busy ... people everywhere, day an' night. Not a chance in the end. Besides, there was no fishin' to be 'ad. Well, not anywhere nearby anyway. Funny the places you come across though. See, I got to near the end of me 'oliday an' I was looking at somewhere I could go on me way 'ome. Lookin' at me map I realised I'd driven through what looked like a really good part of Scotland. Dumfries and Galloway. I was getting pretty frustrated by then, not with the fishin' but with me lack of opportunities. Loads of places were pretty remote and those that weren't didn't seem to offer any opportunities. Bit like fishin' I suppose. Y'know, y' can sit for hours an' get nothing an' it's only when you move on that a big fuckin' swirl goes through the water not five feet from where you were bloody sitting. Anyway, as one last gasp attempt I fought I'd give Dumfries and Galloway a go.

Come to think of it, I think Simon Templar was the name of the character. Might 'ave been the name of the show. No, no, that's not right. The show wasn't called Simon

Templar, that was the character. Still can't get the actor's name.

So, lovely place as it turned out – Dumfries and Galloway. There's only a couple of smallish towns. Dumfries, o'course, an' then there's a place called Dalbeattie an' another called Castle Douglas, but all the rest of 'em were more or less like villages of one size or another. Even Castle Douglas and Dalbeattie are more like big villages than towns, compared to down 'ere. Anyway, all very pretty scenery an' that. So, that's where I spent the last few days of what was goin' to be me last 'oliday and I was getting pretty desperate to use that gun.

Fuckin 'ell! It was the fuckin' Saint weren't it? Simon Templar was in The Saint. Now, I should get the fuckin' actor's name. I fink it was Roger Moore first but that was back in the sixties an' I never really saw them. Nah, there was another one after that. What was it? Nah, it's gone again.

It was by complete chance I got to use me gun. I was in Dumfries ... I'd pretty much fished meself to a standstill. Couldn't face tying another fly on me line. So, I took a chance and booked a little B&B and decided to 'ang about an' see what 'appened. Well, I was in this lovely pub, all real ale an' that sort of fing. The Ship, I fink it was called. Just enjoying a couple of pints, well, more than a couple as it turned out an' talkin' away to the locals – mainly old blokes but all good for a laugh an' full o' stories. It felt a bit weird sittin' there gabbin' on wiv me fuckin' gun in me pocket. Din't want to leave at the guest 'ouse, did I? So, anyway, I stagger out of there at like half eleven, midnight, an' just started to wander, well stagger really, me way back to the B&B. I 'adn't realised that a couple of young lads 'ad started followin' me until I caught their footsteps behind me. I glanced round at them an' realised they 'ad been in the pub. Stood out in there, din't they? Too young an' shifty lookin'.

So, at last, I fought, 'ere's me fuckin' chance. 'Course they were thinkin' the same fuckin' thing, weren't they? They reckoned they were gonna turn over the pissed English cunt somewhere quiet. I'd been in this big park down by the river earlier in the day an' I fought, why the fuck not? There's two of 'em but they don't know I've got me gun, do they? So, I took a little detour into the park, which I figured would be empty at that time o' night. I reckon the lads thought all their Christmases 'ad come at once.

I sobered up dead quick as I walked in – adrenalin I 'spose. So, I was proper alert an' ready. I made sure I kept me pace up and there was still a bit of distance between me an' them. As soon as I 'ad a chance I ducked behind a tree an' pulled the gun from me pocket. The two little cunts came runnin' after me, I think they thought I was trying to do a runner. So, they were proper fuckin' shocked when they come round the tree an' see me still standin' there. Only, now I was 'olding me gun, weren't I? The look on their faces! Oh, it was a bloody delight, it was. Mouf open, gobsmacked they were. One of 'em I could tell 'ad just froze, so I popped 'im first – 'e just crumpled to the floor, the smell of piss and shit risin' off 'im as 'e fell. The other one was shocked into action by that. 'E just turned an' started runnin' at full tilt away from me. Funny, I shoulda missed 'im really, I ain't no gunman but it just felt really natral, y'know? I got 'im in the lower back I fink it was first. Anyway 'e fuckin' screamed an' went down grabbin' round there. 'E was still trying to crawl away, moanin' an' groanin' an' whimperin'. I just walked up, casual-like, an' put one in the back of the 'ead. Then I put me gun back in me pocket an' strolled back to the guest 'ouse.

It was all over the radio an' local news the next morning. Well, it would be ... I don't reckon they get many double shootings in Dumfries. Probably 'ad the local nick shittin' themselves. Not like back 'ome, well London anyway, where it's every fuckin' other day. I was only there for one more night, so I just 'ung about an' watched them run abaht like fucking 'eadless chickens. Great fun.

Then I just packed me stuff, got in the car an' drove 'ome. Back to reality, like. Well, what most people see as reality. My reality ... that's a totally different kettle of fish.

Bloody, Ogilvy! Ian Ogilvy, that was the bloke in The Saint. Come to think of it that was probably made in the seventies so 'e was probably a bit too old by the time Brosnan got the Bond gig.

So, that's kind of me career summed up really. I don't know why I'm wafflin' on about it but I figure you two should know. It's not like I need to unburden or anyfing stupid like that. What's the word they use all the time these days? Bring closure? Whatever the fuck that means. It's nuffin' like that anyway. I don't feel the need to confess to nuthin', well maybe that's it a bit, but you won't get to hear this 'til I'm long gone and then it won't matter a fuck. Well, maybe it will matter to the poor fuckers who came across me path back in those days. If I'm honest, I miss it and I wouldn't change a thing. If you want proper reasons and all that guff I'm afraid I can't give you any. Like I said before, maybe it was just in me.

It's been a funny old life.'

Chapter Twenty-Five

It was early morning and the office was a hive of activity. Days of CCTV footage had needed to be collected and organised and allocated to each officer. Others had been drafted in to help, such was the workload. Every last piece of information about the habits, movements and routines of all three victims had been collated and now the arduous task of trying to find them and follow them had begun.

Rose could do little but wait for the results. Impatience ate away at her but she knew she had to keep it in check. The process could not be sped up and it was important that every possible angle was looked at and analysed. In order to keep busy, she had taken on doing a review of everything they knew and all the information they had so far. She felt it a fruitless exercise but it was the best use of her time that she had at that point. It might also throw up an angle they had missed or a line of enquiry they hadn't followed.

She was still torn between the killer being a member of the public and a serving police officer. In order to double-check the police angle, she decided to check the records of the victims going right back to the first time they appeared on the PNC. Souček seemed the obvious starting point; he only appeared from the time the investigation started into the abuse at the school, two years ago. She wasn't surprised to see several entries from the original investigating team, and she jotted the names down and scrolled up to any more recent entries. The only other entry was the one she had expected to see – PC Williams. She noted his name down anyway and moved on to Seamus Harding.

There were, unsurprisingly, more entries for Harding. He first appeared on the PNC three years previously. Every occasion he had been stopped and questioned had been logged. Each access was accompanied by a note giving details of the officers involved with encounters with Harding. She paid less attention to the entries with notes against them and instead scanned for accesses where there was no explanation given. There was only one and the name that appeared made her stop – with almost a comical double-take. Shaking her head, she jotted the name down with a frown.

Finally, she turned to the Myers file. This time she didn't go through all the entries – and again there were a few – but instead she scanned quickly looking for one name. Again, eighteen months previously, the name she had been hoping would not be there appeared: Detective Constable David Baker.

Rose put her hands to her cheeks and pulled them down over her face. She simply could not believe what she was seeing. And she felt angry that they had not checked all of the records at the time the idea had arisen. They had assumed that if it was a police officer that they would have been looking at the records recently. But then, the murders had all been well planned and executed – she forgave herself the pun – so why wouldn't the killer have been looking and planning for over a year?

She was still having trouble reconciling what she was seeing. David was such a good and dedicated officer. There was nothing in his previous conduct that would suggest any wrongdoing, never mind murder. But she couldn't ignore what she had discovered. There could be a perfectly good and innocent explanation and she hoped there was. And, of course, he had only shown up against two of the three names. He hadn't accessed Souček's file. In order to be sure, she decided to check for the other names on her list against the Myers file, although there had been no duplication between Harding and Souček.

There was one – a Detective Sergeant Andy Carter. Rose knew him; he had left the Thames Valley region and now worked up in Newcastle. He was from that area originally and had decided to return to his roots. He had left about eight months ago. He had been one of the investigating team on the school case so it wasn't a surprise that he appeared on Souček's file notes and it was possible that he had had some involvement with Myers. But he had left no note on the Myers file.

Rose found it odd that there were several occasions when someone had logged into the records of the victims and left no note as to why they had done so. The general rule of thumb was to leave some form of explanation for the access. It was not uncommon to see quick two-word notes like 'address check' appear on the files. But it looked like three officers had accessed these files and left no note whatsoever. She didn't know what to make of that exactly but filed it away as something of interest.

The first person she wanted to check out was Andy Carter. He was the sort that would remember this sort of thing. He often recalled details from cases from years back, remembering names and dates and places. It was possible he remembered checking out Myers' file and why. He was likely to also remember why he had left no note.

She reached for her phone and jumped when it rang before she could pick it up. She swiftly picked the receiver up.

'McPhail?'

'Chief Inspector, this is PC Evans. I think you have another body.'

Rose blanched.

'Where?' she asked.

'We found her in her car, not far from Drayton Parslow. Do you know it?'

'I know it,' Rose answered. 'A woman? And in her car? Are you sure it's another one for me?'

'Yes, Chief Inspector, it looks like she's been shot and there's a note pinned to her chest.'

Rose put her thumb and forefinger to her eyes. 'What does it say?'

'Tax evader, ma'am.' PC Evans was clearly shaken by his discovery.

'OK, preserve the scene … you know what to do, Evans. I'll be there as soon as. Have you put a call into Scene of Crime?'

'Yes ma'am, and we have the area taped off.'

'Good, now give me the exact location.'

PC Evans gave solid and accurate-sounding directions.

Rose sprang from her desk and almost ran through to the main office.

'Rod, with me,' she said without stopping.

Rod got up and quickly followed.

'What is it?' he asked as he caught up in the corridor.

'We've got another one,' Rose said, walking briskly and fumbling for her car keys.

'Oh, fuck.' Rod looked to the ceiling in exasperation.

PC Evans' instructions turned out to be perfect and they found the spot at the first time of asking. It was a tiny B-road not far from the little village of Drayton Parslow. As they pulled up, Rose looked beyond the police tape and could see a Mercedes SUV parked in what could be described as a lay-by but was more like a passing space. The PC's patrol car blocked the road just beyond the cordon and had been joined by another car covering the side of the road Rose was on. She pulled up behind this car and then she and Rod got out quickly and moved to the boot, where they donned gloves and plastic over-shoes. The Scene of Crime van was pulled up behind them just as Rose closed the boot.

She walked back to the van and the driver wound down the window. She had worked on all three of the previous murders and Rose knew her to be very good at what she did.

'Morning, Claire,' Rose said through the window. 'I'd like a quick look before you guys go in. That OK?'

'Morning, Rose. Yes, sure, just don't touch anything. Are we sure it's another one?'

'Pretty sure. That's what I want to check out, but all the indications are it's a fourth victim.'

Claire gave a small nod and Rose moved off towards the cordon, with Rod following behind.

PC Evans was standing just outside the cordoned area; turning and spotting them he moved in their direction.

'Morning ma'am,' he said as they approached.

'Morning Evans. What can you tell me?' Rose said, looking over the PC's shoulder to get a better view of the car in the lay-by.

'I've run the number plate – car belongs to a Mr Graham Johnson of Stewkley. I'm guessing this is his wife. Obviously, I haven't touched anything so we can't be sure of an ID. The car was spotted by a passing motorist on his way into work. He was concerned that the door was open with what appeared to be a sleeping woman inside. He called it in when he got to work.'

'Has the husband been contacted?' Rod asked.

'Not yet ... we thought you would want to do that,' PC Evans replied.

'Do we have the name and details of the driver who called it in?' Rose asked, still surveying the car.

'Yes, ma'am,' Evans said, pulling his notebook out.

'Give the details to Rod here,' Rose said, 'I'm going to take a look.'

She moved past the PC and ducked under the tape, approaching the car from the rear. She could see the driver's door was slightly open. There was no sign of damage to either the rear or sides. Before she fully opened the door, Rose checked carefully along its edge, looking for signs it might have been forced open. There were none. Finally, she carefully eased the door open.

Inside was a woman of middle years, well dressed and presented. Rose got the impression she was a professional of some sort. She and her husband – if the owner of the car was her husband – were clearly comfortably off. The car itself and the fact they lived in Stewkley made that clear. But also, her clothes spoke of a good level of disposable income. She was slumped slightly forwards and towards the passenger seat, the seatbelt being the only thing stopping her falling forwards and across the interior into the passenger footwell. There was a lot of blood covering her blouse on her right-hand side where the note was pinned. Printed in large bold letters were the words: 'TAX EVADER.'

Knowing she shouldn't but unable to stop herself, she reached across the body to where the woman's handbag was sitting on the passenger seat. Lifting it clear, she looked inside for a purse or wallet. She found it in the second compartment she looked in. The woman's driving licence was in a clear compartment at the front. Rose read the details.

She was Patricia Johnson, aged fifty-four, with an address in Stewkley. The owner was indeed her husband. There were no convictions or penalty points on the licence; not that that meant anything, as those details would have to be checked with the DVLA. Rose put the purse back and put the bag on the seat where she had found it. She gave another look around the interior but couldn't see anything else of interest. She turned and walked back towards Rod and the PC, waving to Claire and her team to now take over the scene.

'I've called the guy who called it in,' Rod said as she approached. 'He works in town.'

Rose nodded. 'Organise for one of the team to go and see him, will you? We need to go and find the husband.'

Rod lifted his phone and called the office. Rose moved off to her car, opening the driver's door and sitting down, feet still outside on the tarmac. She put her head in her hands and let out a long, despairing sigh.

'Shit,' she whispered, 'shit, shit, shit.'

Chapter Twenty-Six

'Remind me, what car does David drive?' Rose asked, as they drove towards Stewkley to find Graham Johnson.

'An Audi, I think,' Rod answered, brow creasing.

'And what height would you say he is?' Rose glanced over.

'About five nine, maybe ten. What's this about?' Rod asked.

Rose was sure he was making a connection but without more information than she had she was unwilling to explain.

'Just … something or nothing,' she said vaguely.

Rod looked at her, head cocked, for some time, and then decided to drop it. She would explain in her own time, or wouldn't at all. There was little point in trying to press the issue.

Stewkley was a pleasant, well-to-do village situated between Milton Keynes and Aylesbury, close to the Buckinghamshire–Bedfordshire border and just inside Thames Valley's operational area. Using her Sat Nav, Rose negotiated the quiet, rural roads until they found the Johnson residence. It turned out to be a large, converted farmhouse just outside the village – a residence that underlined the apparent wealth of the couple even further.

Pulling up in the large drive, Rose noted the other cars parked there: a BMW 3 series and another Mercedes, this one a CLS coupe – roughly fifty grand's worth of car, she calculated quickly.

Rod rang the doorbell to the side of the large front door. They both waited patiently for an answer. When none came, he tried again. They could hear the bell ringing through the door, a tune Rose couldn't place but that was vaguely familiar.

'I'll take a look round the side,' Rod said, indicating to their left with a nod of his head.

The right-hand side of the house was taken up by a large garage which went all the way to the high wall on that side of the property. The left of the house was open, with a path leading between two slim lawns to the rear.

Rose rang the bell again and stood back, scanning the windows to the sides and above. Rod came wandering back from the side of the building.

'There's a big high gate that seems to be locked,' he said, as he joined her on the doorstep.

'Let's give it one more go,' Rose said, ringing the bell and then knocking on the door.

They were turning to leave when a teenage girl appeared from around the side of the house.

'Can I help you?' she asked, looking warily at the two officers.

'We're looking for Mr Graham Johnson,' Rose said, raising her ID.

'Oh, he's not here at the moment. Has something happened?' the girl asked, brows furrowing.

'Can I ask who you are?' Rose asked instead of answering the girl's question.

'Amy, I'm his daughter,' the girl answered, brows still furrowed.

'Where is your father at the moment, Amy?' Rose asked softly.

'He's away with work and mum's at work, so there's only me here, I'm afraid. Has something happened?' the girl repeated.

'How old are you Amy?' Rose kept her voice soft, looking closely at the girl's face. She guessed the girl was in her late teens.

'I'm eighteen. Look, what's this about?' Rose could see the impatience on Amy's face.

'When is your father due back?' Rose was hoping to avoid having to break the tragic news to an eighteen-year-old girl on her own if at all possible.

'Not until Monday next week,' Amy replied. 'Look, whatever it is just tell me what you want. If it's important I can get him to call you or something. Or you can speak to my mother … I can give you her work number.'

'Where is your father? Is he in the UK or is he abroad?' Rose asked, hoping he was in the UK. At least that way, there would be a chance he could get back relatively quickly.

'He's in Dubai. Shall I get Mum's number?' The girl was half turning back the way she had come. With a sinking feeling in her stomach Rose felt she was left with no option but to tell the girl what had happened. She just hoped she had some family nearby that could support her until her father could get back. Dubai would mean a long flight and a drive back from Heathrow. The journey would take the best part of a day, assuming there were any flights anytime soon that he could catch. Rose had a feeling there would only be a couple of flights a day.

'No, that's fine – could we come in? I'm afraid I have some bad news,' Rose said, quietly moving towards the girl.

Amy's face paled. 'What's happened?' Her voice was almost a whisper.

'Let's go inside and I'll explain,' Rose said, putting a hand on the girl's elbow and gently guiding her back towards the side of the house.

Once inside, Amy led them to a large living room. The house was expensively decorated with a modern feel which clashed slightly with the Victorian-looking exterior. Rose gestured for Amy to sit on a long three-seater settee that stretched along one wall and then sat next to her and turned so that she was facing her.

'Do you have any relatives that live nearby? I think it might be a good idea if someone were here with you,' Rose said, keeping her voice very quiet and calm.

'My aunt lives in Leighton Buzzard,' Amy said, her deeply creased brow making her look older than she was. 'Look, just tell me, what's happened?'

'Can we have her number? Rod here can give her a call.' Rose hoped the aunt was home and able to get over.

The girl nodded and looked between the two detectives; her expression was unreadable but Rose could imagine what she was feeling. She got up and moved over to a low table in the centre of the room and picked up a mobile. Pulling up her contacts she handed the phone to Rod.

'What's your aunt's name?' he asked, also keeping his voice low.

'Katherine,' Amy replied and moved to sit back down on the couch. 'Now, please, what is going on?'

Rod walked out of the living room, giving Rose a sympathetic look as he did so.

'I am really sorry to have to tell you this, Amy, but your mother was found dead this morning,' Rose said. She wanted to reach out and touch the girl's hand as she spoke but felt it would be unprofessional at that point.

The girl's face went very white and her mouth dropped open. 'What? What…?' She couldn't finish and just shook her head – her mouth opening and closing and a tear running down her cheek. Rose sat silently for a moment, giving the girl time to absorb the terrible news. 'Was it a car accident?' Amy asked, eventually.

'No,' Rose said, 'I'm afraid she was murdered, last night.'

Amy began to sob loudly. Rose's instinct to comfort the girl got the better of her and she put an arm around her shoulder and let her cry. As she felt the girl's wracking sobs begin to subside a little, she moved away from her. 'It looks like your mother didn't make it home last night – did you not wonder where she was?'

'I was out last night … didn't get back until late so I assumed she was in bed.' The girl could hardly speak through her tears. 'And I got up late this morning so I thought she had already left for work. Murdered?'

'I'm afraid so,' Rose said very softly.

'How? Why? Why would anyone…' Amy descended back into wracking sobs.

'She was shot in her car, not far from here,' Rose said. She knew she would get no information from Amy in this state and doubted whether there was much she would be able to tell her in any case. She looked up as Rod walked back into the room.

'Your aunt's on her way over now – she won't be long,' he said, his voice sombre.

Amy nodded. Rose had spotted a box of tissues on the coffee table where Amy's phone had been. She walked over and picked them up, bringing them back to the settee. Amy gratefully accepted one and wiped her face and blew her nose. Her sobbing had quietened but tears still rolled freely down her cheeks.

'Was it a robbery or something?' Amy asked after a long silence.

'We don't know at this stage,' Rose said, unwilling to give the girl any details, least of all that her mother had been murdered by a vigilante serial killer.

They sat in silence for what felt like a long time, the only break being an occasional sob from Amy and a few straightforward questions from Rose. Amy confirmed that her mum was a solicitor for a large firm, dealing mainly with family law, and that her dad was a senior manager for HSBC bank, often away on business. Amy herself had not long finished college and was waiting to go to university to study law. She had no intention of following in her mother's footsteps, instead feeling the allure of criminal law. She wanted to become a prosecuting barrister. She could think of no reason anyone would wish harm on either of her parents; they had few friends but those they had were like family, and aside from a mild spat with a neighbour several years ago they lived quietly in the village.

After about twenty minutes they heard a car pull up in the drive. Rod answered the front door when the bell rang and Amy's Aunt Katherine came bustling into the room.

'Oh, Amy,' she said, rushing over to the settee and sitting on the other side of Amy, immediately pulling the weeping girl into her arms.

'What happened?' she asked, pulling Amy even closer.

'Your sister has been shot, in her car – we assume whilst driving home from work last night,' Rose said gently. Katherine's resemblance to Patricia was unmistakable; she was maybe two or three years younger but aside from that they could almost be twins.

'This is just…' Katherine trailed off, unable to voice what she thought. 'Has Graham been told? He's in Dubai.'

'Not yet, Mrs…?' Rose had stood up and was now in the centre of the room next to Rod.

'Taylor,' Katherine replied.

'Not yet, Mrs Taylor. We can do that, if you prefer?' Rose said, then turned to Rod. 'Why don't you make a pot of tea, Rod?'

Rod nodded and left the room.

'No, no it's fine, I'll call him,' Katherine was saying. 'I'm not sure what time it'll be over there.'

'I'm afraid I don't either but I'm sure he would want to know as soon as possible,' Rose said.

Katherine nodded and turned her attention back to Amy. Rose could have asked the same questions of Patricia's sister as she had of Amy but could see little point; she would likely give the same answers. Instead, she waited silently for Rod to reappear with the tea. As soon as he did, Rose made ready for them to leave.

'Family Liaison will be in touch at some point today,' she said, handing over a business card. 'If there is anything you can think of in the meantime, please give me a call. I am so very sorry for your loss.'

With that they left the pair to their grief.

Chapter Twenty-Seven

The office was busy when Rose and Rod walked back in, with everyone working on either the CCTV footage for the first three victims or looking into what details they could find for Patricia Johnson. Louise had gone to interview the driver who had spotted the body, and Sandra was at Patricia's company to find out when she had left the previous evening and any other information she could gather.

Rose went straight over to Gareth's desk. 'Have you any information on Patricia Johnson?'

'Yes, ma'am,' Gareth replied and clicked open the police database. 'Patricia Johnson was stopped on the M1 eight years ago; she had neglected to pay her road tax. She claimed it was an oversight at the time, stating she had been extremely busy with work and had simply forgotten. She was fined, and paid immediately. Other than that, nothing at all.'

'Tax evader,' Rose said almost under her breath. 'Good stuff, thanks Gareth. Time to get back on the CCTV, I'm afraid.'

Gareth pulled a face but said, 'Yes, ma'am.'

Rose turned to Christine. 'Chris, when Sandra gets back from Patricia Johnson's workplace, can the two of you set about getting as much CCTV as you can gather from the time she left work?'

'Yes, ma'am,' Christine said, never taking her eyes from her screen.

Rose looked around the office. Everyone was glued to their monitors, sifting through hours of CCTV footage. She headed into her own office, sat down and immediately opened the PNC entry for Patricia Johnson, hoping she wouldn't see what she suspected she would. Aside from the traffic officer who had dealt with the incident, one other person had accessed the file. With a deep frown she looked at the familiar name: PC Alexander Williams.

'What is going on here?' she said to the screen.

She sat for some time, fingernails tapping on the surface of the desk. She could not ignore the information that David had accessed two of the victims' files and now PC Williams appeared to have accessed the other two. Were they working together? That seemed a leap too far – two police officers with the same mindset going about targeting and killing people in the name of crimes they hadn't committed. So, why had both names now appeared?

She needed to talk to David straightaway and then have another chat with PC Williams. She felt there had to be a logical and innocent explanation.

Or is it that I want there to be one?

She walked into the open office and over to Rod. 'Rod, I need your opinion on something.'

Rod followed her into her office and sat down. Rose tapped her screen. 'I've been going further back checking who accessed the files for our four victims. Two names have come up: PC Williams accessed Souček's and, having looked this morning, he also accessed Patricia Johnson's file, leaving no notes in the process. The other two were both accessed by David.'

'Our David?' Rod asked, eyebrows shooting upwards.

'Yes, our David.'

'When was this?' Rod asked after a long pause.

'Just over two years ago. PC Williams accessed Patricia Johnson's file fourteen months ago. We can't ignore that something is going on here. What it is or what it means I'm not entirely sure.'

Rod was silent again, trying to think what to make of it. Eventually he said, 'Well, only thing we can do is ask them.'

'Yeah, I want you in the room when I ask David about it.' Rose got up from behind her desk and opened the door.

'David?' she called, waiting for him to look up. When he did, she waved him into her office.

'I need to ask you something,' Rose said when he walked into the office. There was nowhere for him to sit so he stood just behind Rod.

'Sure,' he said.

'Close the door, would you?' Rose waved at the door and waited until he had shut it and turned back round. He looked a little nervous now but Rose suspected he was waiting for a dressing down about something. He looked between her and Rod.

'David, we've been looking at the files for our victims, checking who has accessed them and why. Your name is on that list and I wondered why you hadn't mentioned it before,' Rose said, looking directly at the young man.

'Well, obviously I've looked at the files recently,' David replied, nonplussed.

'I'm talking about some time ago, David. Over a year.' Rose cocked her head.

David looked at her blankly. 'Did I? Which ones?'

'Seamus Harding and Dion Myers. You opened their files but left no note of explanation.'

David still looked blank. 'Their names are familiar now, obviously, but I can honestly say that I had never heard of either of them until they were killed – let alone accessing their records.'

'Are you telling me you have no idea why your name appears against these two files?' Rose pressed.

'None whatsoever,' David said with a shrug. 'They've never come up until they were found killed – I have no idea why my name's there. Maybe it's a glitch in the system.'

'It's one hell of a coincidence, don't you think?' Rod said, turning in his seat to look directly at David. 'That a glitch in the system has happened twice and the people in the files that happen to have a glitch turn up dead sometime later down the line?'

'Well, yes, I see what you mean, Rod, but I can give no other explanation.' David looked uncomfortable; he knew what Rod was implying. 'All I can tell you is I had no idea who those people were until we got the shout for their murders. I have – to my knowledge – never looked at their files until very recently.'

'OK,' Rose said. 'Do you know a PC Alexander Williams. I think he's sometimes known as Big Al?'

'Who doesn't know Big Al in this station? Why?' David asked, looking even more confused.

'Right, OK, thanks David,' Rose smiled very briefly at him. 'I might need to ask you about this again.'

'Yes ma'am, although I'm not sure I'll be able to shed any more light on the subject.' David's expression was both worried and puzzled.

Rose nodded, 'Well, back to the grindstone with you.'

'Yes ma'am.' He turned and left the room.

Rod looked at Rose, 'Do you believe him?'

'Yes, he seemed to genuinely have no idea, did he?' She began tapping the desk again.

'Yeah, I would have to agree. Mind you, if he does have anything to do with this then we've just tipped him off.'

'True, but it had to be done. Right, you carry on out there. I'll go and track PC Williams down again.' Rose got up from behind her desk and Rod followed suit and they walked back into the main office together.

Rose found PC Williams at home. She had got his home address from his sergeant who had told her, when she had gone looking for him, that Williams was on a day off. He looked surprised to see Rose on his doorstep but invited her in politely enough. She refused the offer of tea or coffee.

'Two visits from a Chief Inspector in a week. I am honoured,' Williams said as he sat down, gesturing Rose to a seat opposite.

'It's in connection with our last chat that I'm here,' Rose said. 'Last time, I asked you about your accessing the records for Evžen Souček, if you recall.'

'Yes, of course, I remember. I told you at the time the name didn't mean anything to me and it still doesn't.' Williams sounded a little defensive.

'No, I appreciate that,' Rose said firmly. 'It's just that we've had another murder and I was a little shocked to see that you had also accessed the file for this victim.'

Williams looked nonplussed for a second. 'Another one?'

'That's right … a Patricia Johnson. Name ring a bell?' Rose asked looking intently at Williams.

Williams considered for a moment, just as he had when she had mentioned Evžen Souček. 'No, again, Chief Inspector. It means nothing to me.'

'She was picked up on a traffic offence – no tax – a while back, but you weren't the officer that dealt with that. You accessed the file a few months later. And you have no idea why?' Rose watched Williams' response ... he seemed genuinely confused.

He shook his head slowly. 'No, Chief Inspector, I don't know the name and I can't tell you why I accessed – if I accessed – her file.'

Rose sat quietly for a moment. First David and now Williams appeared to have no clue about their access to any of the victims' files. And yet they had accessed them, or at least they had been accessed using their login details.

'Have you ever let someone use your login to access files?' she asked, hoping that would be the answer and she would have someone else to look at.

'No, I'm careful that way, for this very reason.'

'Anyone know your login details?'

'Not that I'm aware of. I've had the same user name for, well, forever, but the password is changed regularly as per standard procedure.' Williams' voice was firm and to Rose it seemed he was being honest and forthright.

'How well do you know DC David Baker?' Rose asked, trying a different tack.

'Not well,' Williams shook his head, either in the negative or in confusion – Rose couldn't tell.

'Have you ever socialised with him? Seen him much out of work?'

'No, like I say, I don't really know him. Where's this going?' Williams asked, again looking confused and a little annoyed.

'Nothing, just something I needed to ask. Right, thanks Al, I appreciate you giving me the time on your day off.' Rose got up from her seat.

'No problem,' Williams replied, also getting up.

He showed her to the door and wished her good luck with the investigation.

Rose drove back to the station feeling none the wiser. As she climbed out of her car, she was still puzzling over how two serving officers could have accessed every one of her victims' files and have no recollection of doing so, when a voice broke her train of thought.

'Chief Inspector, the very person.' It was Scott Ellis. Rose cursed under her breath.

'I have no comment that I can or will make right now, Scott,' Rose said, moving past the reporter.

'But there's been another murder, Chief Inspector, the fourth in what two weeks? I think it's time the people of Milton Keynes got to hear exactly what you're doing about it. I will print something, regardless. I suggest you give me the official line rather than have me speculate,' Ellis called after her.

Rose stopped walking and turned to face him. 'Scott, there really is nothing I can say right now. I'm sure there'll be an official release very soon. Just be a bit patient – as you've pointed out, we've a lot on our plates. I promise I'll talk to you when I can.'

Ellis smirked at her, 'I'm not very good at patience, Rose. But I'll tell you what, I'll leave it until, say, six-ish? Then I'll have to write something.'

'I can't stop you, Scott, there's no official embargo. I'll see what details we can release and let you know – might not be until after six though.' Rose began walking again.

'Fair enough. But I'm starting writing at six,' Ellis said, turning to leave.

'Oh, and Scott?' Rose called, making him turn. 'It's Chief Inspector, got that?'

Ellis gave her a broad smile, bowed slightly then turned and walked out the car park.

'I will find out who feeds you and when I do…' Rose muttered to herself as she stabbed the keys on the security panel.

Rod raised an eyebrow at her as she walked past him in the office. She waved a forestalling hand at him and walked straight into her own office. With a few taps on her keyboard she had the number she needed, picked the phone up and dialled. The line rang several times and then clicked over to voicemail.

'Andy, it's Rose from down in MK,' she said into the handset. 'I hope life's treating you well. I need to ask you something – can you call me back as soon as you can please?'

She hung up, hoping that DS Carter would call her back soon and would have some memory of accessing Dion Myers' file. She pushed the thought to the back of her mind; he would call when he could and then she would know. Until then, there was nothing she could do.

Rod put his head round the door and she waved him in.

He shut the door before sitting down. 'What did Big Al have to say?' he asked, crossing one long leg over the other.

'Much the same as last time. He had no idea who Patricia Johnson was and could offer no explanation as to why he might have accessed the file,' Rose said with a distracted air. She was still annoyed at Scott Ellis' ability to find out information that her team had only just uncovered.

'So, where does that leave us?' Rod asked.

'It leaves us with three police officers who have accessed the files of four murder victims with no explanation as to why and in two cases with no memory of having even done anything.'

'Three?' Rod frowned.

'Oh, yeah, Andy Carter – you remember him? He worked the school case so had unsurprisingly accessed Souček's file but he also looked at Myers'. I've called and left him a message to call me back. He might be able to shed some light on it.'

Rod nodded slowly. 'I remember Andy. Geordie, wasn't he? Your neck of the woods.'

'That's right. He might have a better memory than our other two,' Rose said.

'All we really have, then, is that two of our coppers looked at the files of four victims, two each. Is that right?' Rod said, raising his hands in a half shrug.

'That about sums it up. But it feels like too much of a coincidence, no, it is too much of a coincidence and neither of them left notes or reasons as to why they accessed the files. Something's not right,' Rose said firmly.

'It could be, you know,' Rod said slowly, 'that if we went through, say, I don't know, a hundred random files on the PNC that we'll find loads of entries like that. People cut corners and sometimes just look at something quick and move on. I'm sure it happens all the time when going through suspect profiles and that kind of thing.'

'Yes, that's true,' Rose replied quietly, 'but I wonder what would happen if we split that one hundred into fifty each and then looked to see if the same name came up twice. I'm not convinced it would. And then how many of the people in those files had come to harm after the same person had looked at them. And all in a week to ten days?'

'Well, when thought about it like that then...' Rod bit his lower lip, something he did when he was thinking, '... there's something in it, isn't there?'

'We have to follow up on it. Let's take a closer look at these two. You take Williams and I'll take David.'

'What do you want me to look for?' Rod asked.

'Anything at all – where he goes on his nights off, where and who he lives with, who he hangs about with – but first check his shifts against the murders; if he was on shift it's unlikely he's our killer.' Rose thought for a second. 'He's too tall if the shoeprints and CCTV is to be believed, but then he could be working with someone else. It's quite possible the prints and CCTV are completely coincidental and have nothing to do with our killer, in which case Williams could be involved.'

'I'll do that.' Rod frowned. 'But really if we are looking at them because they accessed the victims' files then they have to be working together. They only accessed two files each remember so they would have to be sharing that information.'

Rose nodded wearily. 'Yeah I know, Rod, I know, but it's all we've got. Except for a bloody gun that's been used in some Dumfries turf war.'

'Probably over ice cream,' Rod said absently.

'What?' Rose screwed her face up. 'What are you on about, Rod?'

'Didn't they have the ice cream wars up there, years back? You know, rival gangs blowing ice cream vans up and that sort of thing?' Rod said, a little embarrassed.

'That was Glasgow not Dumfries. Besides, with the weather they get in Dumfries, ice creams are only sold on the second Tuesday in June.' Rose laughed.

Rod joined in. 'Fair enough. Right, I'll get on to Williams.'

Chapter Twenty-Eight

Rose set about the unwelcome task of looking into one of her own officers. First, she checked the rota to see when David had been on shift and on call, and matched that to the days and approximate times of the murders. She had hoped to find that he had been on duty for at least one of them, allowing her to rule him out. But she had no such luck. He had been off duty on all four occasions.

Then she plugged his car registration into the Automatic Number Plate Recognition system to see if his car was picked up by any of the myriad traffic cameras that dotted the city, looking specifically at the areas where the bodies were found and the areas they thought the victims may have been on the day they were killed. She went to grab a coffee, knowing the system would take some time to process the information.

She was stirring the milk into her coffee when Louise approached her.

'Could I have a word, ma'am?' she asked quietly.

'Sure,' Rose said, pointing with her spoon at an empty mug.

'No thanks,' Louise said.

Rose gestured her into the office and closed the door behind them.

'What can I do for you, Louise?' she asked, sitting back down.

Louise looked a little uncomfortable and embarrassed. 'It's just…'

'Go on, anything you say I'll treat in strictest confidence,' Rose reassured her.

'Well, you won't be aware of this – we've kept it very quiet – but I've been seeing David, out of work. You know, er, socially.' Her cheeks reddened as she spoke.

'Don't worry, actually it hadn't escaped my attention,' Rose said with a smile, watching Louise's eyes widen. 'Not much gets past me, Louise.'

Louise was quiet for a moment. 'Look,' Rose said to break the silence, 'it's really none of my business what you get up to when you're off duty, as long as it doesn't affect what happens when you are at work. My only concern is how that might affect your working relationship, should you split up.'

'We're keeping it very casual, ma'am. But that's not really what I wanted to talk to you about.' Louise looked even more awkward.

'Oh, right, well what's up then?' Rose asked, frowning.

'Well, it's just, it's sort of connected. You see, I'm a nosey bugger, I can't help it, I've always been that way.' She stopped talking and pursed her lips.

'That is something else I had noticed, Louise. It's a good thing in this job,' Rose said, wondering where this was going.

'Yeah, yeah I know. You see, I stayed over at David's place the other night and in the morning he was in the shower and…' Again, she pursed her lips. Whatever it was she had to say she was clearly finding it difficult.

'And?' Rose prompted.

'I was in the living room and spotted his diary on the coffee table. I couldn't help myself and took a look. I only flicked through a few pages, you know, really just going back over the time we had started to see each other – I suppose I was wondering if he'd put anything about me in there.

Anyway, I was looking through it and I noticed something that kind of worried me.' She lapsed into silence again, looking at the floor then the ceiling – anywhere other than at Rose.

Rose stayed silent this time; a worried feeling was growing in her stomach and she also wanted to give Louise time to say what she needed to say.

Louise took a deep breath. 'He had written the names of each of the victims on the day they were killed – at the top of each page.'

Rose took a moment to absorb this information. Eventually she said, 'All four of them?'

'No, well, I only saw the first three. We didn't know about the latest one at the time,' Louise said, looking directly at Rose for the first time during their conversation. 'It's probably nothing, or at least innocent, but it's been bugging me ever since. I mean, it's just a bit odd, don't you think?'

'This was his personal diary, not a work one?' Rose asked, with a slight frown.

'Yes, it was definitely his personal one,' Louise said, looking uncomfortable again.

'Right. Anything else you can tell me?' Rose asked.

'Not really no,' Louise said, with a small shrug.

'OK, thanks Louise. Like you say, it's probably completely innocent, but you did the right thing in telling me.' Rose smiled reassuringly at the young woman.

'I don't want him to know I told you, if at all possible. I feel bad enough just saying it.' Louise looked intently at Rose.

'Sure, I won't mention your name if I need to talk to him about it. Mind you, it won't take a genius to know who told me. But, leave it with me. I need a little while to decide what to do with this anyway.'

'I know. Thanks, ma'am.' Louise got up from her seat.

Rose nodded and watched her as she made her way back to her desk.

Rose checked the ANPR system but it was still running its search. Exhaling loudly, she rubbed her eyes with forefinger and thumb and stared blankly down at her desk. She had no idea what to make of the information Louise had just given her. She knew there was every possibility of an innocent and rational explanation as to why the victims were named in David's diary on the days they were killed. Louise had no idea when they were written in there or for what reason. And, if David were involved, would he be so stupid as to put the names of his victims in his diary? Still, it was another piece of information pointing at David that had a bearing on the case. She needed to know if Patricia Johnson's name was also in that diary but had no way of finding out right at that moment.

She knew she was going to have to at least talk to David again but didn't want him realising Louise had told her about the diary. The last thing she needed right then was for the team to disintegrate into spiteful little spats about who said what and what right they had to be looking at private stuff in the first place. It was the sort of thing that started with just two people falling out and ended with the entire team at each other's throats, one person backing another and so on. She decided that unless something else more concrete came in against David she would sit on it for a bit.

Rod knocked on her door and she waved him in.

'Williams was on night shift for three of the four, partnered with Dan Townsend,' Rod said, without preamble. 'They were patrolling the far side of town when Harding was likely killed and the centre of town for Souček. He was on a day off when Myers was killed and on day shift for Patricia Johnson – didn't knock off until about eight that night.'

'Right, so he's out, certainly as far as the killings are concerned. I've just had some interesting info handed me by Louise,' Rose said, sounding thoughtful.

'Oh yeah?' Rod asked, taking a seat.

When Rose finished explaining about the diary, Rod sat back and rubbed his chin thoughtfully. 'Could be something or nothing,' he said slowly. 'But that's two things now that young David has to explain away – and two too many in my book.'

'They could all be easily explained away but you're right, two connections starts to look pretty bad doesn't it?' Rose said, looking over at her monitor. 'I've run an ANPR check on his reg. If he comes up as being anywhere near any of the sites where bodies were found then we'll have to have him in… formally.'

Rod nodded slowly. 'We need to tread very lightly on this, Rose,' he said, his voice low and grave.

'I know, Rod, I know,' Rose said exhaling loudly. 'Now I have to see the Super and clear what I'm going to say to Scott Ellis. He reckons he's going to write something tonight regardless.'

'Right, OK, I'll see how we're getting on with the CCTV,' Rod replied, virtually springing up from his seat and out the office before she could say anything else. Rose looked at his back with a small frown on her face.

Chapter Twenty-Nine

Chief Superintendent Abdighani cleared her to be fully open with Scott Ellis. Press speculation would only make things worse, he had reasoned, but warning her to keep any vital evidence from the reporter. *Vital evidence?* Rose had thought. *That won't be hard to hide, there's bloody none!*

She was about to go into the office and make the dreaded call when DCI John Reid caught up with her in the corridor.

'Rose, I was hoping I'd catch you. I have something for you,' he said, smiling broadly.

'Something good, I hope,' Rose said with feeling.

'Well, it's not ground-breaking but it will be of interest to you. Come and see.' He gestured down the hall to where his own team were officed.

Rose followed him to the near-identical office space to her own: a large open-plan office for the main team and a smaller closed-off space for the boss. Reid led her over to a desk where DS Danny Merchant was sitting. Rose had worked a few cases with him in the past and they had got on well.

'Hi Danny,' Rose said as they approached. 'What have you got for me?'

'Hi Rose,' Danny greeted her and flicked a finger at his screen. 'This should prove interesting to you.'

Rose manoeuvred round behind Danny and he clicked the mouse. A video, clearly taken on a phone and by either Harding or Denning, Rose guessed. It showed a very quiet street, probably very late at night or early morning. There was very little sound other than quiet footfalls; Rose thought she could hear soft but heavy breathing but thought it could as easily be the wind. The image quality was poor, either because it was dark or because it was a poor-quality phone camera, or both. For several minutes all that happened was the camera moving slowly along the street. A car door opened and closed not far from whoever was operating the phone but the user didn't turn to look, or if they did they didn't turn the phone.

Suddenly there was a muffled shout and the camera shot up and around, its movements sporadic and wild. There was a brief image of a gloved hand over the face of the camera operator. Rose saw it was Seamus Harding. There was more scuffling and then the phone was dropped and the view changed to that of two pairs of legs with feet shuffling and almost dancing as the two people scuffled. A voice, muted and distant-sounding, said something like, 'That's a gun in your back…' and was then lost in more scraping of feet.

The fighting stopped very quickly and the legs moved off back the way Harding had come. The camera showed only an overcast night sky, with spots of rain landing on the lens and distorting the view. Then a black-gloved hand appeared and turned the view completely black as it closed around the phone. For a very brief second there was a view of a balaclava'd face and just the briefest glimpse of an eye, the colour undefined in the dark. Then the screen went black.

Rose stared at the screen for some time, saying nothing. Danny sat back in his seat and looked up at her. She could sense John Reid looking at her and turned to face him.

'Am I looking at what I think I'm looking at?' she asked quietly and slowly.

'We figure so,' Reid answered. 'It's from the night he was killed. It's Harding if you hadn't guessed.'

'Where's it from?' Rose asked. She wanted to ask why the hell they hadn't come across the footage before but decided against it.

'It's from his phone – the battery was dead when it was recovered and it was pretty badly smashed up, so it's taken us a while to get into it and get all the stuff off,' Reid said, answering her unasked question. 'I admit we looked at the larger files first, assuming they would give us the most information and this is a very small file. It was Danny who spotted the date and opened it.'

'If the killer knew what was on the phone why not destroy it?' Rose asked. Her killer had been very careful up until that point.

'We figured that they were the ones that smashed it up … maybe they assumed that would be enough or were simply not bothered by what was on it,' Danny said.

'Yeah maybe,' Rose replied thoughtfully.

'What did you make of the voice?' Rose asked. It had been very muffled and quiet.

'Hard to say anything really … we're going to have it put through the lab to see what they can get from it. I'll have them send the results directly to you – Danny's already emailed you this video,' Reid said, pointing at the screen.

'Perfect. Thanks John,' Rose said, and laid her hand on his shoulder. 'I owe you one big time.'

'I'm not sure it helps you much – you're not getting an ID from that but it's at least another little bit to add to the pile,' Reid said with a sympathetic smile.

'It's something anyway,' Rose replied. 'Thanks guys. And well done, Danny. Top work.'

Rose updated Gareth that they were expecting something back from the audio labs and then went to make the call she had been dreading. Scott Ellis answered almost immediately and just as quickly put her back up with his quirky and all too cheery tone.

'I was just about to start typing – good timing, Chief Inspector,' he trilled down the phone.

'Let's just get on with it, Scott. I'm not in the mood for the happy-go-lucky reporter routine this evening,' Rose said dryly.

She told him everything, only leaving out the part about the notes pinned to the victims' chests. She confirmed the vigilante angle and even dropped a hint that it might be a police officer without going so far as to say so. She explained that every victim had had some involvement with the police but that none of them had been convicted of any crimes. She finished by saying that they were following a number of leads and expected results in the very near future.

'That is a line I have heard so many times before,' Ellis said, dragging out the 'o' in 'so' for far too long. 'It usually means you haven't a clue, but I won't print that I promise.'

'Please don't,' Rose said tiredly.

'Rest assured I will be my usual, professional self. Do you really think it's someone inside the force?' Ellis was fast on the uptake – she had barely hinted at that angle.

'Honestly, Scott, I don't know. Look I have to get on, unless there's anything else you want to ask?'

'No, no, Rose, you've given me more than enough to go on. Thank you.' Ellis sounded ridiculously cheerful.

'Right, well goodbye, Scott.'

'Bye, Rose,' he said quickly before hanging up.

Rose ground her teeth and muttered, 'Chief Fucking Inspector, you annoying little twat.'

She rubbed her forehead; the mother of all headaches was building behind her eyes. She wanted nothing more than to go home and put her feet up, watch some rubbish TV and go to bed. *Curry first, gotta have a curry.* She decided to see if the ANPR system had come up with anything before she did.

It had. And she wished it hadn't.

Head now throbbing, she moved to the office door and looked for Rod. He was still at his desk filing reports, head down and in a world of his own. She had to call his name twice before he looked up. When he did, she jerked her head back towards her office and moved back inside. Just before Rod came in, she looked around him and noted that David's desk was unoccupied.

As soon as he had shut the door, she asked, 'Has David left for the day?'

'Yeah, about twenty minutes ago,' Rod replied with a frown.

'Right,' Rose sighed. 'You know we said that two connections – coincidental or not – was bad enough?'

'Yes,' Rod said, dragging the word out and making it closer to a question.

'Well, now we have three.'

Rod's brows shot up. 'What have you got?'

'ANPR results. I checked David's number plate against the known movements of our victims – especially where we had spotted them on CCTV – for the dates leading up to each murder. And it's given me three hits.' Rose pulled a face that was sad, bothered and upset all at once.

'Fuck,' was all Rod said, shaking his head.

'Now I need to try and track for the rest of the time but I wanted to see if he came up at all first. So, I have Evžen Souček leaving the library at –' she checked her notes – 'fifteen hundred hours on the day he was killed, and I have

David's car driving past the lights just before you get to the library one minute later.'

'OK,' Rod said. He looked about to say something else but changed his mind.

'Then we have Dion Myers leaving his office for lunch at – what was it? – fourteen thirty on the day he was murdered.' Rod nodded. 'And I have David driving past Myers' office at fourteen twenty-eight, in time to be able to spot him leaving. And finally, I have Patricia Johnson leaving work at eighteen hundred hours on the day she was killed and David driving up the same street at seventeen forty-five.' Rose looked at Rod with a crooked, sardonic smile.

'That is too much of a coincidence,' Rod said. 'What do you want to do?'

'Well, first we have to try and track him for the whole of those days, especially at night. The system hasn't flagged him as being near the carpark when Myers was abducted but that doesn't necessarily mean very much. We need to widen that search for the time we think he was taken. Same for the others. I need you to check what jobs he had on for those dates, to see if we can't rule him out by finding he was legitimately in that area. Then we go from there.'

'OK, I'll get on that now,' Rod said sharply and marched out the office.

Rose got to work with the ANPR system, widening the search areas around the locales and times they thought each victim had been killed. Thanks to the video, they now had the time Seamus Harding had been abducted but couldn't pinpoint exactly where, so she concentrated on the other three.

Rod reappeared within five minutes. 'He was working the spate of burglaries we've been having across town for most of that time, plus a mugging and the attack on that Asian kid out at Willen Lake.'

'So, would he have legitimately been in the areas around where we know our victims were at those times?' Rose asked, hoping that Rod would say a definitive yes.

'Maybe,' he replied. 'I suppose he could have had reason, although all the burglaries were way out of the centre and Willen Lake is also out the way. Again though, I suppose he could have been heading through town to interview someone or something.'

This was not the answer Rose was looking for. She rubbed her forehead. She looked at her screen; the ANPR system was going to take some time to process her requests. She needed a bit of time but felt she had to act immediately or lose what momentum she had left in her.

'Right, bring him in. He's to be held for questioning but not arrested. We don't have enough evidence yet. I'll organise a warrant to search his property – the Chief Super should be able to get that quickly enough. Go round up a couple of John Reid's guys – if they're still about – or someone else you can rely on to be discreet. Not any of our team.'

'Right, which interview room do you want him in when I fetch him?' Rod asked, standing to carry out her instructions.

'Put him in a cell. One – it'll shake him up a bit and make sure we get proper answers from him, and two – I want to wait until we have all the results from the search and the ANPR before I interview him,' Rose said and grimaced, massaging her forehead again.

'OK,' Rod said and looked at her. 'You look knackered, ma'am. Why don't you go home? I can handle this for now. Get some rest and I'll see you in the morning, ready for matey boy.'

'I think I will, Rod, thanks,' Rose said. Her head felt like a large mallet had been taken to front and back with malice aforethought. She lifted the phone to call the Chief Superintendent and organise a warrant, with the thought of home becoming ever more enticing.

***

Rod found Danny Merchant and John Reid still in their office. They reluctantly agreed to join him, mainly because they were having to deal with another officer and also because they were about to go home themselves.

'I have a wife and two kids,' Danny complained. 'I can barely remember what they look like.'

'Oh, you love it really, Danny.' Rod laughed.

When there was no answer at David's door, Rod called his mobile. He took some time to answer but eventually he picked up.

'Where are you?' Rod asked with no preamble.

'I'm out, Rod, why?' David asked.

Rod could here low talking and the clank of cutlery on plates. 'Which restaurant?'

'Bombay Garden. What is it you want, Rod?' David sounded more annoyed than curious.

'Right, you have two options – either you stay there and I come and pick you up or you go straight to the station and I'll see you there. Which would you prefer?' Rod's voice brooked no argument.

'What the hell, Rod? What's going on?' David was sounding more agitated by the second. Rod caught a half-mumbled conversation with someone, explaining the call.

'Don't worry – I can be at the Bombay Garden in less than ten minutes. I'll see you there.' Rod hung up. 'Danny, you come with me. We'll get his house keys before I take him in, then you can run back here and get on with the search. His diary is important so make sure you grab and bag that first.'

Reid was unhappy about being left hanging around but Rod assured him it wouldn't be for long.

Danny agreed to wait outside while Rod went in and fetched David out of the restaurant. Rod walked in and looked around; fortunately it wasn't a big restaurant and he spotted David almost straightaway. His eyes widened when he saw that David was with Louise.

'Shit, so much for discretion,' Rod muttered.

He moved over to where they were sitting. They were hunched over the table muttering to each other so didn't see him approach.

'David,' Rod said firmly but quietly. He glanced quickly at Louise.

David looked up a little startled even though he knew Rod was coming. His expression soon morphed into annoyance.

'Rod, I'm off duty – what the hell is it you want?' David wasn't as quiet as Rod.

'I need you to come to the station with me,' Rod said, keeping his voice very low. 'Let's just go, and I'll explain what I can on the way. Let's not have any fuss in here, eh?'

'The station? Rod, what the…?' David's annoyance now turned to incredulity.

Rod leaned in. 'Look, I have to bring you in. I would rather, and I'm pretty sure you would too, that that was done quietly and without fuss. I can do it formally if you want but you don't want that, do you?'

David shook his head in exasperation. 'No, I suppose I don't. Are you going to tell me what this is all about?'

'Not in here and not right now, no,' Rod said and put a hand on David's shoulder.

'I'll get hold of the federation rep,' Louise said as David stood up. She had been sitting, silently taking in the whole exchange, looking as incredulous as David.

'You do that, Louise,' Rod said and led the way out of the restaurant.

David reluctantly handed his keys over to Danny Merchant and climbed into Rod's car. He was silent for the entire drive to the station. When they arrived and Rod explained that they were going to hold him in a cell overnight he exploded.

'What the fucking hell is this, Rod?'

'It's in connection with the murders. I can't say any more than that at the moment. The boss wants you to be held here tonight while your flat is searched and then we'll question you in the morning. Just ride with it for now. I'm sure it'll get sorted quickly enough.' Rod tried his best to sound conciliatory.

'The murders?' David half laughed. 'Oh, come on? Is this some kind of joke?'

'No, David, I'm afraid it's not,' Rod said gravely.

In the end, David stood meekly while the desk sergeant booked him in and then walked to the cells – cells he had walked suspects to so many times. Rod gave him a sympathetic look as he shut and locked the cell door.

Chapter Thirty

Rose was in early but the team were in before her. There was a buzz going around the office as she walked in. Christine approached her as soon she was through the door.

'Is it true? You have David in the cells?' she asked, sounding almost accusatory.

'Yes, it is,' Rose answered quietly. Rod had called her as soon as he had brought David in and explained that he had been with Louise when they had picked him up so it was no surprise to her that the whole team already knew.

'But why?' Christine was not going to let Rose past without an explanation.

'You'll all be fully apprised as soon as Rod and I have asked him a few questions,' Rose said, raising her voice so the whole office could hear. 'Until then, I'm afraid I can't tell you any more.'

Rod was at his desk and several pairs of eyes turned towards him, some were recriminatory and others outright hostile. He ignored them all. Instead, he stood and moved to the door to Rose's office and waited there quietly.

Rose could see a host of questions starting to bubble up on the faces of the team. She held her hand up to quell them before they started.

'I can't tell you any more, so please don't ask.' She moved past Christine and made her way towards Rod, glancing at Louise as she went. Louise was sitting at her desk, head down and looking pale. Rose sympathised with her; some of the information they had to put to David came from her and the team would not take that news well at all. Rose assumed she hadn't told them and hoped she decided to keep it that way.

She entered her office, Rod following behind and shutting the door.

'The search of the flat is complete,' he said, as soon as she sat down. 'There are a few items they've come back with – the diary, obviously, but also some Doc Marten boots that have some mud on the soles. They've been sent to the lab to see if the print taken at the scene of Seamus Harding's and Dion Myers' murders match and also for soil samples. Then there's a balaclava, black.'

'Whoever was in that video Seamus Harding took was wearing a black balaclava,' Rose said, nodding. 'No gun then?'

'No,' Rod said, sounding relieved. 'I don't think he's that stupid. If it is him, he'll have that stashed somewhere else, I would imagine.'

'Let's keep that "*if* he's the killer" in our minds when we talk to him. We only have a few bits of circumstantial evidence and to be honest I really don't want it to be him.' Rose rubbed her forehead; the headache from the previous night hadn't gone away, but had just dulled into a constant and irritating thump at the back of her head.

'I know what you mean. But there are three apparent coincidences connecting him to the victims which is very hard to ignore.' Rod shook his head. 'It's a shit show that it's one of our own.'

'I take it the boots have been fast-tracked?' Rose asked.

'Yeah, results should be with us in terms of the print within the hour. The soil samples will take longer. Let's hope the print doesn't match.' Rod ran a hand down his face. 'If it does, he's in deep shit.'

Rose grimaced. 'I need to bring the Chief Super up to date. We need someone still working on the ANPR results, to see if there aren't any more hits near the victims.' She looked at her watch. 'David will likely be having his breakfast at the moment so let's hang on for an hour to see if the lab results are back on the boot and if we get any more from the ANPR. Put Gareth on it – he'll be the most impartial. By the way, is Patricia Johnson in the diary?'

'Yes, she is,' Rod said gravely.

Rose sighed. It wasn't looking great but she clung to the lab results helping to rule David out. She really did not want to be doing this but knew she had to.

'You get Gareth on to the ANPR work and chase that lab. I'll go see the Chief Super now and then I'll meet you downstairs in an hour.'

Rod nodded and left the office swiftly. Rose stayed where she was for several minutes gathering her thoughts. When she felt she was as ready as she was ever going to be, she got up and made her way through the office to go see Chief Superintendent Abdighani.

***

The old man grunted as he pushed himself out of his seat. Everything ached these days and he cursed his failing body. He was sixty-eight but felt ten years older. Arthritis and the general stresses he had put his body through over the course of his working life were now taking their toll. Years of smoking had resulted in seriously diminished lung capacity and he found the simplest task often left him out of breath.

Carrying his mug loosely hooked on one finger, he shuffled towards the small kitchen of his little flat where the kettle had just finished boiling. Clunking the mug down on the worktop he grimaced as he pulled the top off the tin that held the teabags; the joints in his hands complained and cracked whenever he had to apply even the slightest pressure.

Tea made, he shuffled back to his chair and picked up the remote from the small table next to his armchair. Settling back in the seat, he switched the TV on. It was only eight in the morning so he knew his choices would be limited but still he scrolled hopefully through the menu, looking for something to watch. He smiled as he spotted a programme about fishing on one of the documentary channels. Pushing the button on the remote, he lifted his tea and sipped contentedly.

As he put the mug back on the table his eyes passed over his phone. It was sitting in its usual place, near the edge of the table, as silent and inactive as it always was. He missed hearing from his kids and – more than any of it – missed hearing his wife chatter away as she always had in the mornings. He wasn't lonely exactly; he was used to his own company and had spent many happy hours and days completely alone during his life. Besides, he had his memories.

'Wot we catchin' today then fellas?' he said to the TV and the empty room.

***

Rod rushed up to where Rose was waiting, ready to go into one of the interview rooms.

He waved a slim brown folder at her. 'Lab results.'

Rose took the folder off of him and opened it. She scanned the results quickly and shut the folder, looking at Rod.

'A match,' she said, no emotion in her voice.

'On both print and soil,' Rod said, his voice as flat as hers.

'Right, let's get started,' Rose said with a sigh.

Rod nodded solemnly and they walked slowly towards the interview room. Just as they were about to open the door Rose's phone began to ring. She glanced at it and held a finger up to Rod then took a couple of paces away.

'Louise, what's up?' she asked.

She listened for a minute and then said, 'No that's fine, you do what you have to. Let me know what's going on later. Yeah I will.'

Rod raised a questioning eyebrow to her when she turned back to the door.

'Family crisis, she's nipping off for the day.'

Rod gave an upward flick of his chin. 'Ready?' he said, turning the door handle.

'As I'll ever be,' Rose said with feeling.

***

Sylvia Manning poured all of her concentration into the task in hand. It had taken her more than an hour to lift the voice track and clarify the few words spoken by Seamus Harding's attacker on the short video. She moved the file over to another piece of software that should clean the track up even more. After clicking 'run' she sipped her tea, knowing it would take a few minutes for the software to do its magic.

She had worked in the audio and visual lab for seven years and loved the work. She felt close to the detectives that her work aided and knew how important it could be that they had clean images and good-quality sound recordings. She also loved the technical conundrums the work often presented her. Lots of the material they dealt with was of low quality and took a considerable amount of know-how to be able to present investigating teams with usable material.

The clean-up software had finished its run. She pulled on some headphones and listened to the results. They were still indistinct but much better than she had before. The voice sounded southern but didn't hold any distinctive accent. There was something about it that bothered her but she couldn't quite put her finger on it immediately.

She clicked open another program that looked at and evaluated voice modulation and frequencies. It only took a minute to get the result back.

'Oh?' she said to herself.

She pulled the headphones back on and listened again.

'Oh,' she said again.

***

The fishing programme had finished. He sighed and looked around the small room.

'Wot the fuck will I do now then?' he muttered to himself.

The flat was small and sparsely furnished – his armchair, a two-seater sofa and the TV being the main points of note in the living room. There was a small kitchen with two cupboards, fridge, cooker and a sink that faced the window. He often found himself staring out that window, running the dish cloth round and round the same cup or plate for many minutes. Then there was the bedroom and bathroom, both equally small and utilitarian.

He quite liked his little flat. He had lived there for nearly four years, ever since his wife had died. When she had gone, he found he hated rattling around their old family home. It was too big for him and held too many memories. Within a month of her passing he had the house up for sale and within two more he had bought the flat.

He picked up his phone and considered texting either his son or daughter, then decided against it. He wasn't very good with the phone and found texting a chore. He knew better than to try to call either of them; they were always way too busy. It was his daughter that he missed the most; she reminded him so much of his wife. But she was the one he saw least of. He knew her job kept her pretty busy but he suspected she had been avoiding visiting ever since her mother had died. His son dropped by every once in a while, bringing his own son along. But again, he suspected it was done more as a chore that needed ticking off a list.

'Fuckin' bollocks to 'em,' he mumbled.

***

DS Andy Carter arrived back at his desk after finishing an interview with a prolific car thief who had managed to run down and seriously injure a pedestrian. The young lad had confessed immediately and, in Andy's opinion, was showing genuine remorse. He sat down and pulled the boy's file over in front of him, readying to send the case over to the CPS for review and for a charging decision. He didn't expect they would take very long.

He was about to start work when a post-it note stuck to his monitor caught his eye. He pulled it off and tsked to himself. He had meant to do that a day or so ago.

'Rose'll have my guts if I don't call her back,' he muttered, picking up his phone. He let it ring until it went to voicemail.

'Rose, it's Andy, you wanted to ask me something? I'm in the office all day today so give me a bell back when you can.'

Message left, he turned back to his paperwork.

***

'It's just a coincidence,' David said for the fourth time. 'I'm telling you I had no idea who those people were until they showed up dead. And I have never accessed their records. And even if I did and I've forgotten about it, the access was made months, even years ago. If I had anything to do with this, wouldn't I have looked at them more recently?'

'The killings were very well planned,' Rod said. 'Maybe planned for years in advance.'

David said nothing. He looked rough, unshaven and with bleary eyes. Rose suspected he hadn't slept very much, if at all, and he was clearly very stressed. So would I be in your shoes, she thought.

'David, you must see that a glitch was very unlikely and that you must have accessed those records. Tell me about the others, the ones you didn't access. Is there someone else? Another officer that helped you check the victims out? PC Williams, for example?' Rose knew David was unlikely to just fold and confess; he would stick to his story and, knowing him as she did, he would not start dropping other people in it.

'No, I told you before –' David's voice was weary – 'I don't really know Big Al, only by sight and I certainly haven't asked him to look anyone up for me.'

'Right, so let's look at something else. Your car has been picked up on the ANPR system, driving within a few hundred yards of three of the victims on the days they were killed. What were you doing near all four victims on those days when according to the rota you were on cases that were several miles away?' Rose passed David the printouts showing the hits from the ANPR system.

He looked nonplussed for a second and then shook his head. 'I'm not sure, I was probably just following something up that took me to those parts of town at those times.'

'Another coincidence?' Rod asked, sitting forward.

David shrugged, 'Yes, I suppose so.'

'OK, so if I accept that you just happened to be driving in the vicinity of three of our victims on or near to the day they were murdered, and that somehow there was a computer glitch on two occasions that puts your name against the files for two victims, can you explain to me why their names are also in your diary?' Rose kept her voice low and calm throughout.

Rod pulled the diary out of the clear evidence bag it was in and opened the marked pages one by one. 'All here on the days they were killed,' he said, pointing to the names neatly written at the top of each page.

David looked blankly at the diary for a few seconds. 'I was trying to see if there was a pattern,' he said with a frown.

'A pattern?' Rod asked.

'Yeah, you know, a fixed number of days apart or tied in with phases of the moon or something.' David waved a hand vaguely in front of his face.

'And you do that a lot when you have a case on?' Rod asked, raising an eyebrow.

'Yes, well no, I mean I just happened to be at home and I was thinking about this one so I jotted the names of the victims into my diary to see if there was a pattern. I think a lot about my cases at home,' David said, shrugging.

'Interesting then,' Rod said, leaning back a little, 'that I have flicked through your diary and I can see no other pages where you have "jotted down" any information about any of the cases you've worked on. So why the sudden change of habit?'

'Like I said, I was just thinking about the case and it occurred to me that I might see a pattern or something if I wrote the names down against the days they were killed.'

'You must see, David, that we're struggling with the number of apparent coincidences here,' Rose said, leaning forward. 'And I can see you really want us to see them as coincidences but I'm struggling myself.' She paused for a moment. 'So, I'm going to put them to one side for a moment. I wonder if you can tell me about the pair of Doc Marten boots recovered from your flat last night?'

'I don't own a pair of DMs,' David replied flatly.

'But they were found in your flat, at the back of your wardrobe – the kind of place you might put something you want kept out of sight,' Rose said, looking David in the eye.

'I just said, I don't own any DMs,' David replied, running his hands through his already dishevelled hair.

'You see, it's just that those shoes found in your flat happen to have a sole that matches with the shoe print found near the bodies of Seamus Harding and Dion Myers. And also, the soil from the sole of those shoes matches the soil from the site where Dion Myers was discovered. What have you to say in response to that?' Rose pulled the lab report out of the folder and turned them around on the desk so David could read them.

He barely looked at them. 'I have nothing to say to that. I have already stated that I don't own a pair of Doc

Martens so I have no idea how these ones got into my flat and certainly no idea how they match the print from a murder scene.'

'That's not a very satisfying answer, David,' Rose said, shaking her head. 'Is it just another coincidence, do you think?'

David shook his head and closed his eyes. Rose let him gather his thoughts. Her phone started to ring but she ignored it.

'While you're thinking about that, perhaps you could also have a ponder on the black balaclava, also found in your flat. Or are you going to assert that you don't own one of those either?' Rose was sure that he would give much the same answer but wanted him to say it anyway.

David stayed silent.

She was about to ask the question again when there was a knock on the interview room door and Gareth came into the room.

'Sorry, ma'am, but there's something you need to know,' he said, indicating she needed to leave the room with him by jerking his head backwards.

'Interview suspended at eleven thirty-five,' Rose said, rising from her seat and looking quizzically at Gareth.

***

'This had better be important, Gareth,' Rose said as she followed him out to the front desk. Gareth held the door open for her and then pointed to an intense-looking woman waiting agitatedly in the reception area.

'This is Sylvia,' Gareth said, as they walked up to the woman. 'She works in the audio-visual labs. You'll want to hear what she has to say.'

Rose shook hands with the small woman in front of her.

'Well, what do you have?' Rose asked, glancing at her watch, making it clear that this had better be very important.

'I've finished the work on the video,' Sylvia said, pushing overly large glasses back onto the bridge of her nose. 'You know, the one from Seamus Harding's phone?'

Rose nodded impatiently.

'Well, the thing is, it's the voice. You see I cleaned it up as much as possible but because of the distance the small phone mic would have been from the speaker and because it was outdoors and Seamus Harding was standing between the mic and whoever was talking, it made it difficult to determine much at first.'

Sylvia spoke quickly but not quickly enough for Rose who made an impatient gesture with her hand. 'Right, so it was difficult. What did you find?' she asked again.

'That's just it, I didn't notice it really, at first, but when I was listening to it something bothered me. So, I ran it through some software that looks at specific characteristics in the voice – intonation, frequencies used, that kind of thing – and that came back with some results that are rather surprising.' Sylvia paused and pushed her glasses up again.

'OK, Sylvia, very interesting. What is your point?' Rose asked, leaving long pauses between her last few words to try and speed the woman along.

'It's a woman's voice,' Sylvia said, her magnified eyes blinking.

'What?' Rose asked, incredulous. 'It didn't sound much like a woman to me.'

'No, it didn't really to me at first. But like I say, I think that's more to do with the distortions on the recording than anything else. But the characteristics are all there when you analyse them. The frequency range in the voice is very probably that of a woman,' Sylvia said, smiling tightly. 'I figured it was probably pretty important that you knew as soon as possible.'

'Yes, thank you Sylvia.' Rose looked blank. She had no idea what to make of this new information. 'Yes, thanks for letting me know so promptly.' She shook the woman's hand and turned back into the station.

Rod and David looked up, startled by the force with which Rose opened the interview room door.

'I need to suspend this interview for the moment. Sorry, David. Rod, I need to speak to you.'

***

The doorbell rang for a third time.

'Oh all right, fuckin' 'ell, I'm comin',' he muttered, trying to push himself up and out of his armchair. It took several attempts.

He rarely answered the door. He never got anything delivered and generally took the view that if someone was ringing his doorbell during the day it was likely to be a cold caller, a charity worker or a Jehovah's Witness. He had no time for any of them and they usually left after two tries.

The bell rang for a fourth time.

'Fuck sake, I'm comin',' he shouted as he made his slow progress down the short hall.

He made it to the door before the bell rang again and fumbled with the key to unlock it and remove the chain. Eventually, he pulled the door open with an angry scowl. The scowl melted into a smile when he saw who was at the door.

'Aw'right, gal. Wot you doin' comin t'see yer old man at this time o' day?'

***

David felt as low and confused as he ever had as the cell door clanked shut. He could not comprehend how his own boss and sergeant had drawn all the crazy conclusions they had from what were really just coincidences. He had no clue as to why he appeared to have looked at the files for any of the victims. And he certainly hadn't been driving past them intentionally on the days they died. And a pair of Doc Martens? He had never owned a pair or a balaclava for that matter.

He tried to think. He knew this was all just some mad misunderstanding. Rose was just desperate and had latched onto anything, no matter how tenuous. He wished now that he had agreed to a federation rep being present from the start but had thought he could easily explain anything they put to him. He would ask for one when they took him back in to the interview room that was for sure.

He realised that he might not have acted particularly differently if he had been faced with the same information Rose and Rod had. He would probably have also felt that there were far too many coincidences for his liking – and then the fact there was also physical evidence. That would have been it as far as he was concerned too. He put his hands to his face and then pulled them down roughly.

Think man...

What do I need to tell them so they see I have nothing to do with this?

Driving near the victims on the day they were killed? Where was I going? What for?

File access? Why can I not remember accessing the files? Why would I even access these people's files?

DMs? How can I have boots linked to the crimes in my flat?

My flat.
Driving.
The diary.
The files. Oh fuck, the files!

He sprang up from the cot bed where he had been perched and leaped the distance to the cell door, banging on it loudly as soon as he landed in front of it.

'Sergeant! Sergeant! I need to talk to DCI McPhail immediately. Sergeant!'

***

'A woman?' Rod said, mouth hanging open comically.

'That's what the lab says,' Rose answered shaking her head. 'Where does that leave us? I mean we had the woman that called Dion Myers but nothing else really. Are there two of them? David and a woman? But what about David? Where does he fit now? It doesn't appear that he grabbed Seamus Harding off the street.'

'Doesn't mean he wasn't waiting in the car. And he still hasn't satisfactorily answered our questions. And we have the boots and the balaclava,' Rod said firmly. 'He has to be implicated somehow.'

'Hmmm.' Rose pulled out her phone to check the time and noticed the missed call from earlier. Absently she opened the phone and looked at who it was. She saw it was Andy Carter. 'Andy's called me back. I may as well call him now – you never know, he might have something useful to tell me.'

She moved off and hit redial. The line rang several times and then Andy answered.

'Rose, you got my message then? Didn't want you thinking I'd ignored you. What's up?' he asked before Rose could even say hello.

'I'm going to test your memory Andy,' Rose said. 'You accessed a file not long before you left here and I need to know if you remember it.'

'Well, I'll try,' Andy said, puzzlement in his voice.

'It was for a Dion Myers. He was half being looked into for fraud, here and in Northampton. One conviction. Ring any bells?' Rose knew it was no more likely that Andy would remember than anyone else she had asked about the files but still it was worth a shot.

Andy was quiet for a few seconds. 'You know that does ring half a bell,' he said slowly. Rose felt her sprits lift a little for the first time in a long time. 'Hmm, no, nothing immediately clicking. The name means something but I can't think what at the moment. Let me have a think, and I'll call you back as soon as it clicks.'

'Thanks, Andy. It was a bit of a long shot. Call me back as soon as you get anything.' Rose rang off, hopes dropping again.

Rod was putting his own phone away when she looked back towards him.

'David's kicking off in his cell, demanding to see us,' he said.

'Well, he's got a whole new set of questions to answer now, doesn't he?' Rose said, moving off back to the interview room.

***

'Hello Dad,' she said, following him into the narrow hallway. 'I was saving you until last but I've had to move things along a little.'

'Savin' me 'til last?' he chuckled. 'Sounds fuckin' ominous, gal. In you go, in you go,' he said, ushering her into the living room. 'Cup o' tea?'

'Sit down, Dad,' she said, taking up a position in the middle of the room and pointing to his armchair.

He looked at her with puzzled eyes but made his way to the seat. 'What's all this abaht, then?'

'Give me a minute and I'll explain,' she said, fishing in her bag and pulling out a piece of white paper inside a clear document wallet. There was a large safety pin attached to it.

The man's frown of puzzlement deepened and then his eyes shot wide open when he saw the gun being pulled from the bag. His gun.

'I found the tapes. When I helped you move in here,' she said, pointing the pistol's silencer at his chest. 'And then I found your gun.'

His expression dropped and he looked at her through lidded eyes. 'Oh. You weren't meant to hear them 'til after I was gone.'

'Well, I did. And the thing is, I figure I already knew anyway. I knew from when I was a little kid that there was something. I was just never sure what exactly.' The pistol didn't waver while she spoke.

'Wot you gonna do?' His voice cracked as he spoke. 'Y' don't need that t' take me in. I woulda just come along if y'd asked.'

'Oh, I'm not going to take you in, Dad,' she said, moving towards him. 'On your knees.'

***

Rose sat in the interview room waiting for Rod to bring David back along. She wasn't sure how she was going to broach her new line of questioning. She could ask him outright who the woman was – he had to be linked to her and the crimes somehow – or she could try and subtly introduce the subject. She was too tired, she knew, to go the subtle route.

Direct and to the point never fails.

Her phone pinged; she glanced down and saw she had a text. It was from Andy Stirling:

'Got it, give me a call back.'

She redialled immediately.

'Andy? What do you remember?'

'I remembered because it was a little unusual. You see I didn't access the file … well I did, but I was doing it for someone else.'

'Who?' Rose sat forward in the chair.

'Louise Carney.'

'What?' Rose asked, no one else had mentioned Louise.

'Yeah, she asked me to have a look at this Dion Myers, said she needed some background for a case she was working. I asked her why she couldn't do it herself and she told her machine was running a report and it was taking ages. I didn't think much of it at the time. Lucky, I have a good memory for names otherwise I'd have been no help to you. What's this about?'

'It's in connection with the murders that have been going on down here. You've probably heard about them,' Rose said, still puzzled. Louise?

'Christ yeah, vigilante or something?' Andy said, sounding grave.

'That's the one,' Rose answered. 'Thanks, Andy, that's very helpful, if puzzling. I have to go – I'm actually in the middle of an interview.' Although I'll be asking a very different set of questions now.

'Right you are, Rose. Let me know how things pan out.'

'Will do, Andy, cheers.' Rose hung up.

She sat for a few seconds tapping the phone against her teeth. Then she dialled another number and waited.

The Duty Inspector answered after a couple of rings.

'Hugh, it's Rose. Is Al Williams on duty today?'

'Not until tonight,' Hugh replied. 'What's up?'

'Can you give me his personal mobile number? I need to speak to him urgently.' Rose felt she had no time for more explanations.

'Sure, give me a tick.' She heard Hugh put the phone down. 'Here you go,' he said after a few seconds and gave her the number.

'Thanks, Hugh.' Rose hung up and immediately redialled.

Al Williams took longer to answer. He had been sleeping, ready for his night shift and sounded groggy.

'Tell me Al,' Rose said, after telling him who was calling. 'Those files I asked you about. Are you sure no one asked you to access them?'

'We've been over this twice, Chief Inspector. I don't recall ever accessing those files. It was quite a while ago,' he said, sounding annoyed to have been woken for the sake of answering a question he had already answered before.

'Are you sure, Al?' Rose pressed. 'DC Louise Carney, for example?'

There was a pause of maybe a half a minute; she could hear PC Williams breathing down the line as he thought.

'Oh bugger,' he said eventually. 'Yeah, now you say that. I think I might have looked something up for her. Her terminal was playing up or something. I would have said but I didn't connect the names with her asking me.'

Rose sighed. 'Thanks Al, I'll let you go back to sleep.'

She hung up and put her forehead on the interview room desk, bumping it softly on the cold surface. *Oh, for God's sake, surely not.* Her head felt light and a sick feeling begun in the bottom of her stomach.

***

'I'm not gonna beg,' he said, knees clicking as he knelt. 'I don't regret a fuckin' minute of it.' His voice had regained its strength and there was no sign of fear from him at all.

'I don't need you to beg, Dad,' Louise said, tying his hands behind his back with cable ties. 'See, I was saving you until last for my own sake. The others were the real work. They were important. You. You're just a piece of vermin I have to put down.'

He made a strained grunt as she tightened the cable ties as tight as they would go.

'Others? Wot you on abaht? Wot others?' he asked, voice still unnervingly calm.

'Don't you watch the news, Dad?' she asked, genuinely puzzled. 'Those four people killed in the last few weeks?'

'That was you?' He tried to turn his head to look at her but she pushed the muzzle of the silencer into his cheek turning his face back around.

'Yep, a right chip off the old block, eh?' she chuckled. 'But no one has worked out why, yet, never mind who. Shall I tell you why, Dad? Do you want to know? Or even care?'

'Yeah, 'course I want t' know,' he said. She knew he was simply asking in order to stall for time but was happy to indulge him. After all, having listened to the horrors he had committed without any sort of explanation or motive, she felt she had to let him know what had driven her to murder four people.

She moved round to face him. Reaching down, she tore open his shirt and pulled the paper out from under her arm. Keeping the gun trained on his face she opened the safety pin with her free hand. He looked at her, confusion in his eyes. She turned the paper round so he could read what was printed there in large bold letters:

'SERIAL KILLER.'

'Wot the fu…' he stammered just as she drove the pin through his chest, plunging the needle through the fat and muscle, pushing hard to force it out the other side. The point emerged on the other side of his nipple. He made a strangled sound in his throat but otherwise didn't react.

'You should be labelled, like the others, before I tell you why. You see I was always going to explain to you and not them. They never found out why I had to do away with them but I want you to hear it.' She looked around the room and spotted a low footstool near the small settee. She pulled it over and perched on it, tilting her head to one side as she stared at her father.

'It was all about prevention, you see? I was doing the job all coppers everywhere try and do –prevent crime before it happens or escalates.'

***

Rose lifted her head from the desk as Rod ushered a hyperactive-looking David into the interview room.

'Rose,' David said frantically as soon as he was through the door. 'It wasn't me – I think I've worked it out.'

'I know, David,' Rose said, gripping his arm. 'Did you ever access files for Louise?'

'Yes, yes, that's what I was going to tell you. I remembered ... she asked me to look into the victims. And those times you've picked my car up on the ANPR – she had called me and asked me to go on an errand for her. I think she set me up.' David's voice was high and everything came out in a rush, words tripping over each other.

'Louise?' Rod said, surprise in his voice. 'Have I missed something?'

'The woman, Rod,' Rose said flatly. 'It's Louise. She asked Andy, PC Williams and David to access the files. I would bet she was the woman that called Dion Myers and the woman in the video from Seamus Harding's phone.'

'Fuck,' Rod said quietly. 'She's the killer?'

Rose nodded. 'Probably,' she said quietly.

'What size shoes do you wear, David?' she asked.

'Ten,' he answered, bewildered.

'What size are the shoes we recovered?' she asked Rod.

Rod closed his eyes. 'Nines.'

'Why the fuck didn't that get checked immediately?' Rose shouted.

'They were in his flat,' Rod said defensively. 'As far as we knew no one else had been there so they had to be his.'

'Louise stayed at mine more than once,' David said, voice quiet and flat.

Rose ran her hands through her hair, exasperation about to boil over. She needed to get control of herself.

She took a deep breath and looked at the ceiling for a moment, thinking.

'We need to find her and fast. She said there was a family crisis – what family does she have in Milton Keynes, David, do you know?'

'Her dad and a brother, I think,' David said, frowning as he tried to recall, his brain feeling like mush inside his head.

Rose's face became hard. 'Right, I want the addresses for both of them. Maybe there's a genuine family crisis, but they need to be checked out immediately. And her place. I also want traffic cameras checked straight away. We need to find her car and track where's she's gone to, if she's not at any of the family addresses.' She paused for a moment. 'She probably doesn't know we're on to her, but in case she does, have an armed response unit ready. Rod, get that organised right now.'

***

'Prevent crime? But aren't you…?' He looked genuinely puzzled.

'Shut up. No interruptions, just listen.' She pushed the gun towards his face. 'I stopped them getting any worse. I realised they were all capable of going on to commit far more serious crimes. That teacher and his protestations of innocence – he was a filthy paedophile waiting to happen. And that peeping tom … it was only a matter of time before he raped someone. Same with the others – if we left them to their own devices they would have gone on to commit serious fraud, and probably ripped the taxpayer off for thousands, given half a chance. All of them were apparently innocent, but I knew better.' She stopped, breathing heavily.

'I don't understand,' he said quietly. 'They were all innocent? Then why 'ave you done this?'

'I told you, prevention. I stopped them before it could get started. You see, ever since I was little, I knew there was something dodgy about your little trips away. When I was about twelve, I convinced myself you were having an affair or something. But then as I got older, I don't know what it was, but something kept telling me there was something very wrong. I put it to the back of my mind but it stayed there – it kept coming up from time to time and I still had no answers. That's probably why I joined the police – I had an insatiable need to know the true answer. And then, when I helped move you in here, I found the tapes. And I got my answers. Suddenly I knew what I had been concerned about for all those years. And it was so much worse than I had ever expected. You killed all those people for no reason.' Her voice broke and she sat quietly for some time, a single tear running down her face.

He dropped his head and sniffed. 'I couldn't explain it t' meself, Lou. 'Ow could I explain it t' you?'

'I don't need your fucking explanations,' she screamed, spittle flying and hitting his forehead. 'The point is I couldn't have stopped it. Even if I'd known sooner, I wouldn't have been able to prevent it. It had already happened. And it kept going round and round in my head – how can I be any good to society if I couldn't see and prevent my own father from killing all those people, in the name of a holiday, for fuck sake.'

She began to sob. 'I couldn't stop it. So, I stopped others. I stopped them,' she mumbled between racking breaths. She inhaled a deep, shuddering intake of breath and let the air out slowly through her nose. His head was still bowed and she stared at the top of his head, a grimace on her face.

***

Rose kept low and to the right of the ground floor flat as she crept slowly forward. They had tracked Louise's car easily enough and had quickly realised that she was heading for her father's address. Rod, David and the armed response team waited a short distance down the road. Rod had tried to insist that he go scope out the flat but Rose had been adamant that she was the one that would do it. She inched closer to the first window and lifted her head enough to be able to look in. It was a kitchen, no one was in inside. She dropped her head and moved further along keeping close to the wall.

The second window looked into a living room and there was Louise sitting on a low footstool pointing a gun at an older man who was on his knees in front of her. She could see his hands were cable tied and the very edge of a white piece of paper pinned to his chest.

She ducked back down and signalled the sergeant in charge of the armed response unit.

It was time to move and fast.

***

There was a loud crack from the front door. She sprang up from the footstool and moved behind her father.

'Bye Dad,' she said quietly and there was a dull thudding noise just audible above the crashing and shouting in the hallway. The old man slumped forward, revealing a small ragged hole in the top of his head.

'Armed police – on the floor! On the floor!'

Epilogue

David and Rose stood a little way back from the rest of the funeral-goers. The weather was befittingly damp and cold. Grey clouds skimmed overhead, depositing light but freezing showers every five minutes or so. Patricia Johnson's family huddled together against the cold and their grief.

'You didn't have to come. You hadn't met them,' Rose said quietly, glancing sideways at the young man.

'I felt I needed to,' he said. 'Part of me feels responsible.'

'You're not responsible for any of it, David. She had the whole station taken in.' Rose laid a hand on David's upper arm. 'As far as we can tell she was generating lists from searches on her own login, looking up lists of names for minor offences, cautions and any other involvement with the police. Then she was using half the station to look up the details. Then she picked out her victims, possibly at random or through some twisted logic. No one would have twigged.'

'Yeah, I know. But I thought I knew her. You know?' He cocked his head slightly.

'You hadn't been seeing her very long. There was no way you could have spotted anything,' Rose said, sympathy in her voice.

'She nearly had me arrested for multiple murders, so no, I guess you're right. I can't have got to know her very well – Jesus, planting that stuff in my flat.' He ran a hand through his damp hair and shook his head. 'What I don't get though is there's no way she's a size nine shoe. The prints and her shoe size don't match.'

'There was a drawer full of very thick socks,' Rose replied quietly. 'You know, the type you get for walking and that sort of thing. She's a size seven – still quite large for a woman – but we think she probably filled the boots out using those. I don't think she was ever planning on running after her victims so the oversized shoes wouldn't have mattered very much. We're pretty sure she was basically trying as hard as possible to give every appearance of a man at the scenes.'

David nodded and looked off into the middle distance. Rose followed suit, sniffing and pulling her jacket collar up against the rain. After a time, she turned back to look at David.

'How did she fix the diary?' Rose asked, shuffling her cold feet.

'She didn't – I genuinely thought I might be able to find a pattern. I caught her looking at it one morning. She must have figured she could use it one way or another. She was right as well.'

Rose nodded and lapsed into silence. Louise had said very little since her arrest but Rose had managed to get her to boast about how she had gone about getting the details of her victims and how she had planted evidence in David's flat, even how she had called him to drive somewhere whilst she was watching her victims from a discreet distance. She had to pull that trick a few times before she was sure his car would be picked up nearby. And she had hired a different car for every murder. The chances of picking it up were slim to none. All in all, she had been a cunning and brutal killer, aided by her knowledge of police work.

'Had she planned to use me as a scapegoat all along, do you think?' David asked after a time.

'No, I don't think so,' Rose said. 'I think she had begun to realise that she would get caught sooner rather than later and you were just … convenient.'

David nodded thoughtfully. 'Why'd she do it? I can't get my head around that.'

'Right now, I really don't know. Maybe it'll come out at some point or she'll never say, who knows?' Rose said, her voice distant as she puzzled over the same question.

'There are more questions here than answers, I'm afraid, David,' Rose said, turning to look at the young man. 'We still have no idea why she shot her father or why she labelled him a serial killer. She's not saying and we've very little to go on. There's a whole new investigation to be had there but fortunately it's not one we'll have to conduct.'

'It's not something I'm going to get over any time soon,' he said, looking down at his shoes.

'No, neither will I,' Rose said as she watched the funeral party move away from the graveside and start to break up. Amy Johnson looked over to where they were standing and gave Rose a tearful wave. Graham Johnson nodded to her solemnly. She acknowledged both of them and turned to leave.

'But then, neither will they,' she said and then tugged David's coat sleeve. 'Come on, I'll buy you a pint. I might even play you some Iron Maiden on the way.'

He looked at her with a questioning expression on his face and then followed her out of the cemetery to her car.

'Who's Iron Maiden?'

Colin's Clan

If you have enjoyed this book and would like access to all sorts of goodies, sign up to Colin's Clan, to receive:

- A monthly newsletter, with humorous anecdotes, new release news and opportunities to interact directly with Colin.
- Competitions for signed copies and a host of other prizes.
- Access to all sorts of secret swag.
- Opportunities to pre-order books at discounted prices.
- Advance notification of events where you can meet Colin.

To sign up visit:

www.colinamillar.com/colins-clan

For more information about Colin A Millar visit:

www.colinamillar.com

Facebook:

https://www.facebook.com/ColinAMillar

Printed in Great Britain
by Amazon